D0174312

Home to WILLOWBROOK

CAROLE GIFT PAGE

A
JANET
THOMA
BOOK

THOMAS NELSON PUBLISHERS
Nashville • Atlanta • London • Vancouver

Published in Nashville, Tennessee, by Thomas Nelson, Inc., Publishers, and distributed in Canada by Word Communications, Ltd., Richmond, British Columbia.

Scripture quotations are from The King James Version of the Holy Bible.

Library of Congress Cataloging-in-Publication Data

Page, Carole Gift.
   Home to Willowbrook / Carole Gift Page.
     p. cm. — (Heartland memories ; bk. 2)
   ISBN 0-8407-6778-1
    1. Title. 2. Series: Page, Carole Gift. Heartland memories;
bk. 2.
  PS3566.A3326H65 1995
  813'.54—dc20   94-43916

Printed in the United States of America.
2 3 4 5 6 — 00 99 98 97 96

———

To my mother, Millie Gift of Jackson, Michigan, who captures her own heartland memories in her beautiful paintings.

And to my aunt, Virginia Pope of Shearwater, Tasmania, Australia, whose passion for life triumphs over every obstacle.

Thank you both, for your love and inspiration, and for helping me catch a glimpse of a nobler, gentler time when life revolved around home and family.

And to my dear friend and colleague, Doris Elaine Fell. Thanks for sharing your editorial skills.

1

*T*HE DEAD *OF a soundless night.*
An endless highway headed nowhere.
Blackness palpable as blood.

Catherine Herrick's black DeSoto was aimed straight-arrow through a drenching Indiana downpour when without warning she felt herself careening across the yellow line, her gloved hands helpless on the steering wheel. Her vehicle skated up rain-slick asphalt like a pebble tossed in play, skittering across a frozen lake bed.

Out of control, airborne, delirious sensation of lightness. Is this what it's like to fly?

Two great white orbs exploded into her vision, canceling out the darkness with their stunning glare. The lights mesmerized her, obliterated her consciousness. Those huge, radiating globes were all she recalled as she plunged over the precipice into a musky, foul oblivion.

A dream.
More than a dream.
Worse than a dream.

Like clockwork Catherine awoke, sitting bolt-erect in bed, drenched with perspiration. The dream was over. She was safe at home in the rosebud room in the old Victorian mansion on Honeysuckle Lane. Her brother's house, with its handsome Gothic arches and ornamental gables, its lush gardens and towering oaks.

But as the cobwebs of sleep cleared, Catherine knew with a wrenching jolt that the nightmare wasn't over after all. It was only beginning, as it began afresh each day. She grasped the truth in painful shards of recollection. Her body and mind were still prisoners of the accident.

Catherine pushed back her covers and hoisted her long, slender legs over the side of the bed. Her feet felt sluggish, awkward like those of a child just learning to walk. She moved her hand to the back of her neck, blotting the beads of sweat that dampened her cropped red hair. Her body warmth made the scent of her lavender cologne sweetly pungent. She pulled at her cotton nightgown, loosening the bodice, welcoming the night air on her moist skin.

In so many ways, she was a child again—a twenty-seven-year-old child learning the tasks a youngster takes in stride. To walk correctly. Speak properly. Read and write. And yes, even how to draw again. How she prayed God would give her back her artistic talent. It was her only prayer. She wasn't comfortable asking God for favors.

A child's cry down the hall sliced into Catherine's groggy musings. Jenny—awakened by her own four-year-old nocturnal goblins. Instinctively, Cath clambered out of bed and padded barefoot to her daughter's room. She knelt beside the bed and placed her palm on Jenny's forehead, under her wispy, strawberry-blonde curls. Moonlight streamed across the child's face. She looked like a Kewpie doll, with round, freckled cheeks and long, thick lashes. "Are you okay, angel baby?"

Jenny opened her blue eyes wide and squirmed away from Catherine's touch. "Mama! I want my Mama!"

"I'm right here, sweet pea."

"No! I want Mama Annie!"

"Here I am, Jenny." The lilting voice came from the willowy figure in the doorway. Annie. Catherine's best friend since childhood. Her brother's wife. Her child's mother. Annie filled all the roles so expertly. Since the accident she had become Cath's caregiver as well.

Catherine stood up, her fingertips lingering on her daughter's curls. "Jenny wants *you*, Annie."

In the shadows Annie offered a wordless glance that spoke volumes. *I'm sorry, Cath. I wish things could be different. I don't mean to hurt you. Still friends?*

Cath hovered in the doorway watching as Annie reached out and gathered the child into her arms. "What's wrong, little princess? Did Jenny have a bad dream?"

"The big doggies chased me, Mommy. They scared me."

"Want me to rock you back to sleep, sweetheart?"

"I want a drink of water."

"I'll get it, Jenny," said Cath, starting for the bathroom.

"No! Mama Annie get it!"

"Don't be silly," said Annie. "Cath can get your drink while I rock you."

Cath brought the water but Jenny turned her head away. Cath held the glass closer, her hand trembling. A trickle escaped over the rim.

Jenny's mouth puckered in rebuke. "You spilled it on my nightie!"

Cath slammed the water glass down on the dresser, rage and humiliation shattering her fragile composure.

Annie caught Cath's arm. "She doesn't mean to be cruel. She's just a child. She doesn't realize . . ."

"She knows I can't take care of her anymore." Cath's voice broke with bitterness. "She hates me for it. I don't blame her. I hate myself."

Annie's grip tightened. "Don't, Cath. It's not your fault you were hurt in the accident. Jenny will come around. And look at you. You're getting better every day."

"Am I?" Catherine pulled away and fled to her own room. Her green eyes wide with unshed tears, she gazed into her dresser mirror as filigrees of light broke through the lace curtains and illumined her elfin figure. The dusky glass reflected a ghostly waif, still bone-thin, complexion pale as eggshell, a frame as fragile as a whisper.

Shortly after coming out of the coma, Cath remembered someone exclaiming, "Lord almighty, this poor creature can't be our Catherine! She was so strong, so stubborn and proud, just bristling with health and energy. Merciful heavens, our dear Cath is gone, leaving this wraithlike soul in her place!"

For the life of her, Cath couldn't recall who had said that. Couldn't even summon a face. Couldn't place the voice. Surely it wasn't Annie. Nor her brother, Knowl. Perhaps her mother. But hadn't someone said Betty Herrick was off in a sanitarium somewhere? Or was Cath mistaken about that too?

People and places, faces and names faded in and out of her memory like relics moldering beneath an endless sea. They popped up, visible for an instant, then were swallowed again by a briny deep—the trackless, shadowed caverns of Cath's mind. Huge chunks of her life had simply vanished, while other parts remained jumbled and strangely juxtaposed, like images in a Salvador Dali painting. Odd how well she recalled the paintings of artists she had studied at the Institute when more practical, everyday details constantly eluded her. The events of her life seemed as surreal and bizarre as the draping, dreamlike clocks in *Persistence of Memory,* that inscrutable Dali painting.

Cath hugged her arms against her chest and leaned into the mirror until her breath clouded its surface. She held her breath and stared unblinking into the sea-green depths of her own eyes, as if she might glean some fragment of truth that would make the random puzzle pieces of her life form a picture she could comprehend. But there was nothing, except shadows and silence.

Would she ever be whole again? A normal person someone could cherish the way Chip, her childhood sweetheart, had once loved her? But Chip, with his regal features and blond good looks, was not a memory she welcomed. Better to leave him buried in the past than to resurrect the pain his memory would bring.

At breakfast that morning, Cath nursed a cup of hot tea with milk and sugar while Knowl and Annie consumed ham and eggs and black coffee and discussed their plans for the day. Cath absently traced the lacework in the linen tablecloth as her gaze moved over the Blue Willow ware in the antique hutch. These days she preferred to remain silent and detached while others conversed. She found their conversations tiring. Her thoughts were always a step behind, leaving her scrambling to fill in the blanks or span the gaps.

Knowl, his wheat-colored hair tousled and his brown eyes animated behind his wire-rim spectacles, was saying something about President Truman lifting wage and price controls—except for rent, sugar, and rice.

"It's about time," said Annie, pouring more coffee. Her dark hair cascaded over her shoulders in crimped ringlets. Now that she was in a family way, her face glowed as her body blossomed. Her flawless skin and classic features reminded Cath of a painting of the Madonna by a Flemish artist. She couldn't recall the name, but she could visualize the portrait in every detail. It was comforting to know her mind still worked at times.

"The president acts like the war's still on," Annie mused.

"To hear the administration talk about it, it is," said Knowl. "Only they're calling it a 'Cold War' now."

"Don't talk about war," said Cath. It reminded her of Chip and Pearl Harbor.

Annie reached over and patted her hand. "We won't, Cath dear. Aren't you going to eat something?"

"I'm not hungry."

"You need to eat. You're entirely too thin. Isn't she too thin, Knowl?"

"Annie's right," said Knowl, chucking her under the chin. "I can't have a sister of mine wasting away to nothing."

"I am nothing," Cath murmured distractedly. She looked around. "Where is my baby?" It was hard now to realize that for weeks after coming out of the coma, she hadn't known Jenny was hers. She had supposed the child was Knowl's and Annie's until Anna Reed—Annie's mother—mentioned in passing that her granddaughter had red hair just like Catherine's. Cath was stunned to learn she had a child, and even more stunned that she hadn't remembered.

"Jenny's in the garden with her grandmother," said Knowl.

"They're cracking walnuts in the gazebo," said Annie. "They want to enjoy the outdoors before the first frost hits."

Knowl pushed back his chair. "Winter will be here before we know it."

"I want to go paint," said Cath, lifting her chin resolutely.

"Fine," said Knowl. "I'll set up your easel in the garden."

"No, I will walk to the woods. I want to paint the colors of autumn." Cath stared Knowl down, answering his look of concern with a curt "Don't worry. I won't get lost."

"I think it would be better if you went to the park instead," said Annie. "There are some lovely things to paint there. Remember how you used to love to paint the old willows?"

"No," said Cath, pushing back her chair. "I don't remember." In her hurry to leave, she toppled her china teacup, spilling its contents in a brown ring on the white linen tablecloth. She grabbed for the cup, uttering an exclamation of dismay as it clattered noisily against its saucer.

"It's okay, Cath," said Annie. "Nothing's broken. You go get your art supplies. I'll clean up the mess."

My whole life's a mess other people keep having to clean up, Cath thought ruefully. She left the table, fighting the silent rage that rose up so often lately, like a knot tightening in her chest, leaving her breathless and feeling so maddeningly helpless.

She gathered her art supplies from the back porch, where Knowl had set up a makeshift studio for her. She tucked her small easel and watercolor paper under one arm and picked up her paint box with the other hand. She paused to gaze out the window at the gazebo in the garden, where Anna Reed was playing with Jenny. Anna was an older, more stately version of Annie, her graying hair rolled back from her handsome face in a graceful chignon. No one would question that Anna and Annie were mother and daughter, in both temperament and physical attributes.

Catherine envied the closeness and easy camaraderie the two women shared. What little contact Cath had with her own mother these days—a scrawled postcard from Betty Herrick mailed from the sanitarium—simply confirmed her fleeting childhood memories. Cath and her mother had never been close and had, in fact, been at odds with each other most of their lives. Yes, she remembered that, remembered the pain.

Cath set down her paint box and reached for the back door handle. "Here, let me do that." Knowl strode over and opened the door for her. He carried her paints down the porch steps and offered her his hand. "I'll drop you off at the park on my way to the newspaper, Cath."

"The woods!" she said stubbornly.

"No, sis. It's too far. You might get lost."

"I'm not a child," she protested, then acknowledged silently, *But I am a child. Worse than a child.*

Wordlessly she climbed into Knowl's new Dodge six-passenger sedan and settled back in the leather seat. She remained silent as he drove down Honeysuckle Lane past the spacious manicured lawns of Willowbrook's most prestigious vintage estates.

In a way that Cath couldn't articulate, all of her feelings were tied to Honeysuckle Lane and the old Reed mansion with its Victorian gables, dome-shaped cupola, and inviting wraparound porch. Its lovely old rooms of velvet and brocade tapped into a deep well of childhood sensations, not conscious memories exactly, but the sense of something familiar and beloved. At the same time, this turn-of-the-century house, built by Annie's Grandfather Reed, represented the source of profound pain, starting with Cath's ill-fated love for Chip Reed—Annie's brother—and the birth of the child he would never know. Cath was sure the townsfolk still talked about it, although she couldn't be sure how much they knew. At first Knowl and Annie pretended Jenny was their adopted child—until Cath barged back into their lives, demanding her baby.

Of course, all of that was in the past, Cath mused darkly, and Annie had won out after all. Jenny called *her* Mommy now. Since the accident, Cath was left broken and struggling to be born anew out of the paralyzing grip of that insidious coma.

"Cath, are you okay?"

Startled, she looked at her brother. "Why do you ask?"

"You looked so lost in thought."

Lost. An apt description, she reflected solemnly. *I'm lost in the bewildering labyrinth of my own thoughts, drowning, trying to make sense of it all.* Aloud, she said simply, "I was trying to remember."

"What?"

"Everything. The past. Our childhood."

Knowl chuckled. "We spent most of our time at the Reed home. Chip was my best friend. Annie was yours. We did everything together. Do you remember?"

"Bits and pieces." Mostly she remembered Chip, with the ruddy face and flaxen hair, the valiant adventurer who yearned to slay dragons and rescue damsels in distress.

Knowl's voice turned guarded. "Do you recall how you felt about Chip?"

"Sometimes." *He was the love of my life. He died. I died. What else is there to say?*

Knowl was driving down Jefferson now, just a block from the park. He glanced over at Cath, his brow furrowed. "Will you be able to get home okay?"

She felt that cold, hard stone again in her chest. "Of course I will. I may be brain-damaged, but I'm not an idiot."

Knowl's tone was conciliatory. "I'm sorry, Cath. I know Annie and I shouldn't fret and fuss over you so much, but we worry about you."

She stared straight ahead. "Don't. It doesn't help."

"What *will* help?" He sounded mildly exasperated.

"I don't know. Nothing. Leave me alone."

"We can't, Cath." Knowl cleared his throat uneasily. "Annie's trying hard, you know. She would give her life if she could turn back the clock to before the accident. But you don't make it easy for her. Especially now, with the baby coming, she needs to be surrounded by peace and harmony, not tension."

Cath looked sharply at her brother but said nothing.

"I'm not saying this to upset you, Cath," he continued. "It's just that from the time we were kids, you were as pigheaded and independent as they come. And that's good. It helped you survive Chip's death and made you strong enough to relinquish baby Jenny to us so she'd have both a mother and a father."

"But I took Jenny back and made Annie run away—"

"No, Cath, *I* made Annie run away. But that's all in the past. The point is, you were able to pick up the pieces of your life and carve out a successful career as an artist. And you'll be able to do all of that again."

Cath bit her lower lip. "No, I won't."

"Yes, you will," said Knowl. He gripped the wheel until his knuckles whitened. "Look at all you've come through since the coma—the intensive therapy and rehabilitation, the seizures and headaches and mood swings. You're beating it, Cath. You're winning. You're almost home-free. But you've got to know when to let the people who love you help you. That's all Annie and I are trying to do."

Cath didn't reply. She had no words to make Knowl understand. How could she be winning when she felt like such a failure? How could she be whole when so many pieces of her were still missing? She had taken this dark journey alone into alien country, leaving her brother far behind. Once their relationship had been marked by fun-loving banter and good-natured sibling rivalry. Now there was this chasm between them neither could span, this constant tension in the air. Why couldn't Cath appreciate all Knowl and Annie had done for her—willing her back to life after the accident, patiently urging her to reclaim her faculties and abilities? Why did she resent them so much? Why did she feel this impenetrable wall around her, shutting everyone out?

Cath felt her eyes moisten with unshed tears. She blinked them back and tightened her lips. She would not let Knowl see her cry.

He pulled the vehicle over beside the curb and stopped, then reached across to open her door. "The park, sis. Be careful."

She gathered her art supplies and climbed awkwardly out of the car. Knowl smiled at her, his fingers drumming the steering wheel. She said good-bye and turned away before he could offer to help. She crossed the sidewalk to the grass and kept walking, without looking back. She would show Knowl how independent she could still be.

Finally she stopped and looked around. Knowl's car was gone. Her shoulders sagged a little with the weight of her easel and paint box. She sank down on the nearest bench, feeling the coldness of the wrought-iron creep through her thin cotton dress. The breeze was chilly. Why hadn't she remembered to wear a coat? Why hadn't Knowl reminded her?

She was too tired to move on. She would paint right here. She set up her easel, propped up her pad of watercolor paper, and removed her palette from the paint box. She squeezed out little mounds of burnt sienna, alizarin crimson, yellow ochre, and cerulean blue. At least she was remembering the names of her paints. Then she opened a small jar of water and dipped in her best sable-hair brush. She gazed at the landscape surrounding her and felt a lurch of disappointment. She had come here to paint the flaming colors of autumn, but it was November now, and most of the trees were bare, or their leaves were dry and dead, the somber color of raw umber.

What's wrong with me? she wondered. *Why don't I see the world as it really is?*

She mixed dabs of burnt sienna and ultramarine blue and began sketching nearby trees and shrubs. But even she could see that her hand moved awkwardly, that the strokes on the paper didn't match the images in her mind. She exclaimed into the gray morning air, "Oh, God, why can't I make it work anymore?"

Bitter tears stung her eyes. Who would ever believe that she, Catherine Herrick, was once an accomplished artist whose work had graced the cover of the *Saturday Evening Post*? She had painted Annie holding baby Jenny and called it *Mother and Child*. It could have been the Madonna and Christ-child. She had poured all her feelings for her baby into that portrait. That painting and others that followed had earned her a reputation as one of America's most promising young artists, "in the tradition of Winslow Homer or Norman Rockwell himself," one critic had effusively proclaimed.

Where is that artist now? Cath cried silently. She tore the paper from her easel, ripped it in pieces, and flung the scraps on the ground. She sat back on the bench and watched the fragments skitter with the breeze over the dry grass.

As she glanced toward the street, a figure caught her eye—a tall, lean man standing by the curb in a rumpled brown jacket, pullover sweater, and jeans. Something in the way he stood—stock-still, as if riveted to the spot—made Cath's gaze linger. He had sharply chiseled features in a long, narrow, unsmiling face. A thatch of reddish-brown hair tumbled over his high forehead, and dark brows seemed to crouch over small, intense eyes that seared mercilessly into Cath. Try as she might, she couldn't pull away from his gaze.

Something about the young man was uncannily familiar—attractive and repellant at once. Did she know him? Was he someone from her past she had forgotten? He watched her as if he knew her, and yet he remained unmoving, staring her down, as if waiting for her to react.

A ripple of alarm traveled along Cath's spine and moved into her throat and chest, constricting her breath. *What if the man is up to no good? He could be a thief, a pervert, a lunatic.* She clumsily put away her watercolors and gathered up her easel, sketch pad, and paint box. She began walking toward home, her awkward gait giving way to a labored shuffle. Surely she only imagined the danger. Her mind often played tricks on her these days, her capricious imagination summoning perils when there were none or ignoring risks that were clearly there. *Relax, Cath. Take a breath. Don't drop anything. Find the rhythm in your walking. That's it. You're perfectly safe.*

She walked a block and looked around. The street was empty. She uttered an audible sigh of relief and kept walking, her pace slowing as her confidence returned. When she was just a block from home, she glanced around again, almost convinced she had only imagined the stranger.

Her heart leapt in her chest. The man was there, walking leisurely behind her, his hands in his jacket pockets, his face expressionless, his gaze still squarely on her.

She hastened her pace, shambling and tripping like a foolish marionette with tangled strings. Her breath grew ragged. She considered dropping her easel and paints on the sidewalk, but that would only tip off the man that she was afraid. She was nearly running now as her fear mushroomed. At last she reached the wrought-iron fence surrounding the Reed estate. She fumbled with the gate and escaped inside, struggling up the expanse of lawn to the sprawling porch. With trembling fingers she seized the knob on the paneled door and scrambled inside. From the safe haven of the marbled hallway, she collapsed against the closed mahogany door. Her chest heaving, she turned the lock and peered out the small beveled window at the street. An automobile rumbled by on the cobbled pavement, and a dog barked somewhere in the next block. But that was all.

The stranger was nowhere in sight.

2

CATHERINE, IS SOMETHING wrong?"

Cath whirled around, breathless. Annie stood in the parlor doorway in a pretty pink frock and white pinafore. She looked every inch the lady of the house, the lovely mother-in-waiting. The thought crossed Cath's mind, *If Chip had lived, this might have been my house and my perfect life and family.* She dismissed the thought with a twinge of guilt. "No, Annie, nothing's wrong," she said quickly. "I just thought I saw someone outside."

"Someone you know?"

"No. A stranger." She set down her art supplies and cast another glance out the window. "He's gone now."

"Didn't you have a pleasant time in the park?"

"Pleasant enough."

Annie came forward and clasped Catherine's hand. "I'm glad. I was waiting for you to come home. I have some good news."

"Good news?"

Annie's face glowed as she removed an envelope from her pocket.

"I received a letter today from Robert Wayne. You remember. My editor friend from California."

Cath nodded. "The one who found a publisher for your book about Chip?"

"Yes, he's the one. Robert was an editor with Sanders and Browne Publishers before the war."

Cath followed Annie to the parlor and sat down in the oak rocker by the bay window. Annie sat in the red velvet Queen Anne chair beside the fireplace.

"After Robert was wounded at Pearl Harbor he started working with the Salvation Army mission in California." Annie removed a sheaf of papers from the envelope. "That's where we met."

"I know you've told me the story before," said Cath, feigning interest. "Sometimes my memories get mixed up." She didn't add that what she remembered hearing of Robert Wayne left a bad taste in her mouth.

"Guess what, Cath." Annie didn't seem to notice Cath's apathy; she was too caught up in the excitement of the moment. "Robert's gone back to New York to work for Sanders and Browne. He's received a wonderful promotion. Senior editor. Can you imagine? He says it's because of the success of my book."

"I'm not surprised. How long has it been on the *New York Times* Best Sellers list?"

"For thirty-six weeks now."

"That's swell, Annie." Cath knew her enthusiasm was forced. Surely Annie knew it too. But how could she be expected to fathom Annie's success as a best-selling author when she herself measured success by how steady she could hold a paintbrush? Why was it that everything came so easy for Annie and so hard for Cath?

"That's only part of my good news," said Annie.

"What else? Tell me."

Annie went on reading, but nothing connected in Cath's mind until she heard the words, *I'll be coming to Willowbrook next week. . . .*

She met Annie's gaze, her brows arching sharply. "What did you say?"

"Robert Wayne is coming to Willowbrook to talk to me about my next book. He thinks Sanders and Browne will be interested. Isn't that simply grand?"

"Your next book?" Cath's mind felt sluggish, confused. Had she missed something? "What book, Annie?"

Annie's face flushed. "I haven't actually said much about it, Cath. I've been working on it privately for months. No one's read it yet—except Robert. I sent him my first draft. It's awful, really. Not at all complete or polished. In fact, I was afraid Robert would hate it. But, Cath, he actually loves it. I just read you that part, didn't I? 'I absolutely love your new book, Annie. It's warm and compelling and deeply spiritual. Even better—if that's possible—than *Pacific Dawn.*' Isn't that a beautiful thing for him to say?"

Cath nodded, but her mind was on something else. "What about Knowl? How will he feel about Robert Wayne coming here?"

Annie looked puzzled. "I'm sure he'll be pleased for me. Why do you ask?"

Cath's eyes narrowed. "Robert Wayne—wasn't he in love with you? Weren't the two of you close when you were living in California? You told me so, didn't you, Annie? Or am I mistaken?"

Annie twisted a strand of velvet brown hair around her index finger. "Yes, we were close. He helped me with my novel, and he helped me during some hard times.'

"Really?"

"Perhaps you don't remember how it was, Cath. The war was raging. We were all grieving over Chip's death. I thought Knowl was in love with someone else. And you had taken Jenny back. I was devastated, ready to give up on life, and Robert was there for me. We cared about each other." Her tone turned emphatic. "But there was never anything serious between us. He knew I was married. He never would have asked me to violate my wedding vows."

Cath raked her fingers through her short tufts of red hair. Before the surgery she had had long auburn locks as beautiful as Annie's brunette ringlets. "But if you hadn't already been married," she said slowly, measuring her words, "Robert Wayne would have asked you to be his wife. You as much as told me so."

Annie lowered her gaze. "He never said the words, but I know that's how he felt."

Cath sat erect. "Then how can you let him come here, knowing he's in love with you? Knowl will never stand for it."

Annie bristled. "Knowl is a reasonable, caring man—"

Cath's voice rose with the heat of her emotions. "Knowl would be a fool to let that man come here. So would you, Annie."

"I don't see it that way."

Cath wasn't finished. "You left my brother once, and he waited for you. Don't tempt fate again, Annie. Isn't Knowl's love more important than your career?"

Annie came over and put a reassuring hand on Cath's shoulder. "Of course it's more important. But Robert Wayne poses no threat to us, Cath. I love Knowl with all my heart, just as he loves me." A smile touched Annie's lips. "Just wait. You'll like Robert. He can be a very charming man."

Cath jutted out her lower lip. "I'll keep my eye on him."

Annie ran her hand over the slight swell of her abdomen. "There's nothing to worry about, Cath. Knowl and I have never been happier, especially now that we're expecting a baby of our own. Be happy for us."

"I am, Annie." But *happiness* wasn't a word she was familiar with these days.

A rustling sound came from the kitchen, and moments later Anna Reed appeared in the parlor doorway. "Jenny's down for her nap, and I've fixed us a little lunch. Potato cakes, boiled ham, carrot salad, and gingercake with whipped cream."

"Sounds splendid, Mama," said Annie.

"Then come along. You're eating for two now, you know."

"How can I forget? You pamper me too much."

"I enjoy taking care of my girls." Anna's smile took in Cath as well. "I hope you're hungry, Catherine, dear. If you don't start eating, you'll blow away with the first good wind."

Cath stood up. "Yes, Anna. My walk home from the park gave me an appetite."

"Wonderful. Did you bring home a painting for us to hang?"

As they headed for the dining room, Cath replied, "No, I didn't paint anything special." She didn't tell them she had ripped her awkward effort to shreds.

As they ate, Anna Reed outlined her plans for the afternoon. "After the dishes are washed, I'm going to sit down and listen to *Ma Perkins*. Then I'm going to the A&P. Would you make a list, Annie? I've checked the cupboards and I know we need Milk of Magnesia, Lux Flakes, silver polish, and Bromo Seltzer. Kitchen matches, too. What else? My mind's a blank."

Cath looked away. She knew that blank feeling all too well.

"Is there anything you need, Cath?" asked Annie.

She shook her head. She preferred not to tax her mind with the exhausting minutiae of daily life. Making decisions, even small ones, wearied her beyond belief. She could not imagine deciding between sugar cookies or oatmeal, puffed wheat or corn flakes, ring liver or skinless franks.

"Would you like to go with me, Cath?" asked Anna.

"No. I have things to do." A lie. What did she have to do except mope about the house and mourn her life? She might pine over old portraits of Chip, or peruse her portfolio of sketches and lament her lost talent, or try to engage her daughter in play, knowing Jenny would run to Annie for comfort. Cath detested herself for not rising above her circumstances and being strong and brave the way she knew Annie would be. But she wasn't Annie, could never be Annie. Trouble was, these days she didn't even know how to be Cath.

"You might get some Fletchers Castoria," Annie was saying, "and some apple butter, and Fels-Naptha Soap. And maybe some chicken for dinner. Knowl loves your fried chicken."

Anna smiled. "I plan to call him at the office and see if he'll pick me up at the A&P and bring the groceries home."

"I know he will if he's not working late."

Anna smiled knowingly. "Trouble is, most days he does work too late. I know that comes with the job—trying to run a newspaper. But it doesn't give him much time with his family."

"We manage," said Annie with a patient smile.

The phone rang, and Annie went to get it. Cath could hear her talking seriously for several minutes, but she couldn't make out the words. Finally, Annie returned. She was smiling, but there was something forced about her cheerfulness.

"Who was it, dear?" asked Anna.

Annie sat down. "It was the doctor at the sanitarium."

"Is it Mama?" said Cath with concern. "Is she okay?"

Annie put her hand on Catherine's. "Yes, she's fine. In fact—" Annie looked meaningfully from Cath to her mother. "In fact, the doctor says Betty is doing well enough to come home. He's releasing her next week."

"Releasing her?" Cath barely whispered the words.

"Isn't that wonderful news!" said Anna, a bit too brightly. "Did you tell the doctor she's welcome here?"

Annie nodded. "Where else would she go? Her son and daughter are here."

A clammy sensation, like the touch of a cold fish, lodged in Cath's chest. "Mama's coming here—to this house?" she repeated.

"She must come here, Cath. Knowl would never turn his mother away. You know how close they've always been."

Anna agreed. "You and Knowl are her only relatives, Catherine. Except for your father, of course."

"And no one's seen him in years," said Cath under her breath.

Annie poured herself more tea. "It will work out quite nicely. We can fix up the guest room upstairs for her. I'm sure she's changed a great deal since she stopped drinking. Why, you might be pleasantly surprised, Cath."

Cath pushed back her chair and fled the room. She climbed the stairs to the rosebud room and slammed the door. Like a child comforting herself, she sat on the bed and rocked, hugging her arms against her chest. Nausea welled inside her, but after a moment the feeling passed.

She had not seen her mother since the accident, and only seldom before that. What would it be like to live under the same roof with Mama again? Had Mama died in her long, hard struggle to overcome alcoholism the way Catherine had died in the coma? What sort of Phoenix had risen up out of Mama's ashes? Truth was, Cath still didn't know the person struggling up out of her own ashes. So how could these two tender new sprigs coexist without crowding each other out? she wondered.

At dinner that evening, Cath felt like a cat caught in a barbed wire fence. She couldn't sit still, couldn't keep her muscles in check. Her little finger twitched; her limbs felt more awkward and jumpy than usual. She kept waiting for Annie to say something. After all, she had plenty of news to share. Which would she tell Knowl first—about Mama coming home from the sanitarium or about Robert Wayne coming to visit?

Instead, everyone listened attentively as Knowl talked on about world and national affairs. "Truman's got it nailed down," he declared between bites of Anna's fried chicken. "America can't return to a policy of political isolationism. The countries of Europe are lined up at our door waiting for aid, and the Soviets are just waiting to see whom they can pounce on first."

He removed his glasses and rubbed the bridge of his nose, the way he always did when expounding on some new idea. "Besides, there's the bomb to consider now. It changes everything. If we don't assume the role of peacemakers in this chaotic world, you can bet your bottom dollar no one else will do it."

"You're absolutely right, dear," said Annie, sipping her tea.

"It's disgusting what Russia is doing," Anna agreed. "They were our friends as long as they needed our help fighting the Germans. Now that the German threat is gone, *they* become the threat. What terrible irony!"

"Roosevelt and Churchill knew it was an uneasy alliance from the beginning," Knowl told her, "but unity was the priority then. It took all three Allied powers to win the war. But we set ourselves up for—well, who knows what?"

"Truman has high hopes the United Nations will keep the Russians in line," said Anna.

"Fat chance of that." Knowl helped himself to the marmalade. "I think they'll use it as a sounding board for their own propaganda."

Cath shut her ears to the conversation around her. She looked across the table where Jenny sat humming to herself and lining up the peas on her plate. *She's got her own little world too,* Cath mused. *We're alike that way.*

Fred Waring was playing on the console radio in the parlor. The distant melodic strains offered a curious counterpoint to Knowl's deep, animated voice. The whole world was his chess game. Strange how he felt connected to and responsible for everything that happened, whether it was in Poland, Russia, England, or Willowbrook. Maybe being managing editor of the newspaper made him feel so involved, as if what he said or did really mattered in the larger scheme of things.

Other than having the same bloodlines, he and Cath were clearly opposites. Knowl thrived on being part of something greater than himself; he seized a cause and threw himself into it wholeheartedly. Cath, on the other hand, felt detached from her surroundings, even isolated. She had no causes anymore, no grand ambitions, no high and lofty goals to consume her. But then perhaps the old Cath had been different.

Still, what difference did it make to Cath that farm prices were up, or that Truman was frustrated over the Republican victory in Congress, or that tensions were mounting with Russia? There were more pressing matters at hand. Cath's sanctuary was about to be invaded; her life was about to change—again. Change had become the enemy. And people, even those one loved, always had a way of bringing pain.

Cath's reverie dissolved at the sound of Annie's voice, saying, "Knowl—I have something to tell you. We're going to be having some houseguests, dear." She told him first about his mother.

"That's wonderful news," he said, sitting back and inhaling expansively. "Mama's been through some terrible years since Papa walked out on her."

"She drove him away," said Cath. "I remember that much."

"That's not the issue," countered Knowl. "What's important is that we help Mama make a new life for herself." He eyed Cath sharply. "Don't you agree, dear sister?"

She stared at her plate. "I can only handle one new life at a time."

Knowl ignored her sarcasm. "Do whatever's necessary, Annie, to make my mother welcome. She cared a great deal about you, from our first days of marriage when we lived with her."

"We'll all make her welcome," Anna assured him.

"But you said *houseguests*. Who else, Annie?"

A trifle hesitant, she told him about Robert Wayne.

"I had no idea you had sent him your new book. I thought the manuscript was still in a preliminary stage."

"It is, but I felt Robert should see it and give me his direction early on."

Knowl's voice tightened. "You haven't even shown it to me yet."

"You're so busy with the paper, I didn't want to bother you."

"Bother me? With such an important part of your life? Of course I want to read your book, Annie."

"You can, Knowl. You will. Wait till I show you Robert's letter. He loved the manuscript."

"That's splendid." Knowl raised his linen napkin and dabbed at his lips. "Still, I don't see why this fellow must come all the way to Indiana. Can't you handle this editing business through the mail?"

"Robert feels we need to talk personally," said Annie levelly. "He feels it's important for the book."

Watching the exchange, Cath read an undercurrent of intense emotion beneath Annie's calm exterior. *She cares more for Robert Wayne than she chooses to admit. You'll be sorry if you let him come here, Knowl!*

Knowl set his napkin down. "All right, Annie. If you're sure it's necessary, tell Wayne to come along. We'll make a place for him—as long as he doesn't get too comfortable here. Actually, I'm curious to meet this chap who befriended you in California. The two of us will have to have a nice long talk."

Annie laughed.

But Cath didn't feel the least bit like laughing.

3

Early on an overcast Sunday morning in mid-November, Knowl and Annie drove to the sanitarium to pick up Betty Herrick. Cath stayed home with Anna and Jenny and waited, arguing with her pounding heart that this was an ordinary day like any other. She sat at the kitchen table and drew faces on clothespins for her restless daughter. Jenny sat beside her, wearing her new ruffled princess dress and black patent shoes. She knew without question she was not to get dirty. Grandmother Herrick was coming to see her.

"Gamma's coming, Gamma's coming!" Jenny sang over and over, even though it was unlikely she had any memory of Betty Herrick. In her childish delight she seized the tiny wood people and danced them over the oak table top. She sang songs for them and pretended they bopped each other over their clothespin noggins.

Anna busied herself at the stove, baking fresh biscuits, sweet potatoes, and a rolled pork roast. The kitchen smelled heavenly. It felt like a celebration. Christmas or someone's birthday. But Cath wasn't celebrating. Cath was Jenny's age again and waiting shamefaced for her mother to come home and tell her all the wrong she'd done.

"Mama Cath," said Jenny, tugging on her arm, "make more people for me."

Cath moved her fingertips over Jenny's spun-gold curls. "We'd better save some pins for the clothesline."

"No! Make me more people. Please!"

Cath picked up a clothespin and drew a smiling face, then walked the little wood man over to Jenny. "Are you a beautiful fairy princess?" she asked in a deep voice.

"Yes, I am," said Jenny, playing along.

"Well, I'm your Prince Charming," said Cath in her most princely voice, "and I'm going to carry you away to my enchanted castle!" Captured by the magic of the moment, she reached out and gathered Jenny into her arms and pretended to carry her off. Jenny screeched and laughed and struggled to get down.

When Cath released her, Jenny pulled at her dress. "Play some more, play some more."

"Okay, but we can't let you get dirty, sugarplum." In truth, Cath felt breathless with exhilaration. For the first time since the accident, Jenny had allowed her to get close. They had laughed and played together like any mother and daughter. Did Cath dare hope for more, or would Jenny sense her eagerness and retreat? The question remained unanswered, for Catherine heard the door open and looked over at Anna in alarm. "It's them!"

Anna removed her apron and headed for the hallway. Jenny ran after her. Cath followed from a distance.

Knowl and Annie entered the foyer with a plain-faced mite of a woman between them. She wore a gray tweed coat over a cotton print house-dress, scuffed oxfords, and a wool scarf over her short, gray-flecked brown hair. A fine network of lines etched a fleshy road map over the angular contours of her face; long years of fighting the bottle were evident in every line. Betty had always had features too sharp and pointed to be pretty, cheekbones too protruding, a mouth too hard, an expression too insolent and brittle to win friends. But her dark eyes still possessed the spunky snap Cath recognized in her own eyes. There was still fire in the soul—a fire that could warm the heart or blister one's sensibilities, depending on Betty Herrick's mood. Betty greeted Anna politely and smiled down at Jenny. "What a pretty little girl."

"She's mine, Mama," said Cath softly.

Betty met Cath's gaze. "I know. I remember. She looks just like you."

The two embraced awkwardly, then Betty stepped back and studied Cath intently. "We're some pair, nearly killing ourselves off, aren't we? Me with the booze, you in that fast car on the highway."

"It was an accident, Mama. It was raining. The street was slippery."

"I know, daughter." She lifted her hand to Cath's hair. "They're gone—those beautiful curls. Such a shame."

"It was the surgery, but it's growing back, Mama."

She ran her hand over Cath's arm. "And you're so thin, baby. You trying to finish off what the accident didn't do? Like two peas in a pod, aren't we? Stubborn and self-destructive as they come."

Cath winced. "That's all past, Mama."

Knowl stepped forward and took Betty's arm. "Maybe you'd like to go up to your room and freshen up, Mama?"

She squeezed his hand and smiled grimly. "No, son, I'm as fresh as I ever was. A tough old gal. Only now I'm sober."

Annie helped Betty off with her coat. "My mother has fixed a delicious dinner for us, Mother Herrick. She's even set the table with her best china, silver, and crystal. Are you hungry?"

"Famished. That sanitarium food was straight from the pit of—" She looked down at Jenny. "Well, you get the picture." She turned back to Catherine and put her hand on Cath's cheek. "You look dreadful, daughter. Worse than me. I expect to look bad. I'm an old woman who spent too many years boozing it up. You're a young lady with lots of life left in you. Get a little sun. Put on some rouge. Paint your lips. Don't be an old maid all your life."

Cath opened her mouth to reply, but her throat closed tight and her tongue felt like sandpaper. She could already feel that panicky, choking sensation coming over her. She had to escape. If she stayed in the same room with her mother, she'd suffocate for sure!

At dinner, Cath remained silent, turning her gaze to the overhead chandelier or the French doors and the parlor beyond, while the rest of the family chatted about the weather, politics, the war, the changing nation, the changing world. "It's all too much for me to grasp," said Betty, stirring cream into her coffee. "When I entered the sanitarium, we were still at war, Roosevelt was alive, and no one had heard of the atomic bomb."

"A lot has changed since then, Mother Herrick," said Annie, "but give yourself time. You'll catch up with all the news."

"I'm not sure I want to." Betty stared off into space, still stirring her coffee. "I went through my own private hell in the sanitarium, but at least I felt safe there. My routine was set. Nothing changed. Every day was like every other. I didn't think about the world facing its own torment, everything in such an uproar, millions being killed, bombs dropping. None of it was real to me."

"So many terrible things have happened in recent years," said Knowl, "it's hard to make it real for any of us who've lived in relative calm here at home. At the newspaper, I work with headlines every day. It's not easy to keep all the tragedies and crises from becoming just so many statistics. Sometimes I forget that every statistic represents a flesh-and-blood human being."

"Knowl's doing a wonderful job at the newspaper," said Annie. "You'd be very proud of him, Mother Herrick."

Betty looked fondly at Knowl. "I am proud of you, son. I knew you'd make a success of your life. I knew no matter who else disappointed me, I could always count on you."

Like me, Mama—the way I disappointed you? Cath bit her tongue to keep her silence.

"Let's pray that we have a better world now," said Anna, offering Betty more biscuits. "Maybe people have learned their lesson and our children and grandchildren will be able to live in peace."

"On that we all agree," said Knowl, holding up his crystal goblet of ice water. "May we all live in peace!"

Cath stared down at the uneaten food on her plate. *I'll never know peace as long as Mama's in this house.*

When they had finished their ice cream with strawberry sauce, Annie offered to help Betty unpack.

"Thank you, but I'll be fine." She looked over at Cath. "Come sit with me for a spell, daughter, while I settle in."

"Of course, Mama."

"Knowl will take your things up to your room, Mother Herrick," said Annie. "We spruced up the guest room for you. I think you'll be comfortable. I put extra hangers in the closet and fresh paper in the drawers. If there's anything else you need, let me know."

"Don't trouble yourself, Annie. If I need anything, Catherine is here to help me. We'll just go on up."

Cath offered her mother a hand up the stairs and showed her to her room. Betty shuffled over to the bed and fingered the eiderdown quilt, then gazed around with silent scrutiny at the oak dresser with its hurricane lamp and ceramic water pitcher, the frilly lace curtains framing the dormer window, and the colorful braided rug on the polished hardwood floor.

"Small, but pretty," said Betty. She walked over to the matching wicker chairs by the window and sat down. "I declare, I can look out on Honeysuckle Lane and see all those beautiful houses with their fine lawns and magnificent oak trees." She looked at Cath, who had taken the other chair. "When we lived in the house around the corner—do you remember that, Cath, or has that memory been erased too?"

"I remember more than I want to."

"Yes. So can I. When we lived there in that big old drafty house that your father let go to ruin, I always dreamed of living on Honeysuckle Lane. The houses on this street were always so much nicer than those on our street." Betty absently straightened the lace curtain. "Our house seemed like an afterthought compared with the Reeds' house. Isn't it ironic that your brother owns this house now? Just think! It's a Herrick house, not a Reed house. I should take some satisfaction in that."

"Why, Mama? The Reeds, the Herricks—we're all family now."

Betty flashed a deprecating smile. "I know. One big, happy family. Is that how you feel, Cath? Like part of the family?"

"Yes, Mama. Knowl and Annie have been wonderful to me."

"And you're satisfied to live like this—in your brother's home, with your best friend raising your child?"

Cath stood up. "I won't talk about this with you, Mama."

Betty reached out for Cath's wrist. "No, daughter, don't go. I won't bring up the subject again. I didn't mean to hit a nerve. I just thought it must be awfully painful for you here."

Cath sat back down. "I have nowhere else to go, Mama."

"The same as me." Betty laughed mirthlessly. "At least we have something in common for a change."

"Is there anything else you need, Mama? I'd like to go to my own room."

"Yes, there is something else." Betty leaned forward and spoke in a confidential tone. "What do you know about your father?"

"My father?"

"When did you last hear from him?"

Cath shook her head incredulously. "Mama, surely you're not serious."

"I'm dead serious, Catherine. What do you know?"

"Nothing. I haven't seen Papa in years."

"He hasn't been in contact with you or Knowl?"

"No. I don't know where he is. And I don't care."

"Of course you care," snapped Betty. "We all care, more than we'll ever admit. Don't you think it eats at Knowl that his father simply took off and disappeared when you were both so young?"

"We don't talk about it, Mama. Papa is dead to us," Cath said coldly.

Betty pulled at a loose thread on her sleeve. "I thought about your father a great deal in the sanitarium. We made quite a pair, you know. He was a no-good louse; I was a shrew. I turned to alcohol; he turned to other women. I don't recall if we were ever happy, but we were certainly good at inflicting pain on each other."

"That part I remember," said Cath dryly. "But why are you thinking about Papa now? He's part of the past."

"No, Catherine." Betty pushed back a stray wisp of hair. "As I pulled myself up out of that terrible fog bank of alcohol, I kept seeing Tom Herrick, my good-for-nothing husband who drove me to drink. Only thing is, the clearer my mind got, the more I had to face the fact that it wasn't just Tom; it was me too. I drove myself to drink. And when I realized that, I couldn't hate him quite as much as I did before."

"Are you saying you've forgiven Papa for all he did to us?"

"Not by a long shot, daughter. I'm just saying I don't think things will be finished in my mind until I've looked that man in the eye and had it out with him once and for all. I couldn't do that when I was a drunk."

"Papa could be dead for all we know."

"He used to come back to town now and then and stay a spell," said Betty. "He was there for Knowl and Annie's wedding."

"Yes, he was there, but I don't think anyone's seen him since. And I don't want to, Mama. That man abandoned us. He didn't love us enough to be part of our lives. Not even a postcard or a Christmas card in years. He's never seen Jenny. I could have died in the accident, and he never came around."

"What if he came back, Catherine? What would you do?"

Cath gazed solemnly out the window at the tree-lined street. "I'd spit in his face."

4

Robert Wayne came to town three weeks before Christmas, on December 7, the fifth anniversary of Pearl Harbor. The first snow of the season was drifting lazily over Willowbrook when Knowl and Annie drove to the train station to meet him.

Cath stayed home and painted Christmas cards with Jenny, while Betty and Anna made holly wreaths to decorate the windows. The festive ambiance belied the old wounds this anniversary opened, but everyone agreed it was better to look ahead to the holidays than back at painful losses.

Cath was discovering new opportunities to connect with her daughter. Jenny didn't mind that Cath's paintings weren't perfect. She squealed with delight over the fat snowmen, laughing Santas, and smiling angels. Actually, Cath had to admit that she was getting better, gaining greater eye-hand coordination. Amazingly, her talent was returning.

But even that realization didn't erase the gloom she felt this evening. Everyone in the house felt it in spite of the forced frivolity, but no one spoke of it, except in the most rudimentary way. Five years ago today the

Reeds and the Herricks had sat together in this very house enjoying Sunday dinner when the horrifying news came over the radio. Pearl Harbor had been bombed. Chip, who was to have come home in just two weeks to marry Cath, died in the terrible inferno, leaving Cath alone to bear his child—a baby he didn't even know existed. That day shattered all Cath's hopes and dreams and began a series of nightmares that still held her captive. She wondered, Was she doomed to pay for her mistakes for the rest of her life?

Today Cath realized she wasn't grieving alone. Anna Reed, who seemed always to rise above the encumbrances of the day, had shed tears when she supposed no one was looking. But Cath had noticed and paused to squeeze Anna's hand. "Are you thinking of Chip?" she asked.

Anna smiled through her tears. "Yes, dear. My precious Chilton. A mother never forgets."

"Neither will I," said Cath softly.

"Of course we won't. We have Jenny. We'll always see Chilton in her."

Yes, it was true. Even now, as Cath sat painting Christmas cards with Jenny, she could see Chip's features in the turn of her nose and the curve of her chin. And her own features were there, too—the auburn hair and freckles coupled with the stubbornness and fierce independence. Even though Cath and Chip had never wed, perhaps she could take solace in the fact that they were joined forever in the person of Jenny—a marvelous blend of the two of them.

"Mama Cath," said Jenny, holding up a blank card, "paint me baby Jesus."

"I don't know if I can," she stammered. How did one paint deity? Jesus was Annie's God. Cath had always made it clear she wanted no part of a God who played so capriciously with people's lives. Besides, Cath reflected somberly, her earthly father had abandoned her; what assurance did she have that a Heavenly Father wouldn't do the same?

"Paint baby Jesus," Jenny said again, thrusting the card into her hand.

"I'll paint you the way you looked as a little baby," said Cath, "and we'll call it Baby Jesus."

"But I'm a *girl*!" protested Jenny.

"And a very pretty one, my Christmas angel!"

Before Cath could put brush to paper, she heard the front door open. Knowl and Annie had arrived with the infamous Robert Wayne, the man who had nearly cost Knowl his marriage. As she headed for the door, Cath wondered how her brother could allow this roguish interloper to invade his happy home. Obviously, Knowl was too charitable and trusting for his own good.

The three were already in the foyer, stamping snow from their feet and removing hats and coats and galoshes. Annie came forward with Robert in hand. "Cath, this is my good friend and editor, Robert Wayne. Robert, this is Catherine, my dearest childhood friend."

Robert, a big bear of a man with broad shoulders, had a way of filling a room just by entering it, as if a small space couldn't quite contain his wide, exuberant gestures or the long strides he made with just the hint of a limp. He had a head of thick brown hair and a solidly chiseled face. Taking Cath's hand in his, he declared in a deep, resonant voice, "Catherine, I'm delighted to meet you. I've heard so much about you."

"I've heard about you, too, Mr. Wayne," she said coolly, carefully extracting her hand.

"Call me Robert," he said with a generous smile. He was bigger than life, with his square jaw, classically handsome nose and mouth, and shaggy brows perched over expressive sky-blue eyes that read one's very soul.

"Robert, then," Cath murmured, feeling a trifle flustered.

She watched as Annie introduced Robert to the rest of the family. He seemed genuinely pleased to meet each one.

Following introductions, they all headed for the dining room where Anna had set out a tempting evening repast of cold turkey, browned sweet potatoes, and hot cross buns with cranberry jelly. The conversation flowed, punctuated by laughter and gleeful exclamations as Robert Wayne shared scores of personal anecdotes and clever jokes. Clearly, the beguiling Mr. Wayne could enliven any gathering by simply being there and being himself. The idea turned Cath's stomach. She had wanted to hate this man, to find all sorts of flaws in his character, or his looks, or his personality. To her consternation, he evidenced nothing she could hold against him. Surely there were countless defects and blemishes; he was simply skilled at hiding them.

As he finished his rhubarb brown Betty, he looked at Cath and said, "You've been very quiet tonight, Catherine. I hope I haven't monopolized the conversation. If so, please forgive me."

"Even if you had, I had nothing special to contribute," she replied. "Especially today."

"Today?" he echoed.

"I'm sure you realize this is a significant day for our family," noted Annie. "And for you, too, Robert, considering you were wounded at Pearl Harbor."

He rubbed his large hands together and nodded. "I haven't forgotten today, nor my fallen comrades, nor the horrors I experienced that fateful morning. That's probably why I talk too much and laugh too loudly. Forgive me for my fanciful ramblings, but I vowed that day would not sentence me to a life of misery and regret."

"Mr. Wayne," said Anna, "you've lightened the moment for all of us and warmed our hearts. Thank you."

"Indeed," said Knowl. "We could all use a little warmth with winter's chill invading our spirits and our bones!"

"I agree," said Annie, too brightly. "I always know winter has arrived when the milk bottles on the porch pop their lids."

"And they did this morning," said Anna. "Two inches of frozen cream on the top of each bottle. I made Jenny a special treat. Poured a little sugar and vanilla over a mound of cream. She adored it."

"You used to make those treats for Chip and me," said Annie. "I can taste it now—so cold and sweet it made my teeth hurt."

"Those were very precious days," said Anna softly. "My Chilton, your papa, and his papa all filled this house with their laughter." She dabbed at one eye, then pushed back her chair and stood up. "Well, children, why don't you take your coffee into the parlor while Betty and I clear the table?"

Cath reluctantly followed Annie, Knowl, and Robert into the parlor. She didn't want to engage in mindless prattle with this stranger, but she considered it her duty to keep an eye on him for her brother. Knowl, for all his knowledge and intelligence, might miss subtle warning signs, nuances in the conversation between his wife and her charming editor.

The four sat down around the fireplace—Knowl and Annie on the love seat, Robert in the overstuffed chair, Cath in the oak rocker. They talked for a while about Knowl's work at the newspaper and Robert's work at the publishing house.

"Isn't it interesting," said Annie, "that you and Knowl have such different jobs and yet you're both editors."

Knowl smiled wryly. "I love what I do, but what I edit today ends up lining trash baskets or doghouses tomorrow. What you edit lines shelves in libraries for years and years to come."

Robert laughed. "And yet who says either will be read?"

They all chuckled. Annie added, "Yet, we are all vain enough to keep right on writing, no matter who reads us."

"Fortunately," said Robert, "you, Annie, are being read by just about everybody. I wish I could say that about all the books published by Sanders and Browne."

"Is the publishing industry in a slump?" asked Knowl.

"Let's just say these are lean years for publishers and booksellers. Low profits. High prices. People still recovering from the war, trying to get back on track. We're all in the same boat, I suppose." He sipped his coffee. "Of course, classics like Charles Sheldon's *In His Steps* always sell well. And Lloyd Douglas's novels are selling like hotcakes. Too bad Sanders and Browne isn't publishing them."

"Do you think my new book will do well?" asked Annie.

Robert nodded. "Religious themes are experiencing something of a boom right now. I think part of it is anxiety over the bomb. We don't know when someone else might set off another one somewhere—for far less noble reasons than to end a war."

"That's why I wrote my new book," said Annie, "to address the anxiety of our times. I wanted to offer some spiritual guidance by sharing what God has taught me in recent years."

"Speaking of your new book, would it be rushing you to talk about the manuscript tonight?"

"Of course not, Robert," said Annie, her eyes dancing.

Knowl stood up. "I think that's my signal to go tackle my own tasks. I'll let you two work in peace."

Cath held her seat. "I think I'll stay and listen. I'd like to hear about your new book, Annie."

"That's very sweet of you, Cath." Annie moved over to make room for Robert on the love seat.

He sat down and removed her manuscript from his briefcase. "I don't want to present your book to the editorial committee until you and I have a chance to do a thorough edit."

"It needs a lot of work, Robert. I don't know where to go with it from here. It's not quite a novel, and not quite an autobiography."

"It's an honest account of one woman's spiritual odyssey. But you have to decide whether to tell your own story or fictionalize it."

Annie looked helplessly from Catherine to Robert. "I don't know. I don't want to betray the secrets of people I love, and yet I can't tell my own story without involving them."

"Am I in your book?" asked Cath, startled at the idea.

"Yes, Cath. I've changed your name, but—"

"And Jenny? Is she there? And Chip?"

"Yes, in a way. I've disguised all of you, but you're there. You're all part of my life."

"I don't want to be in anybody's book," said Cath, her voice rising shrilly. "It's bad enough that my family and the town know what I've been through. I won't have the whole world—"

"It's not like that, Cath. Most of the book is about my own spiritual journey. I promise, I won't say anything about you unless you approve."

Cath's mouth settled into a pout. "I want to read every word before it's published."

Robert flipped through the manuscript until he found a page he was looking for. "I like the way you captured this Jewish man—Helmut Schwarz—the man at the World's Fair who introduced you to Christ. And I like the way you express what happened that day."

In a deeply expressive voice, Robert read Annie's words. "I had spent a lifetime in church singing hymns and reading Scripture, but not until that moment did I realize Jesus wasn't just a historical figure to believe in, but a living person who wanted to share my life. Helmut introduced me to the living Christ who desired to indwell me and fill me with His passionate, justice-loving, life-changing Holy Spirit. I realized God was offering me a relationship, not just a set of age-old rules to follow. He was giving me Himself and all that came with a victorious, risen Savior—unconditional love, undeserved forgiveness, unfailing companionship, unimaginable resources, unparalleled redemption. And because of that relationship and its transforming power, I would never be the same again."

Robert paused, and there was silence in the room. Catherine stirred. "I should go and let you two work," she said, standing up abruptly. After all, who wanted to hear about all that God had done for Annie? What had He done for Cath, except look the other way when she got into trouble!

That night, Cath had a hard time sleeping. She dozed, then dreamed fitfully. She kept seeing Helmut Schwarz, the Jewish evangelist, and then suddenly it was Jesus's face she saw, and Annie's words rang in her mind: *He was giving me Himself . . . unconditional love, undeserved forgiveness. . . .*

Cath awoke with a start and sat up in bed. Aloud she said, "There's no such thing! God doesn't care about me! If He loves me, why do I hurt so much? Why do I feel so alone?"

Restless, her nerves jumpy, she climbed out of bed, slipped a robe over her nightgown, and padded downstairs to the kitchen for a warm glass of milk. She removed a bottle from the icebox and filled a saucepan. As she warmed the milk on the gas range, she heard a rustling sound behind her. She whirled around to face Robert Wayne in the doorway.

"Hello, Catherine," he said pleasantly. "I see you had the same idea."

Self-consciously, she clasped her bathrobe around her. "If I'd known I was going to see anybody—"

He held up his hands appeasingly. "It's all right. I'm in my pajamas too. And if you wouldn't mind sharing a bit of that milk—"

She caught the pan just as it began to boil. "You like warm milk?"

He grinned. "I must admit, it's seen me through some troubling nights."

"Me, too." Cath poured two glasses and they sat down across from each other. "I could make some toast, if you like."

"No, this is enough, thank you." He sipped his milk, then sat back and studied her carefully. "I have a feeling you weren't too pleased about my visit. Am I right?"

Cath nodded. "Nothing personal, Mr. Way—I mean, Robert."

"What is it?" he asked lightly. "You feel protective toward Annie?"

"I feel protective of my brother. I don't think he realizes the deep bond you and Annie share. I don't think Annie realizes it either, or she wouldn't risk having you here."

"You feel she's risking her marriage?"

"Maybe I just have a suspicious nature."

"What do you think I should do?"

Cath turned her glass between her hands. "I think you should leave Annie and Knowl alone. Go back to New York. Do your editing by mail."

Robert eyed her curiously. "Do you think their marriage is that unstable?"

Cath turned her glass too sharply. The hot milk sloshed out on her hand. She blotted it with a napkin. She felt awkward, uncomfortable. "No, my brother and his wife are very happy together. Annie's expecting Knowl's child next May. They have a very good marriage. I just want it to stay that way."

"So do I," said Robert.

"Do you?" She stared him down. "Can you honestly say you don't love Annie?"

He was silent for a moment, sipping his milk. When he met her gaze again, there was a tenderness in his expression that unnerved her. "Of course I love Annie. I'll always love her. But not the way you think. I have no designs on her, no ulterior motives." He paused, as if debating whether to say more. His voice came out hushed and grave. "So far in my life I have loved two women I cannot have—Annie and another woman I loved before the war."

Cath looked at him, waiting. When he didn't continue, she asked, "What happened?"

He drummed his fingers on the oak table top. "While I was at Pearl

Harbor, she left me for another man. In my grief, I turned to alcohol for consolation, and it nearly destroyed me. I'm sure I'd be dead by now if God hadn't reached down and pulled me up by my bootstraps and turned my life around."

"Is that how you ended up at the mission in California, where you met Annie?"

"Yes. We became good friends there. But I knew she was married, so I assure you I never made improper advances."

Cath eyed him coolly. "But you fell in love with her."

He lowered his gaze. "That I couldn't avoid. But, you see, Catherine, since then, I have decided God wants me to remain single, unencumbered by a woman's love. Therefore, I've promised myself to remain unattached and uninvolved in affairs of the heart. Does that reassure you?"

"It's easy to claim how virtuous you plan to be, but the flesh is weak."

A flicker of amusement crossed Robert's face. "I'm surprised to hear you quoting the Bible, Catherine."

Cath lifted her chin jauntily. "I happen to be an expert in the 'flesh is weak' department."

He smiled at her—a smile that rippled through her like a tickle. "Catherine," he said in his most conspiratorial tone, "it sounds like we have more in common than we ever imagined."

5

Six days after his arrival in Willowbrook, Robert Wayne carried Annie's edited manuscript out the door to Knowl's waiting car. Catherine watched from her bedroom window, more than a little relieved to have him heading back to New York. No matter what he had said about his honorable intentions toward Annie, Cath hadn't missed the extraordinary bond the two shared. Surely Knowl had noticed it too and was no doubt pleased to be delivering Mr. Wayne to the train depot and out of his life for good.

Even as Knowl's vehicle pulled out of the driveway, Cath's irritation lingered. Had Annie been so blind she couldn't see what was happening? Cath had seen it. An undercurrent of mutual attraction had sizzled like electricity between Robert and Annie. Didn't they realize they were playing with fire?

If Annie had grown up in a broken home the way I did, she'd never take such liberties with her marriage, Cath reflected as she dressed in her warmest knit sweater and leggings. She forced the nagging questions about Robert and Annie out of her mind as she went about the room gathering her art supplies. *Think about painting instead!* If the December chill permitted, she would set up her easel on the front porch, and, before the cold turned her fingers numb, she would capture the noble trees on Honeysuckle Lane bejeweled with early morning frost.

A half hour after Knowl left for the train station with Robert, Cath left her room and encountered Annie at the top of the stairs. Annie was carrying an armload of laundry for the wringer washing machine downstairs. Cath had her sketch pad and paint box in hand.

"You missed saying good-bye to Robert this morning," Annie noted with the slightest hint of accusation.

"I'm sure he didn't miss me as long as he had you," Cath replied curtly.

"We just had a quick cup of coffee together," said Annie, "since Knowl had to get to the newspaper early. Robert said to say good-bye to you."

"Did he? I saw him leave. I was watching from my window."

"And you didn't come down to say good-bye?"

"Robert's *your* friend." Cath started down the steps.

Annie followed. "I had hoped he could be your friend, too. Why are you so hostile toward him?"

Catherine paused halfway down the stairs, set her paint box on the step, and turned back to Annie. "Can't you guess?"

Annie paused, a step behind Cath. "No, I can't. You've been mean-spirited all week."

"Maybe I see what you don't see. Robert Wayne is in love with you. How do you think that makes Knowl feel?"

"It's not true. We're only friends. Knowl knows that."

"Then Knowl's naive. He doesn't see what a threat Robert is to your marriage."

"Is that what you believe?" cried Annie.

"Yes, and, in fact, I told him so."

"You told Robert?" Annie sounded incredulous.

"Yes, and he denied everything."

As Cath started back down the stairs, Annie reached out and seized her sleeve. "How could you have done that? You've embarrassed Robert and humiliated me!"

"I was just looking out for you, Annie, but if that's the thanks I get—" Cath jerked her arm away and continued down the stairs.

She would never be quite sure what happened next. Perhaps Annie reached out for Cath again, or lost her balance, or tripped on a step, or stumbled over Cath's paint box on the stairs. All Cath knew was that as she reached the bottom step, she heard a commotion behind her and turned around, and stared in horror as Annie came tumbling down the stairs, her laundry flying every which way, her dressing gown tangled around her legs.

Like a ghastly vision out of a nightmare, Annie lay crumpled on the floor, her torso twisted strangely, her eyes closed as if in sleep, and her chestnut brown ringlets falling like gashes across her pale face.

Catherine bent down as Betty and Anna came running from the kitchen. "Call Dr. Galway," she demanded. "Can't you see Annie's hurt?"

Betty hurried to the telephone while Anna came scurrying to the stairs with a blanket and tucked it around her unconscious daughter. Anna pressed her cheek against Annie's forehead and moaned, "Oh, dear God, my darling baby!"

Betty returned to the stairway, breathless. "The doctor's on his way, and so is Knowl. They say we shouldn't move Annie till they get here."

By the time Knowl arrived, Annie was conscious and insisting, "I don't know what all the fuss is about. I'm perfectly fine."

"Dr. Galway will determine that," said Knowl as he gently massaged her forehead.

It seemed like forever before the graying physician arrived. "My car wouldn't start in this cold weather," he told Cath as he unwound his scarf and removed his overcoat from his corpulent frame. With effort, he stooped down and began examining Annie, murmuring—almost crooning—words of consolation. At last, he motioned for Knowl to carry his wife upstairs to the bedroom. He lumbered up the steps behind them without a word about Annie's condition.

Cath waited outside the bedroom door, telling herself it was enough that Knowl and Anna were in there with Annie. A knot of guilt tightened in her chest. What if Annie blamed her for the accident? And—heaven help her!—what if she was right?

When Dr. Galway finally emerged from Annie's room, he put a reassuring arm around Cath and said, "She's going to be fine. No concussion, no broken bones. Just a nasty bump on the head."

Cath hardly dared voice her next question. "What about the baby?"

Dr. Galway's shaggy brows furrowed. "Too soon to tell. The baby still has a strong heartbeat, but Annie did take quite a tumble. The next day or two should tell the story. Annie's to have complete bed rest. Don't let her tell you otherwise."

After Dr. Galway left, Cath took a pot of hot tea up to Annie. One part of her wanted to flee and never face Annie again, but she knew she must, so she tiptoed into the shadowed room and set the tea service on the antique cherry-wood dresser.

Knowl looked over from the large four-poster bed where he sat holding Annie's hand. "Our girl's feeling better," he told Cath, a bit too brightly. "Doc says she's going to be okay."

"I know. I talked with him in the hall."

Lying in that immense bed, Annie looked pale and fragile as a china doll—and terribly vulnerable to the winds of fate. Silently Cath prayed, *Dear God, don't let anything happen to Annie or her baby!* As she served the tea, she met Annie's gaze and murmured, "I'm so glad you're going to be all right."

"They can't keep us Reed and Herrick girls down, can they?" Annie whispered with a wan smile.

Cath and Knowl kept a vigilant watch over Annie all day, Knowl reading to her by the golden glow of the hurricane lamp, Cath humming mindless tunes or playing the old Victrola, and both of them plying her with steaming chicken broth and hot tea.

By evening, Annie's patience had worn thin. She insisted that everyone stop treating her like an invalid. "I'm fine. By tomorrow morning I'll be up and around and good as new."

Cath went to bed that night feeling encouraged, her fears assuaged. Annie would be okay. This whole terrible incident could be forgotten. But sometime in the dead of night, in the midst of slumber, with her mind still steeped in dreams, she heard a sound that startled her back to wakefulness. A knock on her door. She rose and opened it. It was Annie.

The moon cast a pale shaft of light across Annie's face, illuminating tousled russet curls and gray-green eyes glistening with fear. She swayed in the shadows, nearly doubled over and holding her middle. "Help me, Cath. I'm bleeding."

"The baby?"

"I don't know."

Cath pulled on her robe. "Did you wake Knowl?"

"I don't want him to see me like this." Annie seized Catherine's wrist. "Help me to the bathroom. Then call Dr. Galway!"

Cath gave Annie her arm for support and helped her down the hall. Then she bolted for the stairs, taking the steps two at a time. She stumbled in her haste, her coordination still leaving something to be desired. Her fingers trembling, she dialed the physician's number, bleated the news about Annie, then clambered back upstairs, her chest heaving. "Annie," she whispered against the bathroom door, "Dr. Galway's coming. Are you okay?" She heard a long, low moan. "Annie, talk to me, please!"

When Annie didn't reply, Cath tried the door. It opened. Her heart hammering, she stepped inside. The room was warm with an odd, acrid smell. The single bulb over the mirror etched the room with a pallid glare—the washbasin, claw-foot tub, radiator, commode. It was a scene jarringly surreal, like the ghastly, illogical remnants of a nightmare. Annie stood in her blood-soaked nightgown holding a miniature infant in the palm of her hand. The tiny baby was perfect in every detail, from his rosebud lips to his pale white fingernails. His skin was iridescent as porcelain, revealing a bluish lacework of veins.

"Look, Cath," said Annie in a small, stunned voice. "Knowl's son."

Hours later, as dawn seeped in with its faint, cheerless glow, Cath stirred and stretched aching muscles. Amazing. She was in her own bed and had actually slept. She had been so sure she would never sleep again. Her mind turned swiftly to Annie—to the heartrending image of Knowl embracing Annie in wordless grief. Cath felt a wave of rage and revulsion sweep over her. *It's not fair! They wanted this baby! Oh, God, why would You take it from them? Annie's always been good—not stubborn and willful like me. She's always loved You! How could You do this to her?*

Cath lay still, her heart and mind numb, until she heard others in the household stirring. Anna was probably going to the kitchen to fix breakfast; meals were served on time no matter what crises struck. Cath's own mother would be dressing Jenny in her dungarees and brushing her auburn tresses. She was becoming a more devoted grandmother than she had ever been a mother. And Knowl would be rising and tending to Annie's needs, offering the comfort only a husband could give.

Cath winced. She ought to offer comfort too. Annie was her dearest friend; they had shared a lifetime of heartaches and disappointments. If ever Annie needed her, it was now.

Cath rose and dressed, steeling herself for this unwelcome task. Guilt gnawed her. Emotionally thin, she had scant comfort to give, but from somewhere within herself she would muster the courage to face Annie and help her bear her loss.

With shoulders squared, she padded down the hall to Annie's room and knocked gingerly on the door. When Knowl called, "Come in," she slipped inside, her mouth dry, her breath short.

Annie was sitting up in bed supported by feather pillows, her long hair cascading over her shoulders, her eyes shadowed, her lips ashen, her skin like alabaster. She looked vulnerable as a child. Cath went to her and they embraced. "I'm so sorry, Annie," Cath said brokenly. "It never should have happened. Your baby shouldn't have died."

Annie's chin trembled slightly. "It's no one's fault, Cath. It just happened. I have to accept it as God's will."

Cath stared at her in astonishment. "God's will? Why would God want to take your baby when you love Him so much? It makes no sense!"

"I must trust God even when I can't understand Him, Cath."

Catherine looked over at Knowl standing by the wide dormer window. "Is that how you feel, too? Whatever God wants, He takes, and that makes everything all right?"

Knowl gazed back, his face contorted with pain, his hand gripping the velvet sash on the deep vermilion drapes. "I don't know what to think, Cath, but I know God loves us."

Annie reached for Cath's hand, her eyes glistening with a rare intensity. "Listen, Cath, in these past few hours, I've felt as if Jesus Himself were cradling me in His arms, comforting me. How can I think of death when His Spirit fills me with His love?"

Cath stood up and backed toward the door. Her voice came out shrill and uncontrolled. "I came in here to comfort you, Annie, even though I have no comfort to give. I'm not as forgiving as you. I feel angry. And guilty. I blame God. I blame myself! I feel like someone tore something precious out of my own belly."

Annie's hand was still outstretched. "Cath, please—"

"Why don't you get angry or blame someone, Annie? Blame me! Then maybe I'll feel better. Don't just smile sweetly and talk about God's will!"

"Cath, you don't understand—"

Cath shook her head. "You're right. I'll never understand, Annie. I was a fool to think you needed my help. You've never needed anything in your whole life!"

Cath turned and bolted out the door. As she fled down the stairs she heard Annie calling her name, but she plunged on. She could not cope with Annie's strength in the face of her own weakness. She grabbed a jacket from the coatrack in the foyer and bounded out the door and down the yard to the street. She ran blindly until she reached the woods that lay just beyond the fine estates of Honeysuckle Lane.

For what seemed hours, Cath tramped through snow-covered brush and meandered through a maze of frost-spangled spruce, spiring firs, and gnarled, ice-burdened oaks. She watched her breath make puffy little clouds in the air and felt her tears crystallize on her ruddy, wind-whipped cheeks. The brisk air smelled clean and pine-scented. She leaned down and scooped up a patch of pristine snow and touched it to her tongue. The coldness felt dazzling, invigorating.

Cath walked on, slowing her pace, her ribs tight against her air-hungry lungs. Her ears and jaw ached from the cold, but she refused to turn back. She needed to be alone, needed to stand in this silent wilderness and rant and scream and shake her fist at Almighty God. She stopped in a dusky clearing, surrounded by gnarly, sky-high monoliths of oak and elm, birch and poplar, maple and ash.

She walked over to one young birch and ran her hand over the smooth white bark. Even with numb fingers, she managed to peel back a thin sheet and felt the hard, close-grained wood underneath. That's how her heart felt this moment—hard and cold and impenetrable. She stared up at the slate-gray sky and said aloud, "Why, God? How could You do this to Annie? She loves You with all her heart. How could You take her baby?"

Her words sounded small and feeble; the noise she made was absorbed quickly by nature's vast, soundless expanse. She opened her mouth and formed a scream deep in her throat. The sound rose like a geyser, echoing against trees and brush. She gripped the trunk of the young birch, digging her fingernails into its yielding bark. She screamed until her throat tightened, cutting off sound, then struggled to swallow over the raw, swollen tenderness.

Her eyes felt glassy with unshed tears. What was she doing standing in this hushed, crystalline forest screaming at a God who didn't give a whit how she felt? No matter. She had to tell Him anyway. "Do You hear me, God?" she rasped. "I don't understand! Why Annie? She trusts You. Look at her! She won't even fight back. She calls this God's will. She accepts even this from You!"

The tears spilled out, cold as icicles on Cath's cheeks.

"Well, I can't trust You! You could have kept Annie from falling. You could have protected her baby. Now I'll never know if it was my fault, and I'll never stop feeling guilty." Her voice broke with despair. "After this, how do You expect me to trust You and call You Father? Look what my own father did to me—abandoned me, never loved me, gave me nothing but pain! And You're just like him—cruel and spiteful, taunting me, offering crumbs until I hunger for You, and then snatching everything away!"

Cath brushed away her tears with awkward fingers. "Don't You see, God? I wanted to believe the way Annie does. I wanted to feel Your love the way she feels it. But now You've spoiled everything. Now I'll never believe!"

As snow flurries wafted in the silvery sky, Cath turned around and trudged back home. A darkness of spirit settled over her. It seemed she was forever destined to be alienated from those she most yearned to love—friends, family, and even God.

The moment Cath stepped back into the warmth of the Herrick house, she realized how chilled to the bone she was. It would be a miracle if she didn't contract pneumonia. She warmed herself by the fireplace in the parlor, then prepared a tray of hot tea and biscuits and took it upstairs to Annie.

She found Annie in the nursery sitting in the antique rocker beside an empty crib. She was folding tiny booties and kimonos and placing them neatly in a large white box.

Cath set down the tea service and stared at her. "What are you doing?"

Annie looked up distractedly. "I'm packing away the baby clothes. I won't be needing them now."

Cath strode over and snatched away the box. "This can wait, Annie. You aren't up to—"

"I'm fine, Cath." She took back the box. "I've got to keep busy. I can't just sit around and mourn."

"Then let me help you." Cath picked up an organdy bonnet and placed it in the box.

"That was Jenny's," said Annie. "Remember? So many of these garments were hers. Of course, the dresses and bonnets wouldn't have been suitable for a little boy, but the nighties would have done nicely." She pressed a soft flannel gown against her cheek. "I can still smell the talcum scent of Jenny's skin when she wore this."

"How can you think of Jenny now?" asked Cath.

"It helps. We still have her."

"You'll have other babies, Annie."

"Maybe. But not this one. Not my son."

"You said it was God's will."

"It is." Annie's eyes moistened. "But it still hurts."

"Oh, Annie!" Cath knelt on the braided rug at Annie's feet. She set the white box aside and wrapped her arms around Annie's waist. The two clung to each other. Neither spoke. Neither wept. But against her cheek, Cath could feel the soundless, convulsive sobs in Annie's chest.

The next morning, as a fresh snow shrouded the frozen earth, the Reeds and Herricks gathered in the little cemetery behind the church. Bundled in coats and scarves against the icy chill, they circled the tombstones of Jonathan and Alma Reed and their son Jon, Annie's father. In silence they bowed their heads as old Reverend Henry said a prayer over the little cedar chest that contained the tiny, fragile body of baby Jonathan Herrick. Then in thin, ragged voices they sang "Rock of Ages" while Knowl gently placed his son in the dark cavity he'd gouged out of the frigid, unyielding ground.

6

CHRISTMAS CAME AND went with little fanfare, and on its heels, the new year. Everyone in the Herrick house agreed 1947 would be better than the year before. After all, Cath was nearly completely recovered from her accident, and Knowl and Annie would surely have other children. Just as the nation was healing from the wounds of war, so the Reeds and Herricks were healing from their personal wounds.

Annie threw herself into another rewrite of her book. Knowl became busier than ever at the newspaper, writing editorials about the Cold War, rising prices, the housing shortage, and President Truman's foreign policies. Betty Herrick remained sober and became increasingly attached to little Jenny. Anna Reed fixed delectable meals as usual and ran the household in her gentle, unassuming way. And Cath devoted herself to her art, slowly, laboriously reclaiming the abilities she'd lost in the accident.

As spring arrived, Cath spent more time in the park, setting up her easel and painting the blossoming trees and flowers—plump lilacs and daffodils, bright tulips and orchids, sweet pansies and violets. She savored their fragrances, reveled in their lush, rich colors. She was glad to shake off winter's torpor, glad to be roused from its heavy, paralyzing quiescence. In the heat of the sun, her spirits rallied and her energies were rekindled. Her appetite for life was whetted for the first time since the accident nearly a year ago.

She looked better too. She had put on a few much needed pounds, and her thick auburn locks, shorn mercilessly for the surgery, had finally grown back to shoulder-length tresses. Sometimes Cath painted the children who played in the park or invited a passing couple to pause for a quick sketch. Most people were flattered to pose and pleased when she sent them on their way with a simple watercolor portrait in hand. She considered most of these paintings merely exercises, as a musician might practice the scales until he mastered the dexterity to play Mozart or Beethoven. The paintings themselves were temporary, expendable, of little consequence. It was the control, the deftness, the skillful command over line and brush stroke that she coveted, until talent was hers once again.

But she had lost so much ground. Before the accident she had had more commissions than she could handle. These days, no one clamored at her door. She imagined word of her accident had gotten around, and now people supposed Catherine Herrick was little more than a vegetable, surely no longer an artist to be reckoned with or a painter whose works one might wish to own or display.

"Well, I'll prove them wrong, or die trying!" Cath promised herself each day as she headed for the park. "I'll show the art community and the whole world that I'm as good as I've ever been, maybe better. I'll be on top again, no matter what it takes."

But she wasn't quite there yet. For the most part, her current work showed the facility, the grace, the adroitness of her past work. Before, it took five paintings to produce one she was genuinely proud of; now it took ten. The freedom still wasn't there; her hand still couldn't move with the agility, the litheness, the coordination she needed to release the passions behind the brush. She needed to be more limber!

That was the thought uppermost in her mind the day she spotted the young man watching her from a distance. She had been in the park only a half hour or so and was having trouble getting started. Her fingers felt sluggish and stiff, and the painting—a landscape—looked awkward and childish. The perspective was off, and the shapes were displeasing to the eye. She was about to tear the watercolor paper from her easel when she noticed the stranger. Something about him struck her as curiously familiar—his long lean face, his tall lanky frame, his mop of reddish-brown hair, his intense dark eyes. He wore a beard that made Cath think momentarily of Jesus. Yes, Jesus might have looked like this man. Through the ages, portraits of Jesus had always borne striking similarities—the beard, the hair, the sturdy features, the shape of the head. Was that why this fellow looked so familiar?

Cath looked back at her painting. She felt a trifle flushed and uneasy. Would the man come over and comment on her work? She glanced back in his direction, but the man was gone. His sudden absence stirred an odd sensation in her chest, a knot of alarm, as if a cold hand had tightened around her heart. It was the feeling of a memory that lingers just beyond consciousness, inspiring a sense of dread without divulging the reason. *An absurd reaction,* mused Cath, and she quickly chided herself for her foolishness.

The next day Cath saw the man again. He was wearing the same rumpled brown jacket and denim trousers. This time, she forced her gaze to meet his. To her surprise, he ambled over and looked at her painting. "Nice job," he said in a voice that was masculine and lyrical at once.

"Thank you."

He shifted his stance, his hands in his jacket pockets. "I seen you here before."

"I know," said Cath, dabbing at her palette. "I saw you watching me."

"Didn't mean to stare. It's just—you looked like someone."

"Someone you know?"

"Someone I thought I knew. But I was wrong. We never met."

She squinted as the sun hit her eyes. "Are you from Willowbrook?"

He glanced around, as if he needed to see the area again before deciding if it was his home. "No, I'm not from these parts," he drawled.

"I didn't think so." She continued painting while he watched, silent.

Finally he said, "I bet you could paint me real good."

The challenge of capturing the sullen, enigmatic quality of his face intrigued her. "All right," she said. "But you'll have to sit still for a half hour."

"I'll be still as a mouse." He sat down on an iron bench a few feet from her easel and stretched his arms expansively along the back of the seat. He crossed one muscular leg over the other in a confident, take-charge gesture. He could have been a cowboy, with his leather boots showing an Indian design burned into the rawhide. But this was Indiana, so Cath suspected he was a farmer, a migrant worker, or a day laborer, not a cowpoke riding the range.

She fastened a clean sheet of paper on her drawing board and propped it on the easel, then blended raw umber and ultramarine blue on her palette and mixed in a few drops of water. She turned her attention to the man's face, seeing it with an artist's eye. The high, wide forehead under a thatch of unruly hair. The narrow face and prominent cheekbones. The solid jaw under a neatly trimmed red beard. A full lower lip that had settled into a permanent pout. The sharply chiseled nose and thick brows crouching over riveting dark eyes. Cath guessed he was in his early twenties, but his hands were large and calloused from years of manual labor.

"Turn your face to the left and tilt your chin up," said Cath. "That's it. Now don't move until I say."

A wry smile turned up one corner of his mouth, and his eyes twinkled. "Okay if I breathe?"

Cath smiled back. "I'd say no, but I lose more models that way."

He chuckled. "I bet you do."

As she laid in the broad strokes, making sharp, incisive lines, then adding shadows with a light wash, she could feel her excitement building. She was responding creatively to this man—his face, his features, the riddle of the man behind the eyes. This painting would be the one in ten!

When she had finished, she stepped back and scrutinized her work. She felt heady, euphoric. Her old confidence was back. At last, she was at her best again.

The man stood up and flexed his muscles, then ambled over to examine his portrait. "You're good," he said, and whistled. "Good as they get. You somebody famous?"

I used to be, she thought ruefully. "I'm Catherine Herrick. My friends call me Cath."

"Okay. Cath it is." She noticed something shift slightly in his eyes, a shrewd, knowing expression. "Me—I'm Luke. Luke Henry." He reached for the painting. "Can I keep this?"

She held it fast. "I'm sorry. Usually I'd say yes. But I'd really like to keep this one." When she saw disappointment darken his eyes, she said quickly, "But I'll do another one tomorrow if you're still in town."

He moved his jaw thoughtfully, as if he were chewing something. "Sure. I'll be in town a few more days."

"Are you here on business?" she asked, silently scolding herself. She was already violating her "no questions" policy for the sake of a man she simply had to paint again.

"Business? Guess you could say so. I'm working on them new ticky-tacky houses out by the highway."

"You're a carpenter?"

He nodded. "I mostly do the framing."

"That's an important job. Houses are in such short supply these days."

"But those houses are cracker boxes." He made a square with his hands. "All alike, all in a row. All the soldier boys who came home from the war are buying them for their brides." He looked around appraisingly. "They're not like the houses in this neighborhood. These houses got real character. Each one's an original."

"People can't afford big houses anymore," said Cath. "Especially returning servicemen. Even if they could, there are so few elegant old houses left."

Luke turned his gaze toward Honeysuckle Lane. "Bet it would be real nice living in one of them big fancy houses." His eyes drilled hers. "Is that where you live, Cath?"

She felt the hairs on the back of her neck bristle. "Yes," she said in a small voice. She began packing her supplies.

He folded her easel and handed it to her, his hand lingering on hers for a long moment, until she pulled away. "I'll be here tomorrow, Cath," he told her. "I'm glad we met."

She flushed. Each word felt strangely like an embrace.

"I'll try to make it," she said, her discomfiture growing.

She walked home feeling dazzled and distracted. She couldn't get Luke Henry out of her mind. In her imagination she was still sketching him, tracing the sturdy line of his jaw, his chiseled profile, the cryptic expression in his eyes. Who was he? And why did he unnerve her and fascinate her so much?

When Cath arrived home, she found Reverend Henry visiting Anna and Annie in the parlor. He rose and greeted Cath warmly, explaining in his mellow voice, "I'm just paying a social call. Thought you all might have some ideas how we could spruce up the church a bit. That building's stood its ground since 1910, and it's showing its age—same as me." He chuckled to himself, then added, "We've got to appeal to the young folk these days. We need some color and excitement."

"The walls are awfully drab," said Anna. "Maybe a good scrubbing or a little paint—"

Cath set down her art paraphernalia and took the wing chair by the window. "If you want to add color and interest, why don't you have someone paint a mural in the vestibule?"

"That's a wonderful idea," said Annie, "and it would certainly be cheaper than remodeling the church."

Reverend Henry's mottled forehead rippled into a frown. "A mural? Yes, indeed, an idea an artist would certainly think of." His gray, stubbly brows arched. "Are you interested, Catherine?"

"Interested? In painting a mural for the church?"

"Why not? You suggested it."

"It was just an idea off the top of my head," she stammered. "Reverend Henry, you know I'm not a religious person. I hardly ever attend services."

He smiled tolerantly. "But the good Lord gave you a marvelous talent, Catherine. I'm sure He'd be pleased if you used a bit of it to make His house a more attractive place."

Cath shifted uneasily. She considered excusing herself and racing upstairs, but it was too late. She was trapped.

"If not a mural, then I'm sure the congregation wouldn't mind if we took up an extra collection or two to purchase some of your paintings." Reverend Henry paused, his jowls sagging. "Or perhaps I'm a foolish old man. Your work must bring quite a price in the marketplace."

"That's not it," Cath said quickly. "I wouldn't take any money. It's just that I have nothing suitable—" Her voice dropped. "—for a church."

Reverend Henry drummed his thick, stubby fingers on the tufted armrest. "But you will think about it, won't you?"

"Yes, of course," she said lamely. In desperation, she changed the subject. "It just occurred to me, Reverend Henry, that I met someone today who may be related to you."

"Really? Who was it?"

"A man named Luke Henry. He's from out of town."

"Did he say he knew me?"

"I didn't ask him."

The reverend's eyes twinkled and his cheeks reddened. "If he's short and squat like me, we must be related!"

"Actually, he's a tall man. I did a painting of him." Cath opened her sketch book and held up the watercolor rendering. For a long moment everyone gazed at it in absolute silence. Did they like it? Hate it? Finally Cath blurted, "It was rather hurried, of course."

Reverend Henry stood up and examined the portrait more closely. "It's incredible! Do you all see it? He has the features of Jesus!"

"Yes, I saw the resemblance the moment I met him," Cath admitted. "Of course, he's nothing like Jesus—uh, what you would imagine Jesus to be. But the physical resemblance is striking."

Reverend Henry went over and placed his hands squarely on Cath's shoulders. "Would you consider painting a series of panels showing the life of Christ? This man could be your model."

Cath shook her head, flustered. "I'm not sure I'll ever see the man again."

"You don't know where he lives?" asked Anna.

———

"No, not even the town." Flushing, she said, "He did agree to pose for me tomorrow. We're to meet in the park, but he may not even show up."

"Oh, he will show up," said Reverend Henry with a knowing smile. "God will not let him get away."

"That still doesn't mean I'll paint the panels," said Cath. "It wouldn't be right for me to attempt to paint deity when I'm not a believer. . . ."

"Perhaps you believe more than you think you do, Catherine," said the reverend as he examined the portrait again. "There is much more here in this painting than the face of a mere man. You have tapped into something deep inside yourself, my dear, and it shows in your work."

Cath took the painting from him. "I think you see what you want to see," she replied softly.

He caught her slim hand gently in his large, gnarled fingers. "Just tell me you'll consider doing the panels, Catherine, and I will leave it with our good Lord."

She met Anna's gaze, then Annie's. They were both watching her expectantly. She looked back at the kindly, rumpled old minister. "I'll consider it, Reverend Henry. But I'm making no promises."

7

T HE NEXT MORNING Catherine was almost reluctant to return to the park, afraid she would encounter Luke Henry, afraid she wouldn't. She had no desire to paint the life of Christ for Reverend Henry, yet she yearned to her very bones to paint the young stranger again.

She had been painting less than an hour when she spotted him approaching in his slouching swagger, his hands in his pockets, a cryptic expression in his dark eyes.

"I wasn't sure you'd come back," she said, looking up at him with a half smile.

"I should be working," he said solemnly.

"I could pay you for posing for me."

"Naw. I don't want your money. I'll pose for the heck of it."

"You will? That's swell!" She released a full smile. "Why don't we pick up where we left off yesterday."

He sat down on the iron bench. "Remember, I get to keep this one."

"Yes, as long as you let me paint several more."

His eyes narrowed curiously. "Whatcha gonna do with them? I mean, who wants paintings of me?"

Cath considered telling him about Reverend Henry's request. Why not? So she told him, and his reaction was what she might have predicted.

"Jesus? Some preacher wants me to be Jesus? You gotta be kidding!"

"It's your beard and rugged classic features," she explained. "There's nothing mystical about it. You look the way people imagine Jesus to have looked."

He sat back and chuckled. "I never been to church a day in my life, and now people say I look like Jesus. If that ain't something!"

Cath began sketching him with a light watercolor wash. She shouldn't have told him about Reverend Henry's idea. It was too preposterous—and too distracting. She would try another tactic. "It's quite a coincidence," she began.

He looked at her. "What's a coincidence?"

"That you and the reverend have the same last name. Henry. I asked him if he knew you, but he said no. I thought you might be related."

"No, we don't have no preachers in the family, that's for sure."

"No relatives at all in Willowbrook?" she asked.

His brows lowered, shadowing his eyes. "Who wants to know?"

"Just me," she said quickly. "I was curious about what would bring you to Willowbrook from—where did you say you're from?"

His expression remained sullen. "I didn't say. I'm a good ol' Hoosier boy, that's all you need to know."

That sense of unease that had shaken Cath yesterday came flooding back. At moments like this there was something sinister about Luke Henry, and yet just as unexpectedly she would find herself feeling something else for him—a puzzling familiarity, as if she had known him before, or known him always.

What was this disconcerting connection? Was she attracted to him as a woman for a man? No, it was more than physical. It was something that plumbed the depths of her very soul, a sensation so compelling it went beyond words. From somewhere within herself, she understood that, were her passions unbridled, she could love this man or hate him with equal ferocity.

He was watching her, even as she watched him, her brush moving fluidly to capture his image on paper. What was he thinking as he stared at her with those dark brooding eyes?

The questions faded as she became caught up in her work. No model had ever inspired her the way Luke Henry did. Within a half hour she finished the painting and handed it to him. He uttered an exclamation of approval, then gave it back and asked her to sign her name. He stretched for a few minutes and walked out the kinks in his legs, and finally sat down for another portrait.

Cath painted all afternoon, until she was weak with hunger and weariness. She considered inviting Luke home to dinner, then thought better of the idea. It was, after all, Knowl and Annie's house, and Luke was still virtually a stranger. But another thought occurred to her. "Next time, would you like to pose somewhere else?" she asked him. "There's a shed behind the house my brother made into a little studio for me. I paint there sometimes, especially if I'm using oils. It keeps the turpentine smells out of the house."

Luke seemed to have heard only one thing she said. "Your brother?" he repeated, drawing the words out meaningfully.

"Yes. I think I mentioned I live with my brother. Or perhaps I didn't."

"What's his name?" asked Luke, his gaze fixed on her.

"Knowl. Knowl Herrick. He's the managing editor of the *Willowbrook News*."

"Never heard of him."

"He's a wonderful man. I don't know how I would have survived these past few years without him."

"Don't you have parents?" asked Luke. He had moved slightly, changing the angle of his face. Cath stepped forward unthinkingly and turned his chin back to her. He jumped at her touch.

"I'm sorry. You moved. There. That's better."

"You didn't answer me," he said with a hint of accusation.

"Oh, yes, my parents," she said dryly, stalling. Did she dare reveal bits of her life to this man? Then again, wasn't she put off by *his* secretive manner? If she confided a few harmless details, perhaps he would do the same. "My parents divorced when I was young," she said with as little emotion as she could manage. "My mother lives with us now. She was, uh, ill for a long while. My father—I'm afraid I haven't seen him in years."

"You sound bitter."

"I suppose I am. It's not easy growing up without a father."

"Where is he?"

She shrugged. "I don't know. Maybe he's dead by now." The old rage was resurfacing. She couldn't paint when those ancient animosities ravaged her creativity. "I asked you about coming to my studio to pose," she said curtly. "Are you interested?"

"What's wrong with meeting here in the park?"

"Nothing, if that's what you prefer."

"Or you could come to my place," he drawled with a wink.

"Your place?"

"I'm renting a room in a brownstone a few blocks from here."

"No, the park will be fine." She painted in silence for a while. Finally she ventured, "What about you? Do you have family?"

He nodded.

"Brothers? Sisters?" she asked offhandedly.

"A sister."

"You're lucky," said Cath. "I always wanted a sister."

"Did you now?" mused Luke. She couldn't tell how he meant it. Was he mocking her? Taunting her?

"You're a strange one," she told him, her irritation growing. "You act like you have something more to say, and yet you're so—so secretive."

Luke sat forward and drilled her with his gaze. The hard intensity in his eyes stole her breath. "I could tell you things, Catherine, that would curdle your blood," he said in a low, mesmerizing voice. "Oh, I could tell you things—!"

"I'd better get home." She stood up and tossed tubes of watercolor into her paint box and barely rinsed out her brushes. Her fingers felt suddenly awkward and stiff. She dropped several tubes of paint in the grass and bent to retrieve them, but Luke grabbed them up first. He dropped them one by one into her open palms.

"Tomorrow?" he said as if that one word said everything.

"I don't know," said Cath. How long could she tolerate this unconventional man and his unsettling behavior? "I'll see," she said. She gathered her supplies, turned on her heel and started for home. Even when Luke called after her, she didn't look back.

Oh, for the peaceful sanctuary of the Herrick house!

When she arrived home, Annie greeted her at the door bursting with excitement. "Look, a letter from Robert!" She waved the envelope at Cath. "After all these months he's returning to Willowbrook. Coming on the train this weekend."

Cath gazed back without comprehension. "Why?"

Annie chuckled mirthfully. "Goodness, don't you know, dear Cath? He's coming to talk about my new book. He must be bringing a contract!"

"A contract?"

"Yes, silly." Annie clasped Cath's arm. "Robert's tried to get my book to committee for months, but there were always delays. The wait has been excruciating. Now it's over. Robert wouldn't be coming to see me unless they had made a decision."

"I'm glad for you, Annie." Cath knew she sounded distracted, unconvincing. She couldn't help it. She was still reeling from the heady impact of the inscrutable Luke Henry. She darted past Annie and headed for the back porch with her art materials.

Annie followed, the words spilling out about Robert Wayne and her new book. Finally she paused and said self-consciously, "I'm sorry, Cath. I'm so excited about my good news, I forgot to ask how your painting went. Did your Mr. Luke Henry show up?"

"He's not my Luke Henry," snapped Cath.

Annie retreated. "I'm sorry, I didn't mean—"

"No, I'm sorry," said Cath. "He showed up, and I got some marvelous paintings, but the man is so—so different from anyone I've ever met."

"Different? How?"

Cath shook her head. "That's the trouble. I don't know. At times he makes me feel ill at ease, uncomfortable, and yet, when I'm painting him it's as if I were born to paint him."

Annie looked down at the sketch pad. "Let me see."

Cath showed her the watercolor sketches. She knew by Annie's reaction that they were good, better than good.

"These are your best work ever. Even better than your work before the accident. Oh, Cath," Annie implored, "you've just got to do the panels for Reverend Henry."

She ignored Annie's impassioned plea and lined up the paintings to dry beside the large black portfolio that held her best work. Arguing about the matter would just produce hard feelings. When she had put away her paint box and easel, she turned to Annie and asked pointedly, "Have you told Knowl that Robert Wayne is coming to town?"

"No, but I know he'll be excited for me."

Cath didn't reply. Silently she fumed, *The last thing the Herrick house needs is another visit from Robert Wayne!*

Robert arrived on Saturday just before dinnertime. From the bay window Cath saw the taxi pull up in front of the house. She watched the huge lumberjack of a man emerge, unravel to his full height, pick up his leather valise, and stride to the door. He looked entirely too rakish and cavalier in his double-breasted gray flannel suit and swank oxfords. How long would Annie be able to resist his masculine charms? During his last visit he had told Cath he had no designs on Annie and that he intended to live out his life as a bachelor. It was a preposterous claim for a man who exuded such sensuality and virility.

Cath thought about her dear brother Knowl. By comparison, he was lean and lanky with the graceful, sensitive features of a poet. Indeed, he was handsome, but he didn't possess the brawny vitality of Robert Wayne. Cath couldn't help but wonder, *Did Annie notice the contrast and find Knowl wanting?*

Robert was at the door now, knocking soundly. Where was everyone? Betty and Anna were in the kitchen, no doubt, and Annie was probably upstairs dressing Jenny in her best seersucker pinafore.

Reluctantly Cath went to the door and opened it, forcing a brittle smile in place. "Hello, Robert," she said in her most polite tone.

"Hello, Catherine." He stepped inside, set down his suitcase, and enveloped her in his muscular arms before she could utter a word of protest. His massive warmth and the spicy fragrance of his skin stirred something deep within her. For one absurd instant she wished he would hold her like this forever. But just as quickly he released her and offered a tantalizing smile. "Look at you, Catherine," he said in his suavest voice, "you're lovelier than ever. Your hair——!"

Self-consciously she touched her thick, burnished curls and murmured, "It's grown back fully since my surgery."

He winked at her and said confidentially, "I hope this visit we can be friends."

She ignored his remark and said instead, "Come along to the parlor. I'll go get Annie."

He reached out and seized her hand. She turned in alarm. "Wait, Catherine," he said in almost a whisper. "I don't have good news for Annie. She's going to need your encouragement and support."

"What's wrong?"

He put his finger to his lips as if they shared a secret. "You'll find out in due time."

Before Cath could question him further, Annie entered the room with little Jenny. "Robert," she said in pleased surprise, "I didn't realize you'd arrived!"

Cath watched as the two embraced. Robert was an exuberant, demonstrative man. Embraces meant nothing to him, Cath told herself. Just because she had felt something a moment ago in his arms didn't mean he felt it too.

Anna and Betty appeared then, both wearing aprons over their cotton dresses, their faces flushed with kitchen heat. Anna welcomed Robert's greeting; Betty held back and merely nodded a subdued hello. *That's my mother,* Cath mused silently. *Just as suspicious of a man's attentions as I am, thanks to dear ol' Papa. Give him a chance and any man will be as fickle and philandering as Tom Herrick; they'll all break your heart. Robert Wayne's no exception!*

Of course, her darling Chip hadn't intended to break her heart, Cath reminded herself. He had simply convinced her that being engaged gave them the right to express their love freely. He couldn't have known he would die at Pearl Harbor and leave her alone to bear their child in disgrace. He hadn't meant to hurt her, but the wound still festered, especially during the lonely hours of the night when she still longed for his arms. But in spite of everything Chip Reed had been a good man!

And her dear brother Knowl was a good man too, Cath acknowledged. Look how long he waited after Annie ran off to California. Nearly two years. He could have had any woman, especially Annie's older sister, Alice Marie, but he remained faithful, convinced Annie would come back. And, of course, she had. But Knowl was still too trusting for his own good.

"Knowl wanted to be here," Annie was saying.

Cath started at the mention of her brother's name. Her mind had wandered and the conversation had moved on without her. She looked quizzically at Annie. "What about Knowl?"

"I was just saying he has to work late. He won't be here for dinner. He sends his regrets."

"Then may I escort you to the table?" asked Robert, offering Annie his arm.

Cath followed sullenly and took her seat across from them. For Knowl's sake—and Annie's—she would continue to keep her eye on Robert Wayne.

"You've outdone yourselves, ladies!" Robert declared as he helped himself to a slice of roast pork. "This is the best meal I've had since—well, since my last visit! The life of a bachelor leaves something to be desired when it comes to the culinary arts. My sweet potatoes and carrots never turn out this good!"

"You underrate yourself, Robert," protested Annie. "Look at all the meals you helped prepare at the mission. You spent half your time in the kitchen."

He chuckled self-deprecatingly. "I could throw together a kettle of beef stew that tasted a bit like shoe leather, but I never managed a succulent masterpiece like this pork roast."

Cath eyed Robert shrewdly. "Your life in New York must be quite different from your life in California."

He nodded. "I'm happy being back behind my editorial desk, but I regard those few years of work at the mission as some of the best of my life." He cast a fleeting glance at Annie—a look Cath duly noted.

For the rest of the meal Robert kept the conversation lively and festive, sharing fascinating tidbits and humorous anecdotes about life in the Big Apple. The mood at the table remained light and convivial—until Annie asked Robert about her book.

Suddenly his expression clouded. He met Cath's gaze and she remembered his warning, *I don't bring good news.*

"Did you hear me, Robert?" Annie pressed. "You haven't said a word about my book since you got here. I know you've come with news. I can't wait another minute."

He wiped a dab of apricot souffle from his mouth with his linen napkin. "I thought we could wait until after dinner to talk business."

Annie laughed. "Robert, you know full well this isn't business. This is my *life*! I'm dying to know what the committee decided."

Robert took in a deep breath and cleared his throat the way one does out of nervousness rather than necessity. "I'm sorry, Annie," he replied, "but the committee rejected your book."

Annie stared back dumbfounded. Cath waited. No one moved. Finally Annie found her voice and exclaimed, "You mean they want me to do another rewrite?"

Robert lowered his gaze. "No, Annie. I'm sorry. They don't want to publish the book at all."

The tendons in Annie's neck tightened; her eyes were wide with disbelief. "Why wouldn't they want to publish it, Robert? Look how well *Pacific Dawn* has done for them. It was on the Best-Sellers list for months."

Robert nodded. "I know, Annie. It did very well, especially since it was a first novel from an unknown writer."

Tears beaded in Annie's eyes. "Well, I'm not unknown now. Any publisher should be happy to publish my second novel! You yourself said it's as good as the first, if not better!"

"I know, Annie. It's a fine novel."

"Then why?" Tears spilled down Annie's cheeks.

Cath watched with growing discomfort. Now she understood why Robert had wanted to give Annie this news in private. She reached across the table and patted Annie's hand. "It'll be okay. There are lots of other publishers around."

"You haven't answered me, Robert," Annie persisted. "Why did Sanders and Browne reject my manuscript?"

Robert shifted uncomfortably. "The marketing people feel it presents an intensely personal religious theme that will attract a limited readership."

"But what about Lloyd C. Douglas? *The Robe* is certainly a religious novel."

"Also historical. That makes a difference." He sighed. "The publishing industry is facing some lean times since the war ended. They're going with established names—Sinclair Lewis, Taylor Caldwell, Robert Penn Warren."

"But I thought I'd established my name."

"Yes, but to be honest, Annie, sales have fallen since you cut short your promotion tour last year."

"I had to come home, Robert. You know that. And once I'd come back here, I couldn't leave Knowl again."

"Of course not," Robert agreed. "But the publishing industry is a fickle mistress."

"You mean one day you're on top and the next day no one has heard of you?" Annie's voice was thick with sarcasm.

"I'm afraid there's a good deal of truth in that observation," Robert conceded.

Annie gazed around the table, her lower lip quivering. "Then Cath is right. I'll simply have to find another publisher."

"I've already tried that, Annie."

She stared at him. "What do you mean, Robert?"

"I took the liberty of showing your manuscript to several of my colleagues at other houses: Macmillan, Scribners, Knopf, Viking Press. They all agreed your novel wasn't right for their houses."

Annie's expression looked as if it might shatter. "Robert, if they all say my book is unpublishable, what other options do I have?"

"You could publish it yourself," said Cath. "That would show them."

Annie laughed grimly through her tears. "Oh, yes, that would certainly show everyone! But I'm not about to resort to vanity publishing just to soothe my bruised ego!" She pushed back her chair and stood up.

"Wait, Annie," said Robert, clasping her wrist. "Catherine has a point. For this book, self-publishing may be your answer."

"Don't throw me crumbs, Robert!" Annie broke his hold and stepped back from the table. "Excuse me, everyone. I'm sorry. I would just like to be alone for a while."

They watched in silence as Annie hurried out of the dining room. For a long moment they exchanged helpless glances. Finally Cath said, "I've got to go talk to her."

"Go ahead," said Anna. "If anyone can help her, it's you."

Cath went upstairs and knocked on Annie's door. When there was no answer, she slipped inside anyway. Annie was sitting on her four-poster bed weeping.

Cath sat down beside her and remained silent for a time. She gazed around at the dark, sturdy furniture that gave the room a feeling of permanence and stability—the tall cherry-wood armoire in the corner, the antique writing desk silhouetted against the pale primrose wallpaper, the little curio cabinet that held Annie's collection of porcelain dolls they had played with as children.

For a moment, it was as if all the years between had dissolved and Cath and Annie were still sitting on Annie's bed making the blood pact that would bind them forever as best friends. *We, Catherine Herrick and Elizabeth Anne Reed, promise to be best friends forever, and to never like anyone else better, or may heaven strike us dead on the spot.*

But this wasn't 1932. And they weren't little girls anymore. Hurts and disappointments could no longer be remedied by mercurial childhood promises.

After a while Annie dried her tears and gazed at Cath with a rare desolation in her eyes. "It hurts so much," she murmured. "I just can't deal with another loss right now."

"I know."

Annie sniffed. "Tell me I'm being foolish. I shouldn't let this hit me so hard."

"You're not foolish," said Cath. "Your writing means as much to you as my art means to me. After the accident, when I thought I'd lost my talent, I wanted to die."

"It's not just the book," said Annie. "At first it was. The thought of it not being published left me feeling devastated." She hugged a lace-trimmed pillow against her chest. "But suddenly I realized I was crying for something else."

Cath studied her with concern. "What do you mean?"

"Oh, Cath, I was crying for my baby! It's been months since the miscarriage. I thought the grief was past. But suddenly here it is again, as fresh and piercing as if it had just happened."

Cath drew Annie close. "I'm sorry." *Did Annie still blame her? Would Cath ever stop feeling guilty?*

"Why is this happening to me?" Annie asked imploringly. "Why has the pain flooded back? I was managing so well."

"Grief can't be managed," said Cath, groping for the right words. "It just is. It's capricious, ruthless, unpredictable. You just have to plow through it and take it as it comes. I—I learned that when Chip died."

"Yes, that ache is still there too—dear Chip, my only brother." Annie pressed the lacy pillow against her cheek. "Life is strange, isn't it—the way one disappointment triggers old wounds? You think you're walking above it all, and then suddenly you trip and fall into a bottomless pit."

Cath squeezed Annie's hand. "Sometimes I've wondered whether you felt pain the way I do. I guess maybe I thought you were impervious to it all."

"How can you say that, Cath?"

"The way you talk about God always being there for you. You seem to take everything as His will."

"He is there offering comfort," Annie conceded, "but He doesn't spare me pain. How could I expect Him to, when He didn't spare His own Son?"

Cath released Annie and stood up. "Are you going to be okay?"

Annie nodded and even managed a glimmering smile. "I will be, Cath, after I've spent some time alone with Jesus."

Cath walked to the door and hesitated. "If you need anything, let me know." She slipped out without waiting for a reply, feeling mildly disappointed. Why wasn't her consolation enough for Annie? Why did Annie turn every event into a spiritual issue? One thing Cath knew for sure. There was no way she could compete with Annie's Jesus.

70

8

"Let's go on a picnic after church!"

Everyone at the breakfast table stared at Anna in surprise. "A picnic, Mama?" echoed Annie, setting down her china teacup.

"Why not? It's a lovely spring day. Why not treat Robert to a little of our Indiana sunshine? Besides, it would be good for you to get out and forget about your book."

Annie smiled tolerantly at her mother. "Now we know your real reason. You think a picnic will cheer me up."

"Won't it, dear?"

"You know me too well, Mama."

"Well, I think it's a wonderful idea," said Cath, swallowing a mouthful of scrambled eggs. "I may even do a little painting."

"Then it's settled," said Knowl. "Right after church Robert and I will pack the car while you ladies pack the picnic basket."

But after church the sunshine had given way to a cloudy sky.

"What do you think?" asked Knowl as he headed his Dodge sedan home toward Honeysuckle Lane. "Is it going to rain?"

"No," said Cath from the backseat. "It could stay cloudy like this all day without a drop of rain. Let's go on our picnic!"

Jenny clapped her hands and squealed, "Picnic! Picnic!"

"That settles it," said Annie. "Let's go home and get packed!"

Within the hour they were on their way, headed north out of Willowbrook. The gravel road cut a flinty swath through rolling honey-gold meadows and vales of undulating grass as green as shamrocks. After passing miles of ochre cornfields, quaint farmhouses, and cattle-grazing pasturelands, Knowl turned onto a dirt road that led into a thick grove of birch, white poplar, and bigleaf maple. "We're not far from Sawyer's Bend," he told Robert.

"Sawyer's Bend?"

"It's a rustic farming community surrounded by lush woodlands. Watch for Amish farmers trotting along the road in their horse-drawn buggies."

"Sawyer's Bend has some of the most picturesque scenery in this part of the state," said Annie. "Weeping willows sway over a meandering creek that feeds into the Tippecanoe River. It's lovely."

"And so is your way of describing it," said Robert.

"Annie, forever the poet," said Cath.

Knowl pulled over to the side of the road and stopped beside a cozy arbor bursting with wildflowers the color of amethyst. Everyone piled out of the sedan, stretched their legs, and breathed in the sweet country air.

Robert and Annie carried blankets and a heaping straw basket over to a grassy, daisy-fringed knoll while Jenny ran on ahead, chasing butterflies. Knowl escorted Anna and Betty over the uneven terrain and Cath followed with her art supplies.

"This is a perfect spot," said Anna as Robert and Annie spread the flannel blankets on the cool, thick grass.

"I'll get the jugs of lemonade from the trunk and we'll be all set," said Knowl.

While Cath set up her easel near a drooping willow, Betty walked Jenny down by the brook to pick dandelions, and Robert and Annie helped Anna set out the food and utensils.

"Tell folks not to wander too far," said Anna. "This meal is ready to be eaten."

"I'll round them up," offered Robert.

Within minutes everyone had settled themselves on the blankets around tempting platters and bowls brimming with fried chicken, deviled eggs, baked beans, and fruit salad. Knowl held a rambunctious Jenny on his knee. She had already discarded her fistful of golden dandelions to reach for one of Grandma Reed's special treats. Knowl laughed. "This little one is chomping at the bit to get at those sugar cookies and orange slices."

"No, Jenny. You're a growing girl," said Anna. "First you should have some chicken and potato salad."

"No," Jenny wailed. "I want cookies!"

"Oh, look at those big crocodile tears," chided Betty.

"One cookie won't hurt," declared Cath. "After all, this is a picnic, isn't it? We're supposed to have fun."

"She won't eat her dinner," warned Annie.

Cath handed Jenny a cookie. "She's my daughter, and I say she can have a cookie. Does anyone have a problem with that?"

Annie shrugged. "No, Cath, if that's what you want."

They ate in uneasy silence until Robert broke in diplomatically with, "This is wonderful, isn't it? Great food, a little sunshine, delightful company. An unbeatable combination."

Knowl picked up the conversation, mentioning an editorial he was writing for the paper. "People don't realize all that the GI Bill of Rights is accomplishing for veterans. Over a million former servicemen are attending college today, thanks to that bill."

"Our boys deserve all the help they can get," said Anna. "They're all heroes, every last one. And Chip should have been among them."

Cath nodded. "All our lives would have been different if Chip had lived."

Again, a fragile silence. Finally Knowl said, "Looks like we'd better make an early day of it. Those clouds overhead look threatening."

"We can't go until I've painted them," protested Cath.

"Then make it quick," Knowl cautioned. "This is tornado weather."

"Knowl's right," said Anna. "The air is so still."

"They call it the quiet before the storm," said Annie. "Knowl, how many were killed in that tornado that hit Texas and Oklahoma last month?" asked Anna.

"Over a hundred and fifty people, and thirteen hundred were injured."

"I remember the terrible tornado that struck back in 1925," said Betty. "Worst tornado in our country's history. Ripped straight through Missouri, Illinois, and Indiana. My cousin in Princeton died in that one. It killed nearly seven hundred people, as I recall."

Jenny looked up wide-eyed. "What's a tornado, Mama Annie?" Annie pulled the child onto her lap. "Remember the story I read you a while ago? A tornado is what carried Dorothy and Toto to the land of Oz."

Jenny bounced up and down. "Can I go to Oz?"

"Not this time," said Knowl. "It's time for you to go home and take a nap."

"You all go ahead," said Cath, "but I'm staying."

"Don't be stubborn, daughter," said Betty. "A storm's brewing."

"And I want to paint it. The sky may never look quite like this again."

Betty's tone grew strident. "You can't stay here, child. You'll get drenched and catch your death of cold!"

"I'll be fine," insisted Cath. She stood up and headed for her easel. "The storm's still miles away. Will you all just go and let me paint in peace?"

"How will you get home?" asked Annie.

"I'll walk. I'm not the helpless invalid I was last year."

"That's absurd, Cath. It's over five miles!"

"Okay, I'll settle this," said Knowl. He went over and placed a brotherly hand on the nape of Cath's neck. "I'll drive everyone else home, then come back in an hour and pick you up. That'll give you time to paint your precious sky."

Cath smiled up at him. "You always come through for me."

"I still don't think it's a good idea for Cath to stay here alone," said Annie.

"Listen, how about if I stay with her?" suggested Robert.

Cath cast him a defiant glance. "I don't need you to protect me, Mr. Wayne."

He held up his palms in a conciliatory gesture. "I know, Catherine. But I would enjoy keeping you company and watching you paint, if you'll let me."

She turned back to her easel. "Suit yourself." She picked up a brush and dabbed at her palette, pretending to be absorbed in her work. She was hardly in the mood now to paint, but this battle had been too hard-won to forfeit. She gave a perfunctory farewell and hardly turned around when the others left, except to tell Robert he really needn't stay.

Then, suddenly, as she realized it was just the two of them in this pastoral glen, her obstinacy gave way to self-consciousness. How could she possibly paint with the high and mighty Robert Wayne peering over her shoulder?

"You'll probably be bored watching me paint," she noted.

"Not at all, Catherine. I'm a great admirer of your work."

She kept her gaze on her painting, but she could feel his towering frame just behind her. "You've hardly seen my work."

"On the contrary. Annie showed me several of your watercolors just this morning before church. Your sketches of Jesus are magnificent."

"They're not of Jesus. They're of a man named Luke Henry."

"You sound upset, Catherine. Are you angry with me for staying or are you still fuming over what happened at the picnic?"

She frowned. Was there the hint of amusement in his voice?

"I don't know what you're talking about," she said sharply.

"I'm talking about Jenny. I have the feeling you think she has too many mothers."

"The problem is, she doesn't know who her real mother is."

"Annie and the others don't mean any harm. They love Jenny just as you do."

"Maybe so, but when I'm back on my feet, I'm moving out and taking Jenny with me."

"Really? When will that be?"

She looked around at Robert. Was he deliberately taunting her? No, his expression seemed sincere enough. "I don't know when I'll be going.

I have no job, no money. Apartments are impossible to find these days. And, if I found a job, what would I do with Jenny while I worked?"

"Are you that restless and dissatisfied at your brother's home?"

Cath thought a moment. "No, not really. I love that old house."

"You grew up there, didn't you?"

"Practically. It belonged to Annie's family at the time, and her parents were like my own."

"Then you and Annie have always been close?"

Cath nodded. She realized she had become so involved in conversation with Robert that she was no longer painting. She turned to him and said, "This watercolor isn't working. I think I'll walk down by the creek. It's filled with cattails and water lilies."

"Water lilies?"

"Yes. The lily pads are everywhere, spreading across the water like a green and white quilt. And sometimes you see giant green frogs sitting on them and croaking to their hearts' content."

"Didn't Monet paint water lilies?"

"Yes. Often."

"I think I remember one—a water lily pond with a bridge."

"I'm impressed," said Cath. "I had no idea you were an art connoisseur as well as a literary virtuoso."

"The praise is undeserved," said Robert with a smile. "I know little about art, but Monet happens to be one of my favorite painters."

"One of mine too," said Cath. She put away her watercolors, then allowed Robert to carry her paint box and easel while she carried her sketch pad. They headed down the grassy knoll, walking in companionable silence. They were still some distance from the creek when Cath felt the first spattering of rain on her face and arms.

"I'm afraid they were right," said Robert. "The storm is moving in rather quickly. I think we'd better head back to the road and look for cover."

"Drat!" Cath said under her breath.

Clouds that had looked like ripe white cotton fields earlier now moved in dark swirls against a charcoal sky. Lightning spiked the dusky heavens, and thunder rumbled.

"We're being serenaded," quipped Robert, "by the angels' cymbals and drums."

"I don't think I like the song they're playing."

The rain was falling harder now, pelting them with drops the size of dimes. They took long strides through the wet grass. Robert nudged Cath's arm. "Let's cross the road. I see a place over there!"

Cath followed his gaze and spotted a ramshackle farmhouse in the distance. Nearer to the road a deserted barn blackened with age stood beside an empty cornfield. The weather-beaten door stood ajar, and the rusting silo tilted precariously. Cath hesitated only an instant in the downpour, then broke into a run beside Robert. As they ran, hail began to fall, battering them with ice the size of golf balls. Cath felt the sharp sting of ice on her face and arms and heard the clatter of hail hitting rooftop and fields. Just in time they ducked into the barn's musty shelter and collapsed breathless onto mounds of moldy straw.

"If this is Indiana, give me New York," declared Robert as he examined the red welts on his forearms. His chest still heaving, he looked over at Cath. "Are you okay? You've got some welts too."

"I'll be fine, as soon as this storm stops."

"It looks to me like it's settling in for a good long spell." Robert grimaced. "I just thought of something else. Your brother won't know where to find us."

Cath moaned. "If he can even drive in this hailstorm!"

"He'd be a fool to venture out now. Look at the ground. It's white with ice. Miniature snowballs piling up everywhere!"

Cath shivered and sneezed.

"You're catching cold."

"No, it's just the damp musty smell of all this straw."

"I wish I had a coat for you, or the picnic blankets."

"I'm fine," she insisted, tucking her light cotton skirt around her bare legs. She shivered again.

"If you want to move over closer to me, I won't bite."

She moved over beside him but hugged her arms against her chest for warmth. It was ironic that she should find herself trapped with a man she had made such a point to dislike. She cast him an appraising glance.

Did Robert Wayne guess the antipathy she felt for him? Unlikely. He merely returned her glance with a wink and a smile.

For several minutes they listened in uneasy silence to the *crash, clatter, bang* of the white driving sheets of hail. Then, suddenly, the icy barrage subsided and the earth grew unsettlingly quiet, except for the light patter of rain.

"Maybe we should make a run for it," she suggested.

"Where to? We'll just get soaked. Give it a few more minutes."

"I hate this," she said under her breath.

"What? The storm? Or being stuck in this barn with me?"

"The storm. Both. I don't know," she said, flustered.

He met her frown with a smile. "You know, Catherine, we're more alike than you realize."

She gazed at him impassively. "How so?"

He sat forward, resting his brawny arms on his knees. His blue eyes crinkled with amusement. "Well, Catherine, we're both stubborn, strong-willed, and driven by nameless passions that sometimes confound us. We're both passionate about our work and life in general. And we've both acted out of deep pain, anger, and guilt, often to our own detriment."

"I don't know what you're talking about," she muttered.

"All right. Speaking for myself, I came out of the war filled with bitterness, guilt, and rage. At Pearl Harbor I saw my buddies die. I was hit by shrapnel and thought I'd die too, but I recovered with just this limp you see.

"But the wounds inside were harder to heal." He cracked his knuckles, first the right hand, then the left. "I hated the woman who left me for another man when I went off to war. I hated the Japs for blasting so many good men into smithereens. I hated myself because I didn't get a chance to fight back." He paused, a muscle twitching in his jaw. "I felt guilty for surviving when better men died. And I felt like half a man with my busted leg. So I fed off my own rage and drowned myself in alcohol until I was numb."

"So, what the war didn't do to you, you did to yourself."

"Yes. I wanted to die. And I would have, if I hadn't stumbled into that rescue mission in Los Angeles."

Cath picked up a dry straw and broke it between her fingers. "Robert," she said quietly, "why are you telling me this?"

He met her gaze. "Surely you see the parallels, Catherine. You've been wounded by those you've loved who left you—your father, your lover, even your child who calls Annie Mommy. And you've been wounded in body just as I was. The car accident last year nearly stole everything from you."

"But it didn't," Cath said quickly. "I fought my way back to wholeness. I'm well again and painting better than ever."

"Yes, you are," Robert agreed. "But I'm talking about wounds that don't show, wounds of the heart. When we're driven by bitterness and anger, we're on a collision course with our own destiny. Eventually we destroy ourselves."

"Speak for yourself, Robert. I'm doing very well these days, thank you."

He chuckled mirthlessly to himself. "I'm speaking out of turn, I suppose. But I see such pain in your eyes, Catherine. I wish I could help."

"You can help by staying out of my business—and Annie's."

He looked at her. "You still consider me a threat to your brother's marriage?"

"Aren't you?"

"No. I told you so before. Romance is not an option for me. My work is my life."

"Mine too."

"My work, and my walk with God," he added.

Cath looked away.

Robert reached out and touched her arm. "Why does the mention of God make you stiffen and turn away?"

Cath ran her fingers through the thick, matted straw. "I'm just not a religious person like you and Annie."

His hand tightened on her arm. "You mean, you've never experienced that deep hunger in your soul for God's love?"

"God doesn't care one whit about me."

"His love will pursue you all the days of your life!"

Cath looked sharply at him, her voice rising shrilly. "If God loves me so much, let Him give me back my father, and my darling Chip, and my little girl!" She closed her hand around the tendrils of straw until the barbed shafts dug into her palm. "Or even *one* of them! Let Him give me back my father who walked out on us years ago! If God can do that, then maybe I'll believe in Him."

Robert released her arm. "I wish I could free you of your bitterness, Catherine."

She laughed ironically. "What's a little bitterness?"

Quietly he replied, "All bitterness is eventually against God. Until you release it, Catherine, you'll never experience Christ's love."

"You're not in your pulpit at the mission, Mr. Wayne."

He laughed. "No, I'm not, but sometimes I wish I were. I miss that life more than I can say."

"Then why did you leave it?"

"Because I've got publishing in my blood. I just wish there were some way I could do my job and have a ministry at the same time."

Cath gazed out at the sky. "Look, the rain has stopped, but the clouds are turning darker. Especially in the southwest."

"And the wind is picking up," said Robert. He stood up and walked to the open door. "I don't like the looks of it."

Cath joined him. "The air doesn't feel right, Robert," she said anxiously. "It doesn't smell right."

"Those are funnel clouds," he said, taking her hand. "I think we'd better get out of here."

"But where?"

"The old farmhouse. Maybe it has a storm cellar."

They broke into a run across a rutted field strewn with hailstones and through overgrown weeds sodden with rain. The chill air whipped around them and slapped Cath's curls against her cheeks. Brambles caught at her legs, nearly tripping her, but Robert caught her as she sank to her knees in a spiky thicket.

"Come on!" he shouted over the whistling wind.

Even as they ran, the sky darkened and the black clouds that had hovered on the horizon mushroomed above them in a single whirling dervish, its black tail sweeping the ground. "Tornado!" Cath screamed as the twister cut a swath through the landscape, exploding trees and shrubs in its path.

Robert seized her hand and pulled her toward the tumbledown house fringed by windlestraw and witchweed. Its rotting timbers creaked and its drooping porch groaned as dust whorls spun on its broken steps. Its shutters banged against the clapboard frame. A flock of blackbirds flew from its eaves.

"Around back!" Robert shouted. They clambered through wet, prickly thistles and nettles, dodging overgrown brambles and burrs. Just past the back porch they found the storm cellar. Robert reached down and pulled on the heavy, sagging doors. "Pray it opens!" he rasped.

When the rough-hewn panels didn't budge, Robert and Cath each took a side and tugged until the doors creaked open. The voluminous black whirlwind was bearing down on them, sending bits of debris flying everywhere. The buffeting wind nearly slammed the doors shut before Robert could push Cath ahead of him into the dank, cavelike opening. As she scrambled down the narrow steps, the palpable cold of the underground chamber enveloped her. The foul, fusty odor attacked her nostrils. Robert pressed in close behind her and lowered the doors, blotting out the last faint rays of light.

"Robert, where are you?" Cath gasped. The rank air stole her breath and cobwebs crisscrossed her face and arms like gauze.

"Here," he said.

She felt his strong arms circle her as he gathered her to his chest. She sank in relief against his sturdy frame, her head finding solace in the hollow of his neck. How she welcomed the solid warmth of his body against hers. They clung to each other as the earth around them shook. It seemed a thousand locomotives roared overhead, the noise deafening, the vibrations jarring their very bones. Cath could feel the structure above them shudder and convulse. Her heart hammered wildly. Would the tornado rip open their shelter and suck them into its deadly center?

9

AT LAST THE thunderous roar faded and the jolting tremors ceased. The earth fell silent, still once again. Dazed and shaken, Cath and Robert emerged from the storm cellar and gazed around, blinking against the light. The north section of the house that had stood above them only moments before lay in a twisted ruin, its beams and timber scattered like toothpicks amid unspeakable rubble and debris. The barn too lay in splinters strewn randomly over the shorn fields, its weathered lumber oddly juxtaposed with twisted fences and uprooted trees.

Cath clasped her hand over her mouth. "I'm going to be sick," she whispered.

Robert took her in his arms. "No, you're going to be fine, Catherine."

"I can't stop shaking."

He smoothed her hair back from her forehead the way a father comforts his child. "It's over and we're still alive, dear heart. God protected us."

"But what about my baby—what about Jenny?"

His arms tightened around her.

Gradually the waves of nausea passed, but Catherine remained in Robert's embrace, savoring his closeness. A strange stirring of emotions leapt from some secret wellspring within her breast. Incredible as it seemed, Robert had tapped into feelings she didn't know still existed, memories of yearning and desire she thought had died with Chip. *Impossible!* she told herself. The terror of the moment had left her weak and vulnerable, dizzy with fear and shock. Surely that was it. Such a close call with death would leave anyone lightheaded and breathless.

Robert pressed his cheek against her tangled hair and whispered, "Are you all right, dear girl?" Before she could find her voice to reply, he tilted her chin up to his and kissed her tenderly on the lips. For a moment she felt herself respond; then, as quickly, she pulled away and stared up at him.

"Robert!"

His face reddened. He stepped back and raked his fingers through his thick raven curls. "I'm sorry, Catherine. I didn't mean—I shouldn't have—I swear that will never happen again."

Fleetingly she wondered, *Didn't he like it? Did he wish I was Annie?* But she pushed the questions away and started across the scarred field. "We'd better get back to the picnic area. Knowl will be looking for us."

He caught up and fell into step beside her. "I'm praying that Jenny— and everyone else at home—is safe and sound."

She couldn't bear to respond. What if the tornado had swept through Honeysuckle Lane, harming her child, her family? The idea was too abhorrent to contemplate.

Hand in hand, they crossed the wreckage of saplings and bushes, tender flowers and massive oaks. All lay twisted, splintered, in disarray, as if a giant hand had plucked up trees and shrubs by their roots, crushed them with a deadly rage, and scattered the pulverized remains over the ravaged country-side.

When they reached the spot where they'd held their picnic only hours before, little remained of the lush, tranquil vale they'd enjoyed. Cath stared in astonishment at the ravished landscape, its rich green foliage ripped and strewn about like confetti. "We were just here, laughing and talking," she murmured. "Everything was so pleasant and serene. How could everything have changed so quickly?"

Robert took her arm. "Don't think about it now, Catherine."

She stooped down and picked up a handful of wilted dandelions. "Look, aren't these the ones Jenny gathered? They weren't destroyed."

He handed her his handkerchief. "Here, save them, if you wish. Then come along. We must watch for your brother's automobile."

"Oh, Robert, he won't be able to come for us! Look!"

He followed her gaze. Broken branches and limbs crisscrossed the road. "You're right. The streets all over Willowbrook may be blocked. We'd better walk home."

"Oh, I pray there's still a home to walk to!"

For what seemed like endless miles they followed the road into town, grimly pressing on past the skeletal remains of demolished houses, barns, sheds, and shops. The tornado had been a capricious assailant, decimating one structure while leaving its neighbor untouched. Rooftops had been peeled back from their rafters. Some buildings looked like a child's pick-up sticks; others had been reduced to a twisted hovel of masonry, steel, and concrete. Still others remained standing but in obvious ruin. The side had been torn from a two-story apartment building revealing rooms that at first appeared undisturbed—a living room with overstuffed sofa and chairs, a bedroom with a four-poster bed and bureaus, and a bathroom with a claw-foot tub and washbasin with pipes shooting out eerily into thin air.

Cath shuddered and looked away. People were congregating out on the streets—a woman clutching two crying children, an old man in a sleeveless undershirt and baggy trousers wandering aimlessly, a teenage boy already pulling debris off his prized Ford jalopy. No one seemed to know quite what to do or where to go.

No wonder. The tornado had cut a wide swath. Destruction lay everywhere in the piles of bricks and beams from fallen chimneys, buttresses, cornices, and porticos. There was an odd, almost fascinating surrealism about it all. The marquee for the Regent Theater rested atop Kresge's Dollar Store; the A&P's plate glass windows lay in jagged shards amid cans of corn and peas; the storefront windows of Sears Roebuck and J. C. Penney had been shattered too. A smiling, blank-eyed manne-quin protruded from a broken window, its arms contorted in a bizarre gesture of supplication.

Cath and Robert increased their stride, dodging overturned benches and darting past toppled street signs pointing skyward. The storm-laden air, gray with dust and grime rising in faint clouds out of the dross and debris, was unlike anything she'd breathed before. The acrid odor was reminiscent of the oily diesel smell of a locomotive or the sooty charcoal smell of a freshly stocked coal bin, and yet it was neither of those. It was infinitely more pungent and disagreeable.

Cath heard sirens scream in the distance and wondered how fire trucks and ambulances could possibly traverse the cluttered streets. How many people were hurt or trapped or dying?

"We shouldn't have come through town," she said with a shudder. "It looks like the end of the world."

"Just keep walking," said Robert. "This is the most direct route home."

"I never dreamed there'd be so much devastation."

Robert clasped her hand more tightly. "Keep moving, Catherine. We'll be home before you know it."

She stopped suddenly and pointed toward an intersection. "Look, it's Knowl—his car's there beside the road!" She broke into a run.

At the same moment Knowl spotted her and stepped out of his vehicle and opened his arms to her. They embraced, Cath weeping, Knowl studying her intently as he wiped streaks of dirt from her cheeks and demanded, "Are you hurt?"

"We're fine," she replied breathlessly. "We found a storm cellar. What about Jenny?"

"She's fine. Everybody's fine."

"And the house?"

"No damage, except for a few missing shingles. I tried to come for you, but this is as far as I got. The roads—"

"I know. All the streets through town are like this."

Knowl looked at Robert. "Can you drive my sister home? I need to get over to the newspaper."

Cath seized his arms. "Knowl, you can't. You've got to come home with us. We need you!"

He stared hard at her, his temples throbbing, his eyes flashing with a fervency that silenced her. "I've got to get the paper out, Cath. People are depending on it to tell them what damage was done, who survived and who didn't. They need to know what to do now so no one else gets hurt." He gave her a farewell embrace, handed Robert his car keys, and took off down the street toward the timeworn brick building that housed the *Willowbrook News*.

"Be careful!" Cath called after him.

The drive home seemed unbearably long. Cath wanted nothing more than to be back in that beloved old house on Honeysuckle Lane with her family. And until she held her precious Jenny in her arms again, she couldn't put aside the terrible sense of dread that chilled her heart.

"You're still trembling," said Robert, glancing from the road to look at her. His earnest eyes shone with concern.

"I feel as if I'll never stop shaking."

He put his warm hand over hers. "If there's anything I can do for you, Catherine—"

"You've done more than enough already. You saved my life."

"Let's just say God saved both our lives."

"I guess I owe Him one," she murmured.

He nodded. "We all owe Him more than we can ever repay."

As soon as Robert pulled into the driveway, Cath spotted Jenny bounding out the door and down the porch steps. Cath ran to meet her and scooped her up in her arms. The child wrapped her chubby arms around Cath's neck and looked at her with enormous blue eyes. "Mama Cath, did the tornado take you to Oz like Dorothy and Toto?"

Cath kissed her daughter's dimpled cheek. "No, sweetheart. I guess the storm knew the only place I wanted to be was home with you!"

Annie, Betty and Anna came spilling out of the house too. They overwhelmed Cath and Robert with hugs, everyone talking at once.

"We were so afraid you were hurt—or worse!" cried Annie.

"We saw the tornado dip down near town and head toward Sawyer's Bend. It was the most terrifying sight," said Anna.

Even Betty, who rarely showed emotion, was weeping. "We felt so helpless, daughter. Thought you were a goner for sure!"

"Let's go inside, all of us," said Anna. "Catherine and Robert, you go wash the soot off your faces while I go fix something hot and soothing for dinner."

"You take the bathroom, Catherine," said Robert. "I'll wash up in the kitchen. Come on, Jenny. You go with me. Let Mommy have her bath." He lifted the youngster up on his shoulders and carried her into the house.

"Thank you, Robert." She wanted nothing more in the world this moment than to soak in a hot tub away from everyone's anxious questions and worried stares.

In the cozy privacy of the bathroom, Cath turned on the spigot full force and even added some fragrant bubble bath to the water. After a day like she'd had, she deserved to be pampered a little. She disrobed and stepped into the warm, welcoming suds, sinking down until her neck rested on the porcelain rim. She closed her eyes and willed her body to relax, but in her mind's eye she could still see that monstrous black funnel cloud spiraling toward her, devouring everything in its path. She shuddered and blinked against the hideous vision, until another image came to mind. It was Robert. His touch. His kiss. She put her fingertips to her lips and traced the line of her mouth, remembering. Memory mixed with desire as she imagined him kissing her again. But she stopped the fantasy short with a chastening reminder: *Robert Wayne means nothing to you. He's the last man on earth you'd ever want to love. He's everything you're not, everything you never want to be!*

At dinner that evening, as Anna served her tasty creamed chicken on biscuits, Robert recounted the horrifying events of the day, concluding with his and Cath's long walk home through the ravaged town. Cath remained silent, carefully avoiding Robert's gaze. When their eyes did happen to meet, she flushed, her face growing warm. Was he remembering their kiss, giving it more significance than it deserved, or had he forgotten it completely? And why, after the horrendous ordeal they had just shared, did that single, brief kiss hold such prominence in her own mind?

Her preoccupation broke when she realized Annie was asking her a question. "Did you hear me, Cath? Do you think you'll feel like joining us at the Red Cross tomorrow?"

"The Red Cross?"

"Yes. It's too late tonight to venture out, but Mama and I thought we'd see if they could use our help tomorrow. There must be countless families in Willowbrook who've lost their homes. They'll need hot meals and a place to stay."

"I'll telephone Reverend Henry in the morning," said Anna. "Maybe cots could be set up in the church."

"And I imagine the Salvation Army will organize a special soup kitchen for tornado victims," said Annie.

"The soup kitchen's my specialty," said Robert. "Remember, Annie, the long hours we spent cooking and serving at the rescue mission in California? We came up with all sorts of palatable and unpalatable gruel, but most folks seemed to like it. Remember our glorified goulash? Since meat was rationed, we cooked up our own version of hamburger."

"How could I ever forget? And remember our Spam special? You had a way of making it taste terrific. It's too bad you're leaving tomorrow. We could sure use your help."

"Maybe I'll see if I can change my schedule or have my office forward some of my work here, so I can stay over a few extra days."

"That would be wonderful, Robert."

"I can't promise anything. I have to meet this week with a couple of other Sanders and Browne authors in Indianapolis."

Annie's voice grew wistful. "I hate to see you go. I wish you were taking my novel with you."

"I know. I'll try to get back to Willowbrook next weekend and we'll discuss some possibilities. In the meantime, think about what Catherine said about self-publishing your novel."

She shook her head. "I just don't see that as an option, Robert. I'd be taking a giant step backward in my career."

"Hold on! Let's finish this meal in peace," suggested Betty pointedly, "without worrying anymore about catastrophes or careers!"

Everyone smiled knowingly and gave a hearty, "Amen!"

After dinner, Cath took Jenny up to bed, then joined the rest of the family gathered around the parlor radio to listen to news reports on the tornado's devastation. They listened in grim silence for over an hour, until Anna finally turned the dial to a station playing Guy Lombardo. "As Betty said earlier, enough gloom! We need something calming and restful before we retire."

Cath welcomed the pleasant orchestra music. Perhaps the soothing sounds would dispel the nightmares already looming at the fringes of her consciousness. Physical exhaustion had invaded her limbs hours ago, but her mind still raced, resisting slumber.

"You look so tired, Cath," Annie told her. "Why don't you go to bed?"

"Not yet. I'm still too keyed up to sleep."

Annie looked at Robert. "You must be terribly weary too. Would you like me to bring you both some hot tea?"

"I'll do it," said Anna, "and then I'm off to bed."

Cath savored the hot tea with its usual pinch of sugar and cream. She felt more relaxed. Robert and Annie looked more relaxed too. It was just the three of them now, enjoying the parlor's rosy lamplight and Guy Lombardo's melodic strains.

"I wish Knowl were coming home," said Annie, glancing toward the window, "but he won't leave the office until a special edition of the newspaper hits the streets."

"That's my brother," said Cath. "Duty before family."

Annie grimaced. "Don't be critical of him, Cath. I thank God for your brother. He's a wonderful husband."

Cath nodded. "He's a swell brother, too."

Annie's voice grew confidential. "We have a lot to thank God for tonight, Cath."

"Yes, we do," Robert agreed. "Catherine and I had a close call today. I haven't felt that close to death since Pearl Harbor."

"It's twice in one year for me," said Cath. "First, the car crash and coma, and now a tornado."

"I think God is trying to tell you something," said Annie.

Cath met her gaze. "What, Annie? What's He trying to tell me?"

"That He's there for you, watching over you, protecting you."

Cath's gaze remained unflinching. "How do you know He's there, Annie? How is it you and Robert have this wonderful faith, and all I have are doubts?"

Robert walked over and turned off the radio. He and Annie exchanged solemn glances. The room was silent for a long moment, except for the sound of crickets outside and the lonely whistle of a distant train.

"How do I know God is there?" Annie repeated thoughtfully. "The same way I know *you're* there, dear Cath. We spend time together, we talk, we communicate even when we don't say a word. I feel your presence even when we're apart. I feel your love for me and mine for you. I know *you*—your character, your personality, all that makes you Catherine. In the same way I know Christ. We've shared too much together and I've known too much of His love for anyone to tell me He's not there for me."

"But you can't see Him. You can only presume—"

"I see Him in all the ways that matter. I see Him in His Word and in His world and in the hearts of all who love Him."

Cath looked questioningly at Robert. "You feel that way too?"

"Yes, Catherine," he said quietly, his vivid blue eyes as unsettling as they were disarming. "Remember, dear heart, you may not believe in God, but God believes in *you!*"

10

THROUGHOUT THAT WEEK all anyone talked about was the frightful tornado that had devastated Willowbrook. Each day the headlines told the story:

TWISTER CLAIMS THREE LIVES—DOZENS HURT
DOWNTOWN HARDEST HIT—SCORES HOMELESS
RED CROSS TO THE RESCUE HELPING HOMELESS
LOCAL CHURCHES OPEN DOORS TO NEEDY
CITIZENS RALLY FOR WILLOWBROOK CLEANUP
RECOVERY CONTINUES AS COMMUNITY PULLS TOGETHER
PIONEER SPIRIT SEEN IN REBUILDING EFFORTS

Annie, Cath, and Anna spent the week at the church preparing meals and distributing clothing to the homeless. Robert stayed until Wednesday helping church members set up an efficient soup kitchen that provided three balanced meals a day to a hundred needy Willowbrook citizens. Reverend Henry was thankful to have someone with Robert's expertise.

At the midweek prayer meeting he told his congregation, "During this disaster Willowbrook Christian Church is having as great an impact for good on our community as the Red Cross and the Salvation Army!"

But by the end of the week, Cath was exhausted. On Friday morning, still in her dressing gown, she stopped by Annie's room. Sunlight spilled in through the dormer window, giving the room a golden glow. Annie stood before the dresser mirror buttoning her chiffon blouse.

"Better go on to the church without me," Cath told her. "I'm running a little late."

Annie caught Cath's reflection in the mirror and frowned. "You don't look well. You'd better stay home."

"No, I just need a little more time—"

"You need to watch your health, Cath," Annie cautioned. "Your body has spent itself recovering from the coma. Last year you were like a newborn baby learning to walk and talk all over again. Now, after the tornado, it's just too—"

"Stop it, Annie," Cath protested. She stood cradling her arms against her slim body, watching Annie's graceful reflection in the dusky mirror. "I'm perfectly fine, and you know it."

Annie turned and met her gaze. "Do I? You look exhausted. You've got circles under your eyes."

Cath stiffened, facing Annie squarely. "You're my dearest friend on earth, but you can't keep treating me like an invalid." She clenched her hands. "One of these days I'm going to walk out of this house and make a life for myself, and I'll have no one looking over my shoulder to make sure I don't overdo. Until then, I'll decide whether or not I'm up to helping out at the church."

Annie threw up her hands in exasperation. "All right, have it your way. I was just trying to help."

"You're always trying to help." Cath reached over and straightened Annie's lace collar. "It's not that I'm ungrateful. But sometimes I feel smothered by you and your mother and my mother and my brother. I don't feel like a whole person."

Annie studied her quizzically. "What do you mean, Cath? Of course, you're a whole person. The doctors say you've gained back all your—"

"I'm not talking about the accident, Annie. I don't even know what I mean. I just feel like there are so many empty places in my heart and in my life. So many gaping holes. And I don't know how to fill them."

Impulsively Annie drew Cath into her arms and held her close. The fragrance of lilac perfume scented the air, the same perfume Annie's mother wore. "I'm so sorry, Cath. You mean the world to me. Is it because of Jenny? Because she still thinks of me as her mother?"

Cath withdrew from Annie's embrace and gazed at her own sallow face in the mirror. "That's part of it," she admitted. "I've even thought about taking Jenny and going away somewhere, so she would have only me to depend on."

"Take her away?" Annie's eyes widened with alarm.

Cath faced her again. "Don't worry. I know I have nothing to offer my child. It's sad, isn't it? I'm like a puzzle with missing pieces. I don't know who I'm supposed to be, or what I'm supposed to do, or even who I'm supposed to love. As hard as I've worked to recover from the accident, I still feel broken, with all these jagged, hurtful pieces jumbled inside me."

"Oh, Cath, I didn't realize—"

"Of course you didn't." Cath's voice grew ragged. "I don't know why I'm telling you now. It's just that there's still so much pain and anger and hatred churning inside me. How do I get rid of the garbage without getting rid of *me*?"

Annie reached out and smoothed Cath's tousled hair. "Oh, dear heart, you know the answer as well as I—"

Cath raised her hands, palms out. "Don't give me a sermon, Annie, not when I've bared my soul to you. All my life it's been the same story. Everything you touch turns to gold; everything I touch turns to ashes. I can't play by your rules."

"Not rules, Cath. I'm talking about *Him*. Living by His grace, His power, His love. That's the only way I've survived."

Cath examined her fingernails, as if she hadn't quite noticed them before—the delicate cuticles, the pale pink orbs framed by white moons. "Actually, Annie," she said, her voice brightening with a hint of mystery, "I have a special reason for wanting to go to the church today."

She looked up blithely, a faint smile playing on her lips. "I've decided to do the panels for Reverend Henry. I'm going to paint the life of Christ from my sketches of Luke Henry. What do you suppose God will think of that?"

Annie smiled charitably. "I think God would say He wants your heart as well as your talent."

Cath's green eyes narrowed. "Then perhaps He's being a little too greedy. I'm not even sure I can deliver the paintings. Even the masters have considered capturing the face of Christ on canvas an awesome task."

Annie clasped Cath's arms. "I don't mean to trivialize your commitment to the project. I know Reverend Henry will be delighted—and so am I! In fact, I'll wait for you this morning, so we can go and see Reverend Henry together."

That weekend, when Robert Wayne returned from Indianapolis, Cath and Annie picked him up at the train depot. He was dressed in a stylish suede sports jacket and white flannel trousers. *Such a handsome man,* Cath mused silently. Both were eager to talk with him about their projects—Cath about painting the panels of Jesus for Reverend Henry and Annie about moving ahead with the publication of her book.

"I'm pleased you've accepted the commission," Robert told Cath during the drive home. "I know you'll do superb work."

"She's refusing any payment," Annie added as she turned on to Honeysuckle Lane. "Isn't it generous of Cath to donate the paintings to the church? People will come from miles around to see them."

"Stop," said Cath. "You're making me sound like a saint. And we all know I'm not that!"

"Will that young man pose for you again?" asked Robert.

"Luke Henry? I don't know. I haven't seen him all week."

"Can't you contact him? Write? Telephone?"

"No. He works in construction, odd jobs here and there. But I don't know where he lives or where he's from. Come to think of it, I know very little about him."

"How will you paint without a model?" asked Annie.

"I have the sketches. And I'll go to the park again and watch for him. Who knows? Maybe our paths will cross again."

Once they were home and settled comfortably in the parlor, Cath and Annie both spoke with excitement about all the church had accomplished for the tornado victims. "It's thanks in large part to you, Robert," said Annie, "for helping us set up such an efficient operation at Willowbrook Christian. Reverend Henry can't say enough about you, can he, Cath?"

Cath met Robert's gaze with a faint ripple of pleasure and embarrassment. Did he still think about their kiss? Did he see her with different eyes, the way she saw him? Surely not. And yet . . . "Annie's right," Cath agreed quickly. "He's very impressed by you."

"That's kind of him, but I simply did what anyone would do in those circumstances."

Annie reached across the love seat and touched his arm. "Your humility becomes you, dear Robert. Goodness, Cath and I have lost our manners. We've talked your ear off without asking if you'd like something to eat or an hour's rest after your long trip."

"A couple of Anna's hot biscuits and strawberry preserves would suit me fine," he said with a wink.

"I'll get the biscuits," said Cath, standing up. Surely Robert preferred Annie's company to hers anyway. Let the two have their convivial chat. Why should she strive to keep them apart when Knowl seemed so maddeningly unconcerned?

When she returned with a pot of tea and biscuits, Annie was talking ardently about her book. "You know how much it means to me to see my novel published, Robert. Surely you can come up with some plan of action—"

"Actually, I took a few hours to do some research while I was in Indianapolis," he replied, taking the tea and biscuits Cath offered. "I got some good leads. In fact, I'm going to look into a possibility right here in Willowbrook."

"In Willowbrook?"

"You're aware of the denominational publishing house here in town?"

"Yes, of course." Annie accepted the tea but waved off the biscuits. "But it's a very small company, Robert. They operate out of that old brick building on Van Buren that used to house Willowbrook's city hall around the turn of the century. They print tracts and Sunday school material, not books. How could they possibly be of any help?"

"I'm not sure they can," said Robert, sipping his tea, "but while I'm in Willowbrook, I'm going to drop in and have a chat with the president of the company. Maybe it's time they expanded their line into religious books."

Annie looked doubtful. "It seems like such a comedown after being published by such a prestigious house as Sanders and Browne."

"I know, Annie. Sanders and Browne did a fine job with *Pacific Dawn*. But this is a different kind of book. You want your novel published the way you wrote it, don't you? With a secular house, you may end up compromising your work."

Cath poured herself some tea and sat down in the oak rocker by the fireplace. She didn't have much to say when Annie and Robert talked about book publishing; that was their private domain. She wondered if she should just excuse herself and go paint or join Betty and Jenny in the gazebo in the garden.

No, she wanted to stay here. Had to stay. She gazed at Robert, sitting back relaxed, holding his china cup and saucer balanced on his knee. Several strands of ebony hair curled boyishly over his sturdy forehead. Was he the reason she felt compelled to remain in this room? The idea was unthinkable. And yet, inexplicably, she was drawn to the sound of his voice, the curve of his smile, the blue of his eyes.

She bit absently into a biscuit and chewed slowly, remembering the taste of his mouth on hers, the protective warmth of his arms, the deep resonance of his voice as he assured her she would be safe from the tornado.

"Did you hear me, Cath?"

She flinched, nearly spilling her tea. "What?"

"I asked what you thought about Robert contacting the denominational house here in town," said Annie. "Are you all right? You looked so lost in thought."

Cath touched her lips and flushed. "I'm fine. And I have no opinion. When it comes to publishing, Robert's the expert."

Annie set her cup on the mahogany coffee table. "But, Robert, if another house publishes my book, what part will you have in it? You're my editor. I don't want anyone else."

"Don't worry. I'll be here for you."

"But how? You work for Sanders and Browne. They won't want you editing a book for another house."

"That may not be a problem." Robert sat forward and put his cup beside Annie's. He cracked his knuckles thoughtfully. "I've been doing some serious thinking, Annie, not just about your book but about my life as well."

"Your life?"

He looked from Annie to Cath and back again. "When I helped set up the soup kitchen for the tornado victims, all the old feelings and sensations from my days at the rescue mission came flooding back to me—the sense of ministry, of service, of accomplishing something directly for God and my fellow man. I thought I loved editing enough that I could give that up. Now I'm not so sure. If I have to choose between the two, maybe I really belong at the mission."

Annie stared questioningly at him. "Are you thinking about going back to California?"

"All I know is that since the war ended, I've felt such an urgency to do something to make this a better world. Don't you feel it? Catherine? Annie? People are still reeling from the trauma and carnage of warfare and this new threat of global annihilation. They're empty, searching, broken, needy."

Cath looked away. Robert could be describing *her*.

"Just think," he continued, his voice fervent, "we're almost halfway into this century. Think of what has happened so far—two world wars, the atomic bomb, the rise of a monster like Hitler, the annihilation of millions of Jews. Even as we speak, godless Communists are gaining incredible footholds around the world."

When neither Cath nor Annie replied, Robert's tone turned more animated. "The end of this century will mark the second millennium since Christ's death. That has to mean something. I sense it. We're living in extraordinary times—years so precarious and unpredictable that civilization as we know it could be gone tomorrow. And I have a feeling the next fifty years will bear me out. Our world is going to get worse—not better, the way some people claim. We'd better redeem the time. We don't know how many years we have left."

"You're right, of course, Robert," Annie said at last. "But what can we do? What can any one person do?"

He shook his head. "If I knew, I'd be doing it. Meanwhile, I'm searching just like everyone else."

Cath stood up and picked up the tea service. "I'm going out to the gazebo," she announced. "This conversation is getting a little too apocalyptic for me."

11

O N MONDAY MORNING, while Annie drove Robert to his appointment with the denominational publisher, Cath moped about the house, looking for something to do. She was feeling restless, her nerves strangely on edge. She stopped by her mother's room, knowing even as she tapped on the door that she and Betty rarely had anything to say to each other. As she suspected, Betty was sitting in her oak rocker beside her old Philco radio, listening to her favorite melodramas. Most mornings she listened to *Ma Perkins, Helen Trent, Our Gal Sunday,* and *Young Dr. Malone.* In the afternoon she listened to *Stella Dallas, When a Girl Marries, Portia Faces Life,* and *Just Plain Bill. At least she's not drinking,* Cath mused. "Are you busy, Mama?" she asked.

Betty put her finger to her lips. "Just a minute, daughter. This is the best part."

"That's okay, Mama. I'll talk to you later."

She walked on down the silent hallway and descended the steep hardwood stairs with their familiar creaking places. Perhaps she would take Jenny for a walk. But no. Anna had already taken Jenny to the garden to gather lilacs and daffodils for the dinner table. Cath walked aimlessly to the parlor and picked up last night's newspaper. She felt in a state of flux, eager to take swift action and accomplish significant deeds, and yet, something within her held her back; some urgent, crucial part of her felt immobilized. She couldn't articulate the sensation, couldn't wrap it in words to make it real. She knew only that she was growing stagnant—her spirits, her creativity, her very sense of herself as a woman, as an artist, as a human being.

She flipped unseeingly through the *Willowbrook News,* her gaze resting at last on an article titled, "Radio's Future in Question as Television Looms." Without interest she scanned the article. "Radio dealers report fewer sales as television becomes more affordable for the average income. . . . The American Broadcasting Company plans to have five stations in operation by the end of 1948 in Chicago, Detroit, New York, Los Angeles and San Francisco. Plans call for the Chicago station to be finished first. . . ."

Cath tossed the paper aside. She could imagine Betty demanding that Knowl go out and buy her a television set one of these days. Cath had seen one on display in a store. The idea of staring at a flickering little screen showing test patterns, boxing matches, and puppet shows was preposterous, when she could listen to the radio and let her imagination run freely. Surely it was a passing fad and people would soon return to their senses.

As if to prove her point, Cath walked over to the large, cabinent-style radio that stood between the velvet wing chairs and turned the dial. The languid strains of Jo Stafford's "I'll Be Seeing You" filled the room. Cath sat down and allowed the music to stir her senses and carry her back to another time and place—fleeting days when gossamer dreams of Chip made the world seem a magical place. *No, Cath, don't do this to yourself! You can't go back!* Grimly she snapped off the radio. It was true. Those sweet days and romantic dreams were buried in the blood-soaked waters of Pearl Harbor.

Cath gazed around the parlor at the familiar flowered wallpaper, the Monet prints on each side of the fireplace, the red velvet drapes at the windows. An odd thought occurred to her. If Chip was locked away from her in the distant Pacific seas, she herself was a prisoner too. She was locked into time and place, wedged uncomfortably into this time, June 1947, and this place, once the old Victorian Reed mansion, but now the Herrick house on Honeysuckle Lane, in uneventful Willowbrook.

Here was the dilemma. It wasn't Catherine's house. And it wasn't Catherine's life she was living these days. What irony! To have struggled back from the coma only to find herself living a listless, meaningless existence! Incredibly, she was no freer than Chip—and just as dead!

Cath walked around the room with a gnawing nervous energy, her mind leaping from one thought to another. Perhaps it was the tornado and its aftermath that had forced her to see her life with this new, disturbing clarity. Robert and Annie were both seized by a vision greater than themselves. Both felt a profound, energizing calling on their lives—Annie to write books, Robert to publish books and serve mankind.

What was Cath's calling? As far as her place in the Reed and Herrick clan was concerned, she was little more than an expendable appendage. No one truly needed her. No one loved her most or adored her only. Knowl and Annie had each other; Betty and Anna doted on little Jenny. Cath was—well, just Cath. She belonged nowhere, to no one.

With a sudden brisk decisiveness, Cath strode out of the parlor and headed for the pantry where her art supplies were stored. She gathered her paint box, easel, and sketch pad and took long strides out of the house and down the driveway to the street. She walked the half mile to the park with the slim hope of encountering the intriguing Luke Henry, a man who repelled and fascinated her at once.

As she walked she argued silently with herself. She wished she could simply coast along through life and be content with the sane and serene existence fate had dealt her. But then again, nature had never meant her to be passive and docile. Annie had always been the one who longed for a safe, predictable haven; from their childhood Cath had been the one filled with wanderlust, who blithely took risks and cherished adventure.

As she set up her easel on a grassy slope, Cath winced, remembering the fame and accolades of the past. It seemed everyone had wanted her work. After all, how many other artists were commissioned to paint a cover for the popular and prestigious *Saturday Evening Post*?

Now only an old minister in a humble church sought her out. And only to paint panels of Jesus. Oh, for the old days!

But was she happy then? Truly content? She couldn't remember. Those days seemed all too remote, as if they had happened to someone she scarcely knew now.

For a while Cath painted the rich June colors of blossoming flowers and trees while keeping an eye out for the tall, bearded stranger. But when several hours had passed with no sign of him, she realized she might never see him again. Perhaps his business in Willowbrook was done and he had returned home—wherever home might be. A feeling of lament rippled through her. How could she possibly paint the panels of Jesus without her inspiration?

Cath remained at the park until suppertime, hoping against hope that Luke Henry would happen by. This time she would be sure to get his address or phone number so that he could not slip out of her life again. In some inexplicable way, it was as if he held out a lifeline to her. Because she knew nothing about him, his life offered endless possibilities. He could be anyone from anywhere. And yet that wasn't quite true either. He was obviously an Indiana boy, a bit unschooled and rough around the edges. And yet—there was something about him, a riveting, magnetic quality that Cath found mesmerizing.

As she walked home in the warm June dusk, she imagined Luke Henry coming and carrying her off to another life, something grand and mysterious and filled with adventure. Perhaps they would travel the country together, or the world, or the universe. It wasn't that she was necessarily attracted to him physically; no, the connection went deeper, beyond words, beyond reason. She knew instinctively that she had to locate this vigorous young man again, not just for her painting but to satisfy some elusive yearning, as well as a rising curiosity, within herself.

When Cath arrived home, Anna was already calling everyone to the dinner table. Annie and Robert were there, and Knowl was home surprisingly early from the paper. Jenny came running up and tugged on Cath's skirt, urging, "Look at the flowers Grandma Reed and I picked!"

"They're beautiful," Cath praised, reaching out and touching the lush, plump lilacs with her fingertips. She looked over at Knowl. "You're home early, dear brother."

He took his place at the head of the table. "I'm working on an editorial to commemorate the third anniversary of D-Day, and I figured I could find more peace and quiet at home than at the office."

"D-Day?" echoed Annie. "That's right. It's this Friday."

"I want to write something special," said Knowl. "After all, D-Day was a major turning point of the war."

"We lost entirely too many men at Normandy," said Robert, sitting down, "but it was the boldest, grandest amphibious operation the world has ever seen."

Knowl nodded. "If Eisenhower hadn't pulled that one off, we could still be chasing that madman Hitler around the globe."

Anna set a golden baked chicken with cornbread stuffing on the table. "I won't have talk of Hitler spoiling my dinner," she declared. "The war's been over nearly two years. Seems to me it's time we moved on and put it behind us."

"Mama, you don't mean that," said Annie. "We can't let ourselves ever forget it. Your son gave his life in that war."

Anna patted back a wisp of silver-gray hair. "I didn't say forget it. There's not a day goes by I don't think about my precious Chilton." She turned her gaze to Cath. "And I suspect there's not a day Catherine doesn't think about him too."

Cath lowered her gaze. "Chip will always be part of me, just as he'll always be a part of Jenny."

Betty ran her hand over Jenny's auburn tresses. "It's a crying shame this child won't ever know her father. Same way it's a crime my two hardly knew their father, the old scalawag."

"Now, Mama, let's not get into that subject," warned Knowl.

"He's right," agreed Cath. "Our papa is dead to us."

Betty scowled, the lines in her face deepening. "Truth be told, that good-for-nothing Tom Herrick's the one who should have died instead of Chip Reed. Why is it the good die young?"

"The war," said Robert. "It always comes back to the war."

"I don't say forget the war," Anna repeated. "But we all must move on and look to the future, even as we remember the past."

"Well spoken," said Robert, lifting his goblet of ice water. "I'll drink to that. To the future."

They all raised their drinking glasses and said, "To the future."

Silently Cath wondered, *What future? Will I ever find the happiness and contentment Knowl and Annie share?* Unwittingly she stole a glance at Robert. His eyes were on her with an expression that made her set down her glass a little too hard. Water spilled over the rim. She dabbed at it with her linen napkin. "Will I ever stop being clumsy?" she murmured, her face flushing.

But other questions were more pressing. Why had Robert met her gaze at exactly that moment? What was he thinking? Did he feel a secret connection growing between them? Or was she only imagining that searching, enigmatic look in his eyes?

"Well, how did your appointment go with the publisher?" Knowl asked Robert as he handed him the candied sweet potatoes.

"Quite interesting, actually. You know Annie joined me—"

"I knew she was driving you."

"Since I was pitching her book, it seemed right for her to be there."

Annie took a hot roll and passed the basket on. "I'm glad I went. It was an extraordinary day."

Cath noted the excitement pass between Robert and Annie. "Something important must have happened," she remarked. "I see it in your faces."

"Are they going to publish your book?" asked Knowl.

"Not exactly," replied Robert, "although with some modifications their equipment could produce books as well as tracts and Sunday school literature." His eyes took on a shrewd, knowing gleam. "But we did learn some rather intriguing news."

Annie joined in, her tone buoyant. "The publisher wants to move to a larger facility in another state, closer to the denominational headquarters."

Knowl shrugged. "I don't see what that has to do with—"

"He wants to sell the Willowbrook facilities," said Annie.

Robert cut in with an awkward chuckle. "What Annie means is that if anyone were thinking of starting his own publishing company, this would be an extraordinary opportunity."

Cath stared at Knowl and Knowl stared at Annie. Levelly he asked, "Did I hear you correctly, sweetheart? You're thinking of buying a publishing house?"

"It's just a fanciful dream, darling," she assured him. "Of course we wouldn't be foolish enough to risk such a venture. Still, the terms are very tempting, aren't they, Robert?"

He nodded, his broad, handsome face ruddy with an intensity Cath had never seen before. "You'll all have to indulge us our moment of whimsy," he said with a curious blend of apology and wonder. "At the moment all things seem possible. I'm sure when we've had time to sort it out, we'll see the obvious failings in our little plan."

"Now it's a plan, is it?" said Knowl wryly. "A minute ago it was just a fanciful dream."

"Tell us," urged Cath, "what sort of bizarre plan are you two concocting?"

Annie pressed her palms against her blushing cheeks and rolled her eyes heavenward. "Goodness gracious, it's nothing. Just silly talk. Robert mentioned that if we had our own publishing house, we could print whatever we pleased without compromise or capitulation. I said I thought it was a wonderful idea, and I would be pleased to invest my royalties from *Pacific Dawn* in such an enterprise."

Cath took on a mildly mocking tone. "And what will this wonderful publishing operation be called? *Herrick* House?"

Robert looked at her with a sudden, beaming smile. "Why not, Catherine? That's a splendid name!"

Knowl turned to Annie. "You aren't serious, are you? You'd pour your money into something so implausible?"

Annie sounded impatient. "No, Knowl, of course not. As I said, it's just a frivolous little notion."

"Robert," said Cath, "surely you wouldn't consider such a venture. You've talked over and over about going back to the rescue mission in Los Angeles."

He nodded. "I've even written my friend, Marshall Briggs, director of the mission. He knows I'm interested in returning. But, frankly, my real desire is to combine ministry with editing and publishing."

Annie reached across the table for Knowl's hand. "Don't worry, darling. We're only fantasizing about buying our own publishing house. As tempting as the prospect is, we know it's not feasible. But for a few sweet hours, let us dream."

Robert met Knowl's gaze and said candidly, "Unless, ol' boy, you'd like to form a partnership and help us turn that dream into reality."

Knowl was silent for a long moment. Finally he said, "If you're serious, you must realize a wild scheme like this will take a whole heap of praying for all of us." He paused. "But I'll tell you this much. If God wants us to own a publishing house, I'm willing to let Him do the convincing." He looked Robert in the eye. "Before I take this matter up with the Lord, tell me just how serious you are."

"Dead serious."

Cath sat back stunned—not so much at the idea that her brother might contemplate buying a publishing house but that Robert Wayne might become a permanent fixture in Willowbrook. For weeks now she had denied to herself that Robert was inching his way into her heart. If he became an everyday part of her life, how could she possibly quench these tender yearnings? And how could she endure the ache of knowing he could never be hers because in his heart Annie would always be his true love? As much as she hated the thought of Robert leaving, the idea of him staying here with Annie was unthinkable.

"Do you have any idea what's involved in running a publishing house?" Knowl persisted. "Purchasing the facility would be just the beginning. You'd need a staff, people who knew what they were doing."

"Robert would be in charge," said Annie. "He's had years of publishing experience."

Knowl stared hard at Robert. "So you'd leave New York? Give up Los Angeles? Come here? Why? Willowbrook has nothing to offer a big city man like yourself."

"You're wrong," said Robert, his blue eyes resolute. "I think I could find everything I want here in Willowbrook."

12

Catherine wasn't sure when the conversation about buying the publishing house moved from fanciful banter and conjecture to serious consideration, but by the middle of June it had entered the realm of actual possibility. Robert stayed on in Willowbrook to explore the prospects with Knowl, and when the two weren't mapping out strategies, Robert depended on the telephone and U.S. mail to keep up with his editorial obligations at Sanders and Browne.

On Monday, June 16, Knowl announced at dinner the news Cath dreaded hearing. "Robert and I have gone over all the figures. By pooling our resources, including Annie's royalties, we can cover the down payment on the Van Buren facility."

"You've decided to buy it?" asked Cath in alarm.

"No," said Robert. We're still praying about it, but things are looking good. I suggest we spend some time in prayer right now."

"Good idea," said Knowl. Annie echoed his sentiments.

Cath wasn't about to get roped into a prayer meeting. She scooped

Jenny up in her arms and announced, "If you'll excuse me, I'm going to tuck my daughter into bed."

Robert gave her a knowing glance. "We'd love to have you join us, Catherine. I'm sure the good Lord would appreciate hearing a few words from you."

Cath shook her head. "I doubt the Almighty would welcome anything I might say. We're not on the best of terms."

Robert smiled that smile of his. "I'm sure He'd be pleased to change those terms any time you're willing."

"Thank you, Robert, but not tonight." Holding sleepy-eyed Jenny against her breast, she turned on her heel and headed for the stairs. Her face felt warm and her heart was pounding. Why did that pompous, self-assured man have such an effect on her? Or was it his words that needled her, piercing her best defenses? Moments later, as Cath pulled the covers up around Jenny's dimpled cheeks, the child looked up with her innocent angel eyes and murmured, "Say my prayers with me, Mama Cath."

"You say them, honey," said Cath, biting back her impatience.

Jenny jutted out her lower lip. "You say them with me."

Dutifully Cath recited, "Now I lay me down to sleep. . . ." The words continued from her lips, but she blocked them out of her mind. She didn't want to think about asking God to take her soul if she should die before waking. It was just a child's rhyme, after all. Why then did she feel the power of the words weighing so heavily on her tonight? Why at moments like this did she feel pursued by heaven itself? Surely God—if He existed—had better things to do than concern Himself with a stubborn Indiana girl named Catherine Herrick.

The next morning Cath made a decision. She would get busy and complete the panels for Reverend Henry without Luke Henry as her model. She wanted this assignment behind her. In fact, she never would have accepted such a commission if there had been others to consider. Painting deity was better left to those with a penchant for religious art. Truth be told, focusing her creative energies on Jesus was taking a toll on her peace of mind. To capture Christ on canvas, she would have to know Him intimately, and that was something she wasn't prepared to do.

Why should she? God had never been more than an irritant in her mind. He represented condemnation and judgment. She didn't need that. She already felt guilty enough for bearing a child out of wedlock. Secretly she wondered if God had allowed Chip to die at Pearl Harbor because of their sin. She would never utter the words aloud; the very thought pierced her with unspeakable shame. But the notion was always there at the back of her mind, grating against her conscience like sand in the eye. And hadn't she compounded her sin by surrendering her maternal responsibilities for Jenny to her brother and Annie? Even now, Jenny turned for mothering first to Annie or Anna or even Betty; rarely did she seek out Cath.

These thoughts played randomly through Cath's mind as she sat at the breakfast table poking listlessly at her scrambled eggs. Finally, Anna put her hands on her hips and declared, "Goodness, Catherine, did I overcook your eggs? You haven't eaten a bite."

"No, Anna, they're fine," Cath replied, promptly swallowing a mouthful as if to prove her point. "I was just thinking about the paintings for the church. I need to get them done."

"That's wonderful," said Annie as she poured a cup of tea. "I was afraid you might change your mind about doing them."

"Of course not, Annie. You know I wouldn't go back on my word." Cath looked across the table at Knowl, who sat jotting down some figures on a notepad. "Dear brother, before you leave for work, would you go to the attic and retrieve my art books from the Institute?"

He looked up quizzically. "What, Cath? I'm sorry. I was working out some more calculations for this publishing venture we're considering."

Cath repeated her request and he nodded. "Just give me a minute until I finish up here."

"I can get them for her," said Robert, standing up. He was wearing a crisp white shirt and pinstriped trousers and looked roguishly handsome for so early in the morning.

"The attic is dusty," Cath warned as Robert followed her upstairs.

"I'll take my chances," he replied.

She waited on the landing while he climbed the steep, narrow stairs up to the attic. "There's a light just inside the door, and my books are in a box marked 'Chicago Art Institute.'"

A minute later he came lumbering down the stairs with an immense cardboard carton in his sturdy arms. "I see now why you sent a man to get these. They weigh a ton."

"I know. You can take them to my room, if you will."

He strode on down the hall, pushed open her door with his foot, and set the box on the floor in the middle of her room. He looked at her with a smile as he brushed the dust from his hands.

"Oh, goodness, you did get dirty," she cried. Impulsively she wiped at the streaks on his shirt front, then drew her hand back as she felt his muscled chest beneath the smooth material.

"Don't worry, I'll just change my shirt," he assured her. He glanced around her room, his curiosity evident as he scanned her watercolors and sketches that claimed every inch of wall space. His gaze took in the easel in the corner, the palettes festooned with mosaics of dried oils, and the stacks of unfinished canvases propped everywhere. "I don't think I've ever been in your room before," he noted. "You have some fine work here."

"Thank you," she murmured uneasily. Somehow, having him glimpse her personal living space and all its accoutrements made her feel as if he had caught her undressed. "It probably smells of linseed oil and turpentine in here. You won't want to stay long."

He picked up a canvas—a moody, impressionistic portrait of Jenny—and scrutinized it for several moments. "This is especially nice," he told her. "It's brimming with mother-love."

"Really? I never considered my maternal instincts particularly noticeable."

"Your feelings are more evident than you'll ever know," he said obliquely, and winked. "You're a very passionate person, Catherine. You shouldn't fight it so hard."

"Fight it?" She laughed nervously. "Really, Robert, you're speaking in riddles."

His deep azure eyes penetrated hers. "You push everyone's love away: God's, your family's—" There was an unsettling moment of silence as he left the sentence unfinished.

Cath took the painting from his hands. "I suppose you'll be heading back to New York soon," she said, flustered, the back of her neck growing damp. "And I know you've still got business to talk over with Knowl."

"I won't be leaving yet, Catherine," he said meaningfully. "Not until we've finished investigating this publishing deal. Then I'll be deciding whether to stay in New York, head for California, or move to Willowbrook." He paused, his eyes searching hers. "What would you think of me coming to Willowbrook?"

Her cheeks flamed. "It means nothing to me either way," she said curtly, then immediately regretted the sharpness in her tone. More gently she said, "It has to be your decision."

He tilted her chin upward. "Are you still worried about my feelings for Annie?"

She moved away from his touch. "Shouldn't I be? Love has a strange power. It can take us by surprise when we least expect it."

Softly he said, "Are we still talking about Annie and me?"

"Who else?" She stooped down and began removing the art books from the carton. "Thank you, Robert, for getting my books. I won't keep you—"

"I get the message," he said with a smile. "I'll leave you to your research. But sometime I'd like to see the rest of your paintings. I'm a great fan of your work."

She looked up quickly to see if there was any mockery in his expression, but he looked absolutely sincere. She felt a flush of pleasure color her cheeks. "Thank you, Robert. These days I need all the fans I can get."

When he had gone, she settled into her oak rocker by the window and began thumbing through her treasured old books one by one. They smelled faintly musty. These thick volumes had been her constant companions during her years of study at the Art Institute. Slips of paper, ribbon, and old postcards still marked the pages that contained her favorite paintings. If her memory served her right, she would find countless paintings of Christ by the masters.

Sure enough, the books contained religious art that spanned the centuries, from medieval to contemporary. Cath was always captivated by the renderings of the Flemish, Renaissance, and Baroque masters. Nothing could compare, of course, to Michelangelo's monumental paintings in the Sistine Chapel, nor to the exquisite beauty of Leonardo da Vinci's *The Last Supper*. But there were other works that fascinated her as well—Rembrandt's magnificent etchings, El Greco's mystical, haunting portrait of Christ, Botticelli's detailed, richly colored paintings, and Giotto's timeless Byzantine portraits.

Every depiction was different; some showed Christ with a sinewy, ethereal grace; others captured the earthy, gritty reality of a flesh-and-blood man. Some presented a Savior with almost effeminate beauty; others portrayed Him larger than life—an imposing giant of a man with rippling muscles and flowing robes.

And yet there was a startling consistency in all the diverse representations of Jesus, as if every artist in every era and culture had known instinctively how Christ looked. But was it really so surprising? Hadn't Annie and Knowl and the others recognized the likeness of Jesus in her sketches of Luke Henry? Even Cath saw the resemblance, and yet, how did she know His likeness? Did recognition come from her years of studying the religious art of the masters? Or was it something else, something that transcended mortal wisdom and broached the realm of the spirit?

Cath closed her art book and set it beside the other dusty tomes. She could feel a headache coming on. She was becoming too introspective. Annie was the one who thrived on the philosophical, not Cath. She never should have agreed to do the panels for Reverend Henry. Who was she to compete with the works of Rubens, Raphael, Giordano, Tintoretto? Who was she to imagine she could fathom the nature and person of Christ?

She stood up and felt stiff, lightheaded. How long had she sat here perusing her books? Hours perhaps. She ambled into the hallway, still a trifle dizzy, and heard the grandfather clock in the hallway downstairs chime the hour. Noon! Anna was probably preparing lunch already.

Cath felt a pinch of chagrin. She should offer to help set the table or toss a salad. At rare moments like this it struck her that she and Annie were both so caught up in their literary and artistic pursuits, they had abdicated their household responsibilities to their mothers. Anna, especially, thrived on running the house and utilizing her culinary skills. And even Betty seemed to have blossomed as she cared for her little granddaughter. Still, Cath reflected as she hurried downstairs, now that she was well again, she should help more with the chores.

But not this time. Anna was already placing a plate of corned beef hash and a bowl of fruit salad on the table. She looked up at Cath with a welcome smile. "You're just in time, dear. Lunch is ready."

"I was going to offer to help."

"No need. Everything's ready. Just call everyone."

"Where's Annie?" she asked.

"Probably in her study writing. You know Annie."

Cath smiled. She knew Annie. They were two of a kind.

When Annie, Betty, and Jenny had been rounded up and everyone was seated at the table, Cath asked Annie a question she never thought she would ask. "Are there any verses in the Bible that describe Jesus?"

Annie smiled with obvious satisfaction. Cath knew why. The intractable Cath usually bristled at the mere mention of the Bible. Now she was actually inviting Annie to spout Scriptures. It was amazing to what lengths of desperation Reverend Henry's commission had driven her!

"After lunch I'll show you some verses," Annie told her with unmistakable delight.

"Don't get carried away," said Cath dryly. "Just a few should do."

After lunch Cath and Annie settled in the redwood swing on the sprawling, wraparound porch. The air was humid, and flies buzzed with a droning lethargy. Cath could feel the sweat bead on her skin, making her blouse and skirt cling uncomfortably. The pungent fragrance of freshly mown grass tickled her nostrils. She sat back and crossed her arms on her chest while Annie thumbed through pages of her well-worn Bible.

"I think we should start with Isaiah 53," she said.

"Isn't that the Old Testament?" asked Cath. "I want verses about Jesus."

Annie nodded. "Isaiah predicts the birth of the Savior and describes Him with astonishing detail. Just listen."

For he shall grow up before him as a tender plant,
And as a root out of a dry ground:
He hath no form nor comeliness;
And when we shall see him,
There is no beauty that we should desire him.
He is despised and rejected of men,
A man of sorrows and acquainted with grief.
And we hid as it were our faces from him;
He was despised, and we esteemed him not.
Surely he hath borne our griefs,
And carried our sorrows:
Yet we did esteem him stricken,
Smitten of God, and afflicted.
But he was wounded for our transgressions,
He was bruised for our iniquities:
The chastisement of our peace was upon him,
And with his stripes we are healed.

Annie read on, finishing the chapter, but Cath had heard enough. "I wanted physical description," she said, her voice wavering with unwelcome emotion. "I don't want to hear how Christ was wounded and despised and rejected for my sins."

"But it's true," said Annie. "Can't you picture Him? He had no physical beauty. Thorns pierced His head; blood poured from His wounds. He was beaten and spit on. His naked body writhed in agony on the cross. Imagine His eyes as He endured such torment and humiliation for your sins and my sins—"

"But He's also a God of wrath, isn't He?" argued Cath. "I've felt His anger and disapproval plenty of times."

Annie's voice was gentle. "Are you sure it wasn't your own anger and disapproval you were feeling, Cath?"

"I don't know," she admitted grudgingly. "All I know is I've never felt close to God like you do. I've always felt He abandoned me just as my father did years ago."

Annie was silent a moment, her eyes scanning the well-marked page in her Bible. Finally she said, "May I read just a couple more verses, Cath? From Isaiah 54?"

Cath shrugged, and Annie began reading Isaiah 54:7-8:

> For a small moment have I forsaken thee;
> but with great mercies will I gather thee.
> In a little wrath I hid my face from thee for a moment;
> but with everlasting kindness will I have mercy on thee,
> saith the LORD thy Redeemer.

Cath blinked back uninvited tears; her chin quivered. She stiffened her crossed arms against her chest and clenched her hands into fists. If Annie thought she was going to convert Catherine on the spot, she was sadly mistaken. "What do those verses have to do with me?" she muttered, avoiding Annie's gaze.

"Everything," said Annie. "Some day, Cath, you're going to have to confront God's love for you, and respond to it. He won't let you rest until you do. And neither will I."

Cath stood up abruptly and wiped the moisture from her eyelids. "Thanks for your help, Annie," she said, her tone deliberately polite. "I think I have all I need now to begin the paintings for Reverend Henry."

But it wasn't true. In the days that followed Cath realized she desperately needed her model, the strange and elusive Luke Henry. But how could she possibly locate him when she knew nothing about him except his name? The only connection she had with him was the place where they had met in the little park nearby.

So each morning for the next few days Cath packed up her art supplies and walked several blocks over to the park. She sat for hours under the warm June sun painting flowers and trees and passersby while watching for the tall, bearded young man. But there was never any sign of him.

By Friday, Cath was ready to give up. Obviously Luke Henry had disappeared from her life forever. She would have no choice but to muddle through with her commission, using her old sketches of Luke.

And then, that very afternoon, as she was cleaning her palette and putting away her brushes, she looked up and to her amazement spotted that familiar rangy frame and winsome bearded face. Like a ghost from some Shakespearean tragedy, Luke Henry was standing on the corner in rumpled brown work clothes, watching her with a grave intensity.

13

"**H**ELLO, LUKE," SHE said, her heart quickening as he approached. He shuffled toward her, in no apparent hurry, his thumbs hooked on his leather belt. He was dressed in brown; the shirt had saddle-stitching and trim the color of camel hair; it was a western shirt, and he was wearing the same weathered cowboy boots he wore before. His face was tanner and his red beard a little scruffier than she remembered.

"Howdy, Cath," he drawled, looking her over with an approving grin. "How come I had a feeling you'd be here?"

She smiled. "I don't know. Lucky guess?"

"I suppose so. Long time no see."

"I've been here," she replied with deliberate nonchalance. "Where were you?"

"Busy."

"Working?"

"Yep. I had me a whole lot of work repairing houses damaged by the tornado. Didn't have time for sitting and chatting or posing for pictures."

"You've been working right here in Willowbrook all this time?"

"Yeah, mostly here in Willowbrook." He brushed back a thatch of auburn hair from his ruddy forehead. "There's a whole lot of rebuilding to do downtown. And I worked a few days in Nappanee and a few more in Logansport."

"Is that where you're from?"

"Naw. Who cares? It don't matter where I'm from."

Cath groped for the right words—questions that would extract information without sounding too intrusive. "Working away from home must be hard on your family."

"I get home," he replied, sitting down beside her on the wrought iron bench. She moved over to make room for his strapping frame. "In fact," he said, "I've been home this week."

Her curiosity was mounting. "Really? I thought you said you were working here."

"I was, until the past coupla days." He paused, his expression clouding, as if he couldn't decide how much to say. Finally he told her in a confidential tone, "Someone in my family took ill. I had to stick close to home. Take care of things."

"I'm sorry. Is it someone close?"

"Yep. Real close."

"I hope they're better."

"Not much, but I have to get back to work and bring in some dough while the work is plentiful."

"Did you work today?"

"Yeah, but I took off early."

"Any special reason?"

He sat forward and clenched his large hands together as if he were crushing some invisible object. "Yeah," he muttered. "There's a whole lot going on. I got a serious decision to make. Maybe this is the time to do it. I been feeling restless and outta sorts a coupla weeks now."

"Because of the illness in your family?"

"Yeah. And because it's June. June's bad for me."

"What happened in June?"

He spat out the word. "D-Day."

"Someone you loved fought at Normandy?" she asked softly.

His gaze met hers with an unsettling directness. "Yeah. I did."

She stared at him in surprise. "Really? I didn't think you'd be old enough."

"I was nineteen. Old enough to die for my country like lots of my buddies did."

"For some reason I never thought you were in the war. You never mentioned it before."

He continued massaging his hands, nervously squeezing each round knuckle. "I don't talk about it. Nothing to say. It's over. I lived. Lots of others died. Thinking about it does things to me I don't like."

"What things? Maybe if you talked about it—"

His voice sounded thin, barely in control. "Makes me feel like a man with the heebie-jeebies tied up in a bearskin rug. I wanna kick and scream, only I can't budge. I'm trapped like a bug." He looked at her, his eyes narrowing. "I hate feeling trapped."

"I know how that feels," said Cath. She paused, wondering how much about herself she dared share. Somehow confiding in Luke seemed like a natural thing to do. "Last year about this time I was in a car crash," she began, her voice wavering. "It left me in a coma for a long time. When I came out of it, I was helpless as a baby."

Luke's eyes widened. "God's truth?"

"Yes," said Cath. She could feel the tension shooting through her muscles even as she recalled those days. "I had to learn everything over again. It was as if my body and mind had become my enemies. They wouldn't work right. I had to fight them. It was like a battle, like a war, and finally, after a long time, I won. I survived. But it changed me too. I can never go back and be the person I was before."

"That's just how I feel," said Luke, his voice growing animated. "I survived the war, but something inside me didn't survive. It's like I saw things no man should ever see. I experienced things nobody should ever experience."

Cath sensed that for the first time Luke's guard was down. He wanted to talk. Needed to talk. "Tell me about it, Luke," she urged.

He hesitated, then drew in a deep breath and stared back at his hands. Finally he spoke, and as the story emerged, his fingers moved with a brisk, agitated energy, presenting a physical accompaniment to the words erupting from his lips.

"They called it Operation Overlord—a tidy little name, huh? Nothing bloody-sounding about it. Anyway, General Eisenhower set zero hour for Monday morning, June 5. Only thing is, the morning broke with heavy winds and high seas, so Ike postponed the invasion. All day the channel was rough, the skies gray.

"All us guys were on edge. I was with the 29th Infantry Division, and most of us hadn't seen action before. Heck, we hadn't even seen France. My stomach churned all day like I was on the starting line for a race and no one was giving the signal. We had to kill time. Some of the guys shot dice or played cards on jeep hoods, using their invasion money as stakes. Others stood off by themselves smoking and thinking. Some were praying, folding their hands like children saying grace. It's strange. Some who cussed the loudest turned into regular holy Joes. Others sang like they were on *Talent Scouts*. One big bearded Scot sang, 'Don't Sit Under the Apple Tree with Anyone Else but Me.' I can still hear it in my head—those silly words with that heavy brogue. The next morning I stepped over his bloody body on my way up the beach."

Cath instinctively put her hand on his arm. She could feel a tremor where her palm rested. "I'm sorry, Luke. It must have been terrible."

He went on talking as if he had forgotten she was there. "I can still see it in my mind like one of them moving picture shows. The channel was pitch-black with waves of landing ships loaded with men and guns, bulldozers and tanks. Our PT-boats sped around us, watching out for Germans. When we reached Omaha Beach we had to rush the shallows and uproot the steel spikes before they tore open the bottoms of our boats. Our division was one of the first to hit the beach. Every one of us was scared spitless, only we were too dumb to admit it. We figured nothing could touch us; we'd just march in there, scale them cliffs, and take France back from the Germans."

He raked his hand though his russet hair and lowered his gaze. "Next thing I knew I was slogging through sludge with a thousand other guys, walking straight into an artillery barrage, and men were dropping everywhere, falling in their tracks, and the only way I knew I wasn't dead was I was still walking, climbing over the bodies of guys who looked like me, looked younger than me, except they were dead. And suddenly I knew I could be dead just like them the next minute. I wanted to turn tail and run. I wanted to curl up and bawl like a baby. But I just kept plodding up that bloody beach through twisted bodies and debris, knowing the next bullet might be meant for me. I remember wondering how the day could dawn like any other ordinary day when I was crawling on my belly through the pit."

Luke stopped and heaved a sigh, then shuddered. "This is why I don't talk about it," he said, sniffling. "Some things should never be put in words. Words make it real all over again."

"Maybe so," said Cath, "but when we don't talk about the bad things, they grow bigger and take more space inside us and don't leave room for the good things."

He looked at her. "What good things?"

"I don't know. You have to figure that out I'm still trying to answer that question myself."

His gaze remained riveted on her with a solemn scrutiny. "You're a good person," he said at last. "If someone needed your help, you'd be there for them, wouldn't you?"

She studied him curiously. "I suppose so. Why do you ask?"

"I just needed to know. It helps. It makes things clearer for me. Makes me see what I gotta do." He stood up and brushed the stubborn locks back from his forehead.

Cath stood up too. "Are you leaving already?"

"I gotta. My ol' clunker—that rattletrap down the block—needs some gasoline."

Cath followed his gaze to the dented Ford pickup parked by the curb in the next block. "I didn't know you had a truck. I've always seen you walking."

"I like walking, and the park's close to my brownstone, but my truck gets me home and to my jobs . . . when it's running."

"When will I see you again?" she asked quickly. "I really want to paint you again."

He reached out and took her hand and pressed his palm against hers, lining up the fingers one by one. Her hand looked like a child's against his. He flicked his wrist and closed his hand over hers.

Cath let out a little breath of surprise and tugged gently.

He held her fast. "I could take you with me," he whispered.

"What?" Had she heard right?

"Come with me, Cath. Someone needs you."

Her heart started pounding with alarm. "What are you talking about?"

"You're a good person, Cath. You let me talk to you. You let me say things I never said to nobody else."

She pulled harder, but his grip only tightened. "Please, Luke, you're hurting me."

He pushed her forward and began walking her along the sidewalk toward his truck. "You said you'd be there if someone needed you. . . ."

"I meant my family, Luke! I don't know you!"

He bent his face close to hers. "You know me better than you think. Just wait. You'll see."

As they approached his truck, she pivoted sharply, yanking her hand from his. He grabbed for her, but she shoved him away and broke into a run. Her heart hammered with panic as she realized the park was empty. There was no one to rescue her!

Luke was at her side in seconds, his warm, earthy scent filling her nostrils as he circled her slim frame with his strong arms. He held her head against his broad chest as if comforting a child, and murmured, "Don't fight me, Cath. I care about you. It's gonna be all right, I promise."

"Let me go," she whimpered.

He reached out and opened the passenger door and hoisted her up into the cab of his truck. Before she could react, he slammed the door and strode around to his side and climbed in. He looked at her as he turned the key in the ignition. "You gonna be okay?"

Tears slid down her cheeks. "Please don't do this."

He shifted into drive and swerved into the traffic lane, gunning the engine. She clutched the door handle.

"Don't you jump out," he warned. "You'll get hurt."

Her words came out in a sob. "Where are you taking me?"

"You'll see."

"I—I thought you were my friend!"

"We're more than friends," he said cryptically.

"No, we're not. I never led you on."

He kept his gaze fixed on the road. His pickup was clearly a vintage model. It rumbled and clattered and wheezed over Willowbrook's narrow cobbled streets. The cab smelled of fuel, old leather, and stogie cigars—the kind Cath's father smoked years ago. She hated that rank, odious smell. It turned her stomach even now. "It's too close in here. I'm going to be sick," she warned Luke.

"Open the window a crack. Just a crack."

She cranked open the grimy glass and inhaled the warm spring air. She considered flinging open the door and jumping out, but they were going too fast now. She might roll under the wheels and be killed. Better to take her chances with Luke.

Or was she only fooling herself? Maybe her life was as good as over already and she was too blind to see it—the way the troops had been too blind to see they were racing to their deaths at Normandy. Had that terrible day twisted something in Luke's mind, turning him into a madman out for retribution?

Cath stared in alarm at the road ahead. Luke was taking the highway out of town, heading south, entering farm country where the barns were old and decrepit, unpainted, the weathered wood the color of charcoal, except those barns that were plastered with advertisements for Burma Shave, Mail Pouch Tobacco, or Texaco gasoline. The traffic would be light on those unpaved roads that carved endless ribbons through acres of cornfields with rows of green stalks stretching to the horizon and reaching for the sky.

A person could get lost in those cornfields. A person could become invisible in those vast, anonymous croplands. That bucolic countryside, so lush and pristine, could hide a multitude of sins. One slim girl would be no match against a solid, vigorous man who had seen death, who knew it intimately, who had survived but was not the same.

"Where are you taking me?" she demanded, her voice small and uneven.

His gaze remained fixed on the road. A vein in his neck pulsated. "I told you, you'll see."

She wondered, should she try to reason with him, shame him, bully him, flatter him? What in heaven's name would persuade him to take her back and undo this hideous thing that had begun, this appalling betrayal that could end only with disastrous consequences? "I thought you liked me, Luke," she said in a voice light and conciliatory. "I thought we wanted the best for each other."

He looked over at her with a stricken expression. "I do like you, Cath. I like you more than I can say. That's why I gotta do this my way. I don't know how else to do it. I'm not good with words like you. If I tried to tell you, if I explained, you might run away and never let me get close to you again. And I can't let that happen, Cath. I've come too far for that. Don't you see? Too much is at stake."

Her tears started again. "I don't know what you're talking about, Luke. I just want to go home. Please? Please take me home and I'll never tell anyone what you've done. We'll pretend this never happened."

He reached over and gripped her hand firmly in his. "No siree! This is happening, Cath, and we gotta see it through until it's done. It's meant to be. I knew it the first time I saw you last fall sitting in that little park painting, your hair as red and glowing as the autumn leaves. I knew then this day would come."

She gaped at him, stunned. "You saw me—last fall?" A flash of memory shot through her mind like a lightning bolt. She covered her mouth in horror. "You—you're the stranger who followed me home that day. But you didn't have a beard then."

He rubbed his bristly chin. "This was just stubble then."

"You've been following me all this time? Deliberately watching me?"

"I had to know what you were like before I—" His voice trailed off.

"Before what?" pleaded Cath.

He ignored her question. "I watched you go in that big rich man's house, and I said to myself, 'She's a rich girl who hides in her safe, grand house and she doesn't know what the rest of the world is like. She doesn't know there are people like me living in ticky-tacky houses with no carpets on the floor and no fancy cars in the driveway.' And I thought,

This girl doesn't even know we're part of each other; we're living in the same world and she doesn't know I exist. And I knew I had to change that."

"Is it money you want?" she cried. "If it is, my brother will—"

"No, it's not money!" He spat out the words. "This isn't about money. And as for your brother—" He paused and glanced at her from the corner of his eye. "Tell me about your brother. Does he look like me? Is he anything like me?"

"No. He's the finest man I know. Capable, responsible, loyal, caring."

Luke drummed his fingers on the steering wheel. "Is he like his papa?"

"No," said Cath flatly. "He's everything my father never was."

Luke made an annoyed sound low in his throat. "That's downright mean-spirited. I got half a mind to—" Suddenly, the engine coughed, sputtered, and died. The weather-beaten truck rolled to a stop in the middle of the gravel road.

"Thunderation!" stormed Luke. "I forgot the gasoline!"

He jumped out of the truck and stomped to the front and lifted the hood. Then he slammed it down and tramped around and grabbed a gas can out of the truck bed. He got back inside and looked at Cath. "I gotta go get some gas. There was a farmhouse a coupla miles back with a rig or two. I'll hike back and siphon some off if I have to."

"What—about me?" she asked haltingly.

He chewed on his lower lip for a long moment. "It won't do leaving you here. You'll run away or hitch a ride with the next car going by." He glanced around, whistled with satisfaction, then lapsed into a singsong, hillbilly twang. "Well, if there ain't an old tumbledown barn just yonder. Looks to me like a good place to rest a spell."

He went around, opened her door, and pulled her out. "Come on. The sun's hot and I got a long walk to take. I wanna be back on the road before dark. We got miles to go before we sleep." He grinned. "That sounds downright poetic, don't it?"

"Please, Luke," she begged, "let me stay here in the truck. There's nowhere to go and no one around. Look, no other car's been on this road in an hour. I won't leave, I promise."

"We'll do it my way, Cath," he said, gripping her arm. "Let's go."

They tramped across a grassy field brimming with golden dandelions, ragweed, and thistles. She allowed him to nudge her forward through the thick, overgrown meadow, its crop long since snuffed out by the spiky witch grass and nettles. When they finally reached the gray, sagging, antiquated barn, she saw that it was little more than a deserted shed. It was empty except where weeds had grown up between the uneven floor boards. It smelled of moldy straw and must, and something foul that Cath couldn't quite place. Perhaps an animal had died here, or rats or birds or other animals had nested here and long since abandoned their lair.

Luke pulled a red bandanna from his pocket and grasped Cath's arms. "What are you doing?" she cried.

"Sorry, girl. It's gotta be this way." He jerked her wrists behind her, crossed them, and wrapped the bandanna around them, tying it snugly.

"No!" Cath pleaded. "Don't tie me up. I'll be good. I'll stay right here."

He wasn't listening. He unbuckled his leather belt and whipped it through the loops, then stooped down and wound it around her ankles until she lost her balance and nearly toppled. He stood up, gripped her around the shoulders, and lowered her to the floor. She felt the rough, splintery wood pierce her skin through her thin cotton blouse and seersucker skirt. "Why are you doing this to me?" she moaned.

He bent down beside her on one knee. "I'm sorry if I hurt you. I know you're not comfortable. I'll see what I can do."

"Comfortable!" she retorted. How could he speak of her comfort at a moment like this?

"I'll be right back." He turned and left the barn. She could hear him running through the thick, dry weeds. He was back a minute later with a worn mohair blanket and the rumpled brown jacket he had worn the first day she saw him. He spread the blanket on the floor and rolled her onto it, then folded the jacket and tucked it under her head. "Is that better?" he asked.

"Let me go," she wept.

He leaned down close to her and wiped the tears from her cheek. "You're a good girl, Cath, and soon you'll understand. You'll see I had no other choice. Someone needs you, and I'm the only one who can make it happen. Trust me, please."

"You keep saying that," she cried. "Who needs me? Just tell me. I'll understand."

"I wanna believe that, Cath, but I can't take no chances. I gotta go now, but I'll be back as soon as I can." He bent over and lightly kissed her cheek. "Remember this. I care about you more than you'll ever know."

He got up, gave her one last lingering glance, then took long, purposeful strides out of the barn.

"No, Luke, wait! Don't go!" She twisted and squirmed against the restraints that held her fast. Neither the belt nor the bandanna would budge. She could hear the *swish-crackle* of Luke's boots cutting a swath through the overgrown thicket.

Surely he won't leave me here! she thought wildly.

But as the sound of his footfall faded in the warm, alfalfa-scented air, she knew her only connection with the world outside was gone. Breathless, succumbing to a mounting wave of hysteria, she screamed, "Don't leave me here, Luke! Please don't leave me alone!"

14

CATH LAY STILL, listening for some sound that would tell her she wasn't alone. She heard nothing except the distant *caw-caw-caw* of crows, the random twitter of robins and wrens, and the blood pounding in her own temples.

What if Luke never returns? What if no one ever finds me? She imagined someone wandering into this stinking rat hole of a barn years from now and finding her skeleton still bound by an old bandanna and leather belt. Would anyone have the slightest idea who she was or why she was here? She could picture the case remaining on the police logs for years to come, a mystery forever unsolved. She thought of Jenny growing up without her real mother. Chip was gone, and now she'd be gone too. Jenny would be an orphan. Would her daughter think Catherine had left her on purpose? What did a child understand of death?

The thought that she could die here prompted a visceral reaction low in Cath's belly and propelled the taste of vomit into her throat.

With terror pumping fresh adrenalin into her veins, she stretched and strained and wriggled and writhed against her restraints. She could feel her wrists and ankles growing raw, but her bonds remained secure.

No use fighting it. I'll just expend all my energies.

She forced her body to relax on the hard floor. The coarse mohair blanket prickled her skin. She could smell Luke Henry's scent in the jacket under her head. Until today, she had liked that woodsy, virile smell.

Don't panic, she told herself. *Relax. Think of other things and maybe you'll figure a way out of this.*

She thought about her family—precious little Jenny. And Betty, Knowl, and Annie. And Anna Reed, always so strong and supportive, more a mother to Cath than Betty Herrick had ever been. Cath had become so accustomed lately to thinking of herself as an outsider, an extra appendage in the Herrick household. But now as she pictured that cherished house on Honeysuckle Lane filled with the people she loved, she knew how much a part of her they were.

What would they think when they realized she was missing? Perhaps even now they were making that grim discovery. When she didn't return home by nightfall, Knowl would go to the park looking for her. He would find her easel and watercolors and know that something was wrong. He would look for her, ask passersby if they had seen her, perhaps even file a missing person report with the police. Annie would say, "Let's stop and pray for her, that God will be with her wherever she is."

Cath blinked back tears at the thought of Annie's prayers. *Help me, God,* she prayed silently, *and I'll do anything You ask!*

She stared up at the bleak, rough-hewn rafters laced with gauzy cobwebs. She could see daylight through the spaces in the weathered timber. A patch of faded sunlight spilled in through the open doorway. Night was rapidly descending. With no lights or lanterns, the barn would soon be pitch black. Would there be a moon tonight? She couldn't remember.

The thought of lying in this moldering barn in total darkness stirred a deeper, primal terror within her chest. This fusty, primitive box was her prison, her coffin, the last thing on earth her eyes would see.

I'm not here, she told herself. *I'm not really here at all.*

She recalled another dark, terrifying place—the storm cellar she shared with Robert Wayne during the tornado. She had been frightened then, but it wasn't the same. She had felt Robert's comforting arms around her, savored the solid strength of his chest against hers, and had taken solace in the reassuring sound of his voice. He had been her protector, her safe harbor, her refuge in the eye of the storm.

Oh, Robert, if only you were here now, your arms around me, your forceful voice chasing away the shadows! Oh, Robert, I love you so!

Cath broke off her reverie with an incisiveness that left her breathless. What was she thinking? That she loved Robert Wayne? Her mind must be playing tricks. She was delusional! Surely what she felt for Robert Wayne was not love—was, if anything, the opposite of love. He irritated her, infuriated her, mystified her. But that wasn't love. Love was what she had felt for Chip Reed. Love was not something she expected ever to experience again. Chip was dead, so, for Catherine Herrick, romantic love was dead as well.

But the idea persisted, teasing the edge of her consciousness. *Am I in love with Robert Wayne?*

She refused to take the question seriously. This was no time to analyze her love life. What life she had left was perhaps tenuous at best. Night was closing in with a palpable, inevitable finality. Already she could no longer distinguish the deepening sky from the rafters and beams overhead. Rising like a nocturnal symphony was the ratchety song of crickets accented by the haunting call of hoot owls in faraway, unseen trees. The air was growing chill, a breeze rustling the weed-choked grasses surrounding the drafty barn.

I am not here. I am somewhere else, free from worries and care.

Lightning bugs flickered in the darkness. Cath fixed her gaze on them, grateful for even these tiny beacons of hope. She remembered how, as children, she and Annie and Chip and Knowl had captured fireflies and put them in milk bottles. It was a rite of summer. They would watch in fascination as each tiny bug flitted against the glass seeking an escape route while its luminous wedge of green light glimmered like a pulse. They would watch those fragile, frantic creatures until their lights grew dim and went out. Thinking about it now—now that she too knew what it was like to be helpless and trapped—Cath wondered if they as children had ever realized the fatal consequences of their actions. How could they have been so heartless, so unfeeling? Would they have been less cruel if they had realized what they were doing?

Forgive them, for they know not what they do.

Who said that? Cath wondered, and immediately she knew. Jesus had spoken those words, although she couldn't remember exactly when. Then it struck her. He was on the cross, wounded and dying, and more concerned that God forgive His enemies than punish them.

He was wounded for our transgressions. . . .

Words from Annie's Bible played in Cath's mind like phrases in a musical score. *He was bruised for our iniquity. . . .*

She had fought against those words when Annie read them that day on the porch. She hadn't wanted to burden her already guilty heart with thoughts of a suffering Savior. But now, as she lay bound in darkness and cut off from the rest of the world, her defenses crumbled. She felt a curious bond with Jesus. Innocent, he suffered at the hands of others. Innocent, she too was suffering now at the hands of another.

But wait. She wasn't truly innocent. All of her life she had carried the weight of her guilt and shame. Guilt over not being lovable enough to keep her father at home, guilt over surrendering her virtue to Chip because she needed to be convinced of his love for her, guilt over giving up Jenny because she doubted she could be a good mother to her child, guilt even over the possibility that she had caused the accident that cost Annie her unborn child. For most of Cath's life she had operated on a principle of guilt.

But Jesus Himself, at the worst moment of His life had said, *Father, forgive them. . . .*

Cath felt a strange sensation of calm sweep over her. She lay still, surrounded by silence, by darkness. It was as if she had left the reeking closeness of the dingy barn and had on some transcendent level moved into another dimension. The screen of her imagination was the only thing that existed now. She saw herself standing at the foot of a cross, staring up into the face of Jesus. He looked like all the paintings she had ever seen of Him, and yet there was infinitely more etched in the sturdy planes and angles of His face. Her hungry eyes traced every feature—the straight bronze nose and flaring nostrils, the bristly beard glistening with sweat, the tangled, matted hair where a wreath of thorns pierced his bleeding brow, and the parted lips whispering her name.

Catherine, I died for you. Will you live for Me?

And his eyes—dark, knowing, steeped with compassion, penetrating to her very marrow. She could not look away, could not break the connection between Christ and herself. His dying was suddenly a very personal event in her own life. She was bound to that death, part of it, an unknowing partaker in His execution. That death was woven into the fabric of her being, written on the landscape of her own consciousness. Before the spark ignited that flamed Catherine Herrick into being, Christ had already been hammered to that tree so that she, forgiven, could live free. Free of guilt. Imagine.

He had said, *Father, forgive them. . . .*

She was standing at Golgotha staring up at a cross that cut a black swath through a salmon-pink sky; she was alone with a dying Savior. She smelled the sweat soaking His flesh, heard the noise low in His throat as He sucked for air, saw the rivulets of blood streaming down His arms, and tasted the bitterness of vinegar on His parched lips. She could feel His pain searing the callousness of her own heart.

"Why are you doing this?" she cried.

He fixed His gaze on her. *Because I love you.*

Tears welled in her eyes. "I didn't ask You to. I've spent my whole life trying not to think of You, trying to scour the imprint of You from my bones." Tears rolled down her cheeks. A knot of anguish tightened in her throat. "Oh, God, I never wanted to believe I made You die! How can I bear such guilt?"

Familiar words wrote themselves on her heart. *He is despised and rejected of men; a man of sorrows, and acquainted with grief: and we hid as it were our faces from him; he was despised, and we esteemed him not.*

Cath's body heaved with sobs. "I'm sorry, Jesus. I was wrong to reject You. I'm sorry I made You hurt. I'm sorry for all You suffered for me! I don't want to run anymore or hide my face from You any longer."

135

Father, forgive them. . . .

"Will you forgive me, Lord?" she whispered into the darkness. "Will you take away my guilt and make me free?"

Surely he hath borne our griefs, and carried our sorrows . . . the chastisement of our peace was upon him, and with his stripes we are healed. . . .

Tears of repentance flowed freely, and with them came a cleansing such as Catherine Herrick had never known before.

At last she slept, wrapped in Luke's grimy mohair blanket—the peaceful slumber of the forgiven. Until she felt someone shaking her.

"Come on, Cath! Wake up! Are you all right?"

She opened her eyes. A circle of blinding light flashed across her line of vision. Shapes and shadows began to emerge. Someone was bending over her with a flashlight and loosening the bandanna around her sore wrists.

"Come on, Cath. Thunderation, I didn't mean to be so long. I been walking most of the night. Took longer'n I expected to get that gasoline. Cath, you hear me, girl?"

A man's voice, urgent, agitated. Familiar and yet foreboding. God help her, it was Luke! Luke Henry. The dank, pungent smells of wood and straw crowded in, along with the horrific reality of where she was and what was happening.

In the name of heaven, she was still in that ancient, decaying barn, still bound hand and foot, still the prisoner of a madman!

15

"P<small>LEASE LET ME go,</small>" Cath rasped.

"You're loose. See? Here's the belt and bandanna." Luke held them up like absurd trophies and chuckled. "Come on, Cath. Let's go!"

He reached down and helped her to her feet. She swooned against him, dazed. Her muscles cramped; her limbs felt prickly, unresponsive, stirring the familiar sensations of helplessness and desolation that had overwhelmed her after she'd awakened from the coma. Incredibly, she was awaking now to a nightmare even more terrifying.

"I have to go to the bathroom," she murmured as she gingerly rubbed her sore wrists.

Luke gave her a long, desultory glance, as if trying to decide whether her request was only a ploy. Finally he said, "There's bushes out back. I'll wait here, but don't you try running. We've come this far. I'm not about to let you get away now."

Cath was back minutes later, feeling shamed and humiliated. How dare this man force her to take care of such private needs in an open field like an animal! Anger flared inside her with the pyrotechnic sizzle of Roman candles. She wanted to lash out at Luke Henry, sink her fingernails into his cruel flesh, make him hurt the way he was hurting her.

She glared at Luke as he shook out the mohair blanket, doubled it into inept folds, and swung it over his shoulder. She imagined herself tackling him, slamming a rock into his temple, leaving him for dead. But even as she played out the scenario in her mind, she realized how implausible it was. She had no strength to topple him, no rock to disable him. And no telling what vile acts he might attempt if she infuriated him.

As she trudged sullenly beside Luke back to his truck, Cath thought again of Christ, glimpsed in her mind once more the dying Savior. He had allowed men to pound nails into His open palms, had not cursed those who raised Him high on that rugged tree between earth and sky, had in fact murmured His love in the face of their vicious taunts. Jesus had turned from His own nakedness to the needs of a dying thief. He had willingly died a hideous death for those who despised Him.

Cath could never comprehend such love. But from somewhere within her stirred the desire to capture that love on canvas, to make His sacrifice as real to others as it was now, this moment, to her, however feeble her attempts might be. Silently she prayed, *Dear God, now that I've tasted Your love for myself, please let me live long enough to paint the panels of Jesus for Reverend Henry.*

As she settled into the grimy cab of Luke's truck, Cath's nostrils revolted against the stale air heavy with gasoline fumes and the faint odor of Luke's sweat. She shrank from Luke as he slid in behind the wheel and jabbed the key into the ignition. He turned it over until the ancient engine coughed and sputtered and heaved into a slow, labored crawl over the bumpy road. Staring ahead out the dirt-streaked windshield, she pressed her slim body against the passenger door and clenched her hands between her knees. Her summer skirt and blouse were rumpled and torn, her bare arms and legs crisscrossed with scratches.

"You hungry?" asked Luke when they had traveled a few miles.

Cath hadn't thought about hunger, although her empty stomach churned and knotted with pain. No, it was the thirst she was aware of.

Her tongue felt thick and dry and seemed to have fused with the roof of her mouth so that swallowing was agonizing. "Water," she managed.

"I thought of that," said Luke, sounding proud of himself. He reached down beside him and produced an old red thermos, the kind factory workers carried in their big black lunch pails. "I filled this when I helped myself to the gasoline."

Cath seized the thermos, fumbled impatiently with its thick brown cork, and drank lustily. The water was warm and had a dull metallic taste, but she welcomed its healing stream over her parched mouth and throat.

"There's a little place along the highway where we can catch breakfast," said Luke, eyeing her appraisingly. "If you promise to be good."

"I will," she whispered, and she meant it.

They wheezed along a few more miles, the old rattletrap truck grunting and groaning with every mile it claimed. Cath knew they were heading east. She watched the sun transform itself from a pale pink wafer on the horizon to a shimmering fireball overhead. The dilapidated vehicle jounced over rutted, gravel-lined roads and endless strips of highway black with sun-softened tar. They passed acres of swaying cornfields and vast stretches of yellow-ochre wheat fields, where tender grain undulated under a dazzling sun. In and out of view swept quaint clapboard farmhouses nestled on wide green lawns and brown tracts of earth with sagging barns and tilting silos.

"When can we eat?" Cath asked at last. What if Luke had only mentioned stopping for food to mollify her?

"Soon," he said. "We're almost there."

"Where?" she entreated. "Where are you taking me?"

"You'll see." He looked over at her with what seemed genuine concern. "This isn't what you think, Cath. I didn't mean to scare you last night. You hear? I'm not trying to hurt you. I care about you more than you know."

"Then let me go home."

"I can't. Not until—"

"Until what? Tell me, Luke! I can't stand this!"

"I know. I'm sorry. We'll be there soon, and you'll understand. Please don't hate me for what I'm doing."

Familiar tears of anger and frustration brimmed in her eyes. "How can I not hate you for doing this to me?"

The pulse in Luke's jaw throbbed. He spoke out of an unexpected torment. "I know I've messed things up, Cath. I didn't mean it to turn out this way. You gotta believe me. I'm doing this for you as much as for anybody. You'll see."

Privately Cath mused, *If I ever get out of this alive, I'd just as soon see you dead, Luke Henry!* She paused and cried silently, *Dear God, don't expect me to be generous and forgiving like You. I'm too human for that!*

After driving another mile or two, Luke turned onto an asphalt road that cut a narrow swath through a modest burg with a handful of rustic brick buildings skirted by narrow sidewalks. The storefronts bore handmade signs proclaiming Foy's Food Market, Peck's Cut Rate Drugs, Weatherwax Appliance, and Carter's Lumber.

"That's the place," said Luke, pointing toward a nondescript restaurant with chintz cafe curtains extending the length of its plate glass window. A white painted sign overhead with scrawled letters read *Dew Drop Inn.*

Luke helped Cath out of the truck and, with his hand firmly on her elbow, directed her toward the screened door. "Be good," he warned under his breath.

They entered the homey eatery and sat down at a small checkered oilcloth-covered table. A stout, gray-haired woman handed them menus and said she'd be back in a minute. Cath tried to catch her eye, but the woman looked harried, disinterested. Someone behind the counter was calling her, saying something about a meat loaf sandwich. She padded back to the counter, shaking her head. "I told you already. We're out of meat loaf!"

Cath stared blankly at the menu. The words swam meaninglessly. She needed to eat, but her mind registered only that she was back among honest-to-goodness people who had no idea she was living a nightmare in their midst. These bustling, ordinary folk had the power to rescue her—to summon the police or overtake Luke by force—but how could she let them know she was the prisoner of this deranged man?

She stared at the paper napkin under the stainless steel flatware. Perhaps she could scrawl a message to the waitress, but how, and when? Did she dare jump up and scream or try to run? Or would Luke turn violent and hurt some innocent bystander?

The waitress was back, her pencil poised over her notepad, wisps of gray hair straying over her fleshy jowls. She looked like somebody's grandmother, like a woman who would generously offer comfort if she suspected someone was in distress, but at the moment she had too many customers and not enough time.

"It's the noon hour," she told Luke. "Rest of the day we're hardly busy. What can I get you?"

He ordered egg salad sandwiches and lemonade for both of them. Cath considered speaking up and ordering something else, then thought better of it. Why make a fuss over a mere sandwich when her life was at stake?

"Plain or toasted?" asked the woman, her gray eyes sweeping from Luke to Cath.

"Plain." Cath tried to say more with her eyes, tried to hold the woman's gaze with her own silent scream for help, but the waitress simply jotted something on her pad and was gone.

Luke looked at Cath and smiled. For an instant he was the old Luke who posed for her, who had actually reminded her of Jesus, who had taken her into his confidence with tales of his exploits and losses at Normandy.

"This is better, isn't it?" he said.

Cath wasn't sure whether he meant the restaurant, or her, or something else. She shivered inwardly and kept her hands folded tightly on the table. If they could continue this innocuous facade long enough, perhaps she could figure out a way to escape.

"This is the way I imagined it," he continued brightly. "The two of us having a pleasant trip. This is swell."

She nodded, watching her knuckles whiten, the bones vivid under her skin. She could hear a high, shrill sound in her head. It had started out faint at first, but now it was growing louder, filling the cavity of her skull. The noise was building to a crescendo, forming a pressure behind her eyes, turning her forehead feverish. She clamped her dry lips together, knowing the sound was building to a scream. The pain swelling behind her eyes was blinding as a lightning bolt. Remotely she understood that if she lost control and allowed the terror to vent itself, she might never recover, might shrink back into the fetal ball she had been during the coma. *Oh, God, not that!*

"Two egg salads," said the waitress, allowing the stoneware plates to clatter on the oilcloth table top. "And two lemonades. Anything else?"

Look at me! Cath wanted to shriek. *Can't you see I'm sitting with a lunatic? Help me!*

"We're all set," said Luke with his boyish grin. "Everything's hunky-dory."

Cath forced down her sandwich, knowing she would need the strength it offered, but when she swallowed, the bread knotted into doughy clods and the lemonade burned the parched lining of her throat.

"This is real nice, Cath," said Luke, beaming. "I'm getting real excited now. We're almost there."

"Where?"

"You'll see. You're going to be real surprised. More surprised than you've ever been in your whole life."

"I don't like surprises, Luke," she told him shakily. "Please tell me now. Why are you forcing me to go with you?"

His thick brows shadowed his small dark eyes, turning his expression malevolent. "Don't say that. I'm not forcing you. It's just—if I told you, you wouldn't come."

"Yes, I would, Luke. Just tell me."

He concentrated on his sandwich, devouring it, ignoring her. She retreated, nibbling her sandwich too. It was no use. Luke was not a man to be reasoned with. But then, what kind of man was he? Cath didn't want to find out.

When they had finished eating, Luke paid the check and tossed a couple of coins on the table. "We're leaving now, Cath. Don't try anything," he warned. Grimly he escorted her out of the little beanery and back into the cab of his truck. Cath heaved a sigh of dismay. What a fool! Her only chance to signal for help was gone.

They drove the next half hour in silence. Cath chastened herself for not doing something at the restaurant to summon help. Whatever happened now, it was her own fault for not extricating herself from Luke Henry's clutches when the opportunity presented itself. The old Cath, before the accident, would have been more ingenious, and infinitely more daring.

After a while Luke turned off the asphalt road onto a two-lane highway. Cath's hopes rose that they might eventually enter a large city with lots of people milling about, offering her another occasion to escape. Sure enough, she spotted a sign that said, FORT WAYNE—10 MILES.

"Is that where we're going?" she asked, masking her eagerness. "To Fort Wayne?"

"Not quite," said Luke obliquely, and lapsed back into silence. Cath's hopes plummeted when, several miles later, he turned off onto a narrow dirt road that wound among a tangled maze of overgrown bushes and trees. Luke's tumbledown truck bounced over sunbaked hillocks and craggy gullies where spring rains had washed away the earth.

"This road is jarring my teeth loose," Cath complained.

"We're almost there," said Luke. He turned onto another road where a thin layer of gravel covered the tightly packed earth. They passed several houses—small, boxy structures with peeling paint and broken shutters. Exhausted jalopies sagged in unpaved driveways and weeds ran rampant in cracker-box yards. The gravel road led to a forested area of sturdy oaks and pines rising up from a tangle of underbrush, wildflowers, raspberry bushes, and thriving sumac.

Beyond the foliage in a narrow clearing sat an old barn, a shed, a chicken coop, and a squat frame farmhouse made of rough-hewn timber with a black tar paper roof. The front porch looked like an afterthought with its spindly railings and tacked-on gingerbread trim. Unattended lilac bushes obscured any view from the narrow, unadorned front windows. Chickens strutted about the yard with a smug air of ownership.

Luke pulled into the driveway and parked behind a black mid-thirties Ford sedan. He looked over at Cath and said, "Come on."

She stared at the drab structures. "Is this where you live?"

"Could be." He got out and came around to her side and opened the reluctant, creaking door. She climbed down from the cab and walked with him wordlessly through the uncut grass to the porch. She scaled the steps cautiously, taking note of the broken slats. As Luke knocked soundly on the door, Cath breathed a sigh of hope that whoever was inside would have more good sense than this crazy, deluded man, Luke Henry.

After a moment the door swung open and a tall, thin sprig of a girl stared out blankly at Cath. No more than a teenager, she had soft, finely etched features framed by tousled auburn hair. Most striking were her full, pouty lips and large brown eyes as deep and tender as a doe's. She was wearing a worn housedress that looked large on her slim frame. Looking from Cath to Luke, she asked in a mildly accusing voice, "Who's she?"

"None of your business," said Luke. "Where's Ma?"

"Inside."

"Go tell her I'm home."

"Tell her yourself." The girl turned and, moving with a slow, languid grace, disappeared down the hall.

Cath mused that the girl looked so delicate, a strong wind might blow her away. In fact, the waiflike creature didn't seem to take up any space; one moment she was there, the next she was gone.

Luke nudged Cath into the cramped living room with its nubby, maroon davenport, two spindly end tables, and an old maple rocker in one corner. Several Norman Rockwell prints hung on the walls in modest dime-store frames, and a curio shelf held several inexpensive knickknacks. A round rag rug with alternating circles of maroon and white covered most of the hardwood floor. Cath wondered why. The hardwood floor was the room's only attractive feature.

"Ma!" Luke called, sounding impatient.

Cath felt the knot of fear in her stomach relaxing. Nothing about this little farmhouse seemed threatening. Had Luke simply brought her home to meet his mother like a young man wooing his best girl? It seemed improbable, and yet . . .

"Luke! Goodness, when did you get here?"

Cath turned at the sound of the woman's voice and gazed into the lined face of a plain, middle-aged woman with wispy gray-blond hair and faded blue eyes. Wearing a gingham apron over her modest housedress, the woman looked as if she might once have been pretty had not hard work taken a heavy toll. She stared a long moment at Cath, the color draining from her face. "Luke," she uttered in disbelief, "you didn't! Oh, merciful heavens, is this the girl?"

"It's her, Ma. Sure enough."

The woman wrung a dish towel in her thick, white hands. "I told you it would never work, Luke. I told you not to do it."

"I had to, Ma. You know it had to happen sooner or later. We don't know how much time we got."

Cath felt the hairs on the back of her neck rise. This woman sounded as unbalanced as Luke. "I don't know what this is all about," she began unevenly.

The woman fixed her gaze on Cath, her pale eyes registering concern and regret. She tucked her towel into her waistband and reached for Cath's hands. "I'm sorry, dear. I plumb forgot my manners. It's just—I never expected this. I'm Laura Henry, Luke's mother."

Cath withdrew her hands and held them at her sides. "This is bizarre—Mrs. Henry, or whoever you are. I don't know what I'm doing here." Her voice rose shrilly. "I want to go home now. If you have an ounce of kindness, you'll let me use your telephone—"

Laura Henry stared at her son. "Luke, you didn't tell her?"

"No, Ma, I couldn't. She wouldn't of come."

"Then how did you get her here?"

"I just—took her."

Laura Henry looked back at Cath and covered her mouth with her hands. "Oh, mercy, child. What you must think of us!"

Cath felt suddenly as if she had found a friend. Perhaps the whole world wasn't insane after all. Tears sprang to her eyes. "I just want to go home. Please let me go."

Laura urged Cath over to the davenport. "Sit down, dear. Let me get you a sandwich or a glass of tea."

"I don't need anything but a telephone," Cath protested.

Laura Henry's eyes shone with sympathy. "Don't worry, child. Luke will take you home. I'll see to it myself."

"No, not Luke!" Cath couldn't imagine riding anywhere with him again. "I—I'll call my brother."

Luke stepped in, his voice booming with conviction. "No, Ma, first she's gotta—"

"That's enough, Luke. You've already botched up everything. Let me handle this." Laura Henry reached over and touched Cath's arm. "There's someone you better see, dear. Just for a few minutes. Then, if you want, you can go."

Cath looked around uncertainly. "Who? I don't know anyone here."

"Come with me," said Luke, starting for the hallway.

Cath looked questioningly at Laura.

"It's all right. Go with him."

With misgivings, Cath followed Luke down the narrow hallway. As he paused at a closed door and reached for the knob, Cath noticed the frail, auburn-haired girl peering out sullenly from another doorway. But as soon as Cath's eyes met hers, the girl drew back inside and closed the door.

"In here, Cath," Luke whispered as he pushed open the door. With mounting anxiety, she stepped into a small, dark bedroom that smelled of urine and Lysol disinfectant, illness and death. The shades were drawn and the air was close enough to feel. It pressed in on her like an unwelcome blanket—stale, stifling, stealing her breath.

It took a moment for her eyes to adjust to the darkness. Slowly the shadows became shapes—a dresser, a nightstand with a ceramic water pitcher, a bed. Someone was sleeping in the bed.

Cath stepped back and whispered to Luke, "Someone's sick. I don't want to intrude."

"You've come this far," he said meaningfully. He crossed the room and rolled up the shade, allowing the stark noonday sun to spill in with a startling, eye-blinking glare, revealing a cramped room shorn of frills or adornment.

Propelled by a force beyond herself, Cath walked over to the bed and stared down at its sleeping occupant. It was only an old man with sagging jowls and mottled skin, his thinning, gray-streaked hair unkempt, and spiky brows shadowing his eyes.

She moved closer to get a better look at his face, and suddenly, as a shaft of sunlight illumined his features, the random pieces of a monstrous puzzle began falling into place. She knew this man. He was as much a part of her as she was of him. She turned in astonishment to Luke and cried, "This is my father! You've got my father!"

Luke sprang forward, wrapping his fingers around her wrist. She shook off his grip. "How did you do it?" she demanded. "Where did you find him? Did you kidnap him too?"

Luke gazed at her with a solemn, knowing expression, his eyes misting, turning red around the rims.

"Do you hear me?" Cath's voice rose, bordering on hysteria. "Tell me! Why is my father here?"

For a long moment Luke said nothing. Then, his dark eyes piercing hers like nails, he replied, "Because he's my father too."

16

T HE OLD MAN stirred. "Who's here? That you, Luke?"

"It's me, Papa." Luke hesitated, shifting from one lanky leg to the other, then added, "I brought someone to see you."

The craggy face turned, the folds of pale flesh around neck and jowls adjusting themselves on the pillow. The clouded eyes moved from Luke to Cath. With the light of recognition, the frail man's eyes filled and glistened like rhinestones in raindrops. He moved his mouth, his lips thick and sluggish as he groped for words. "C-Catherine?"

"I'm here, Papa." The words came out instinctively. Inside, Cath was numb, her mind frozen and blank as an Alaskan tundra. This was not real—this man, this dark, smelly, oppressive room, the echo of her own breathy, light, incredulous voice. From somewhere else she was watching this surrealistic scene unfold. From somewhere else she was safe and unfeeling, knowing this had to be a dream.

"I knew you'd come, daughter."

Her father's voice. That deep, gravelly voice had echoed down the corridors of her memory since childhood. That familiar tone, those distinctive inflections had so blended with her own voice she didn't know which was which; her father's voice played in her head, argued with her, condemned her for all the wrongs she'd ever done, reminded her of all the love she'd never known. This old man in this house of strangers had her father's voice.

It's not possible. My father's gone, dead; he's been dead to me for years! Had Luke hypnotized her, worked some powerful alchemy to create this convincing apparition?

Cath felt her knees buckle. She reached out and clasped the maple headboard. Surely this dream had played itself out. At any moment she would awaken in her familiar room in her brother's house on Honeysuckle Lane.

The old man held out a trembling hand to her and rasped, "Kn-Knowl—is he all right?"

"Yes," said Cath. "Knowl's fine." *It is Papa*, she acknowledged silently. *He remembers his son.*

She allowed his warm, unsteady hand to envelop hers. Her father's touch. Flesh and blood connection. Jolting loose long buried memories of the towering, handsome man of her childhood, the swaggering, golden-tongued salesman dressed in his fancy suit, a beaming smile in place as he strutted out the door with his Fuller Brush satchel. Always coming and going. Coming and going. Mainly going. And finally gone.

When had she last seen him? At Knowl and Annie's wedding seven years ago. He had looked old even then—his handsome mane of red hair streaked with gray, his rugged face lined beyond his years. But that slightly bloated, bombastic, middle-aged man had nothing in common with the pale, broken figure lying in this bed.

"And—your mother?" he asked hoarsely. "Is she—okay?"

"Mama's fine." Cath wanted to say, *When did you ever care how Mama was?* But she bit back the words. "Mama stopped drinking," she said instead. "We all live together now in the old Reed house on Honeysuckle Lane. Knowl bought it for Annie. It's a wonderful home." *Nothing like the house Knowl and I grew up in around the corner.* "And we're all very happy together." *No thanks to you, dear Papa!*

"Happy? That's good." His eyes closed, and his hand fell away from hers.

"Let him rest," said Luke, urging her toward the door. "Come on. Mama will want to see you." He led Cath down the hall to a tiny kitchen, where Laura Henry was placing glasses of tea on a stained oilcloth-covered table. "You better sit down and have yourself something cold to drink," she told Cath. "It's warm in here, and you'll need some refreshment."

"I don't need tea. I need answers," said Cath, bristling.

"You'll get your answers." Laura turned and removed a tray of biscuits from an old black enamel oven. "You like biscuits with sorghum syrup?"

"Yes, but—"

Luke pulled out a spindly white chair from the table. "Here, Cath. Sit. Mama will tell you the whole story about your papa."

Cath sat down and sipped her tea. The back of her neck was wet with perspiration. Even the front of her blouse was damp. The cold tea felt good going down her throat.

Laura Henry sat down across from Cath. "Luke, go get Bethany Rose. She needs to hear this too."

Luke left and was back a moment later with the pretty waif of a girl who had first answered the door.

"Cath, this is my sister, Beth," said Luke, pulling out a chair for her. "She's seventeen and going to be a senior in high school. She likes to draw and paint just like you do."

Bethany remained standing, her smoldering brown eyes scrutinizing Cath. "What's this about, Mama?"

"You sit down and you'll find out."

With a defiant toss of her head, the girl sat down, her reddish-brown hair cascading around her shoulders. Luke sat down too and propped his elbows on the table, as if eagerly anticipating his mother's words. "Go on, Mama. Tell the story."

Laura Henry fixed her faded blue eyes on her daughter. "I didn't plan to tell you this way, Bethany Rose, but this here is Catherine Herrick, from Willowbrook. She's your half-sister."

"I got no sister, Mama," Bethany protested.

"Yes, you do," said Luke. "You just didn't know."

Cath set her glass down hard on the table. "This is impossible."

Bethany sat forward, her dark eyes flashing. "What's this about, Mama? Why is she here seeing Papa?"

"He's not just our papa," said Luke. "He's her papa too."

"I'd like to know what's going on!" declared Cath. "From the beginning."

"Listen to me, children," said Laura, "and I'll tell you."

The room grew still, except for the droning of a black fly buzzing around the biscuits. Cath felt the blood pumping in her chest and beating with a pounding pressure through her temples. The warm air was charged with a tension as prickly as heat lightning. She didn't want to hear their words. She sensed already that Laura Henry's story would change everything about the way Cath saw herself and her life and her family. This ordinary, plain-faced woman was going to rewrite the history of Catherine Herrick with her terrible, irrevocable revelation.

Laura pushed a wisp of silvery hair back from her face. "Long time ago I lived on this farm with my folks, just the three of us. We were poor even then, but with hard work we got by. When they took sick, I quit high school to help with the chores. After they died I worked the farm alone. I was barely nineteen when a man came by selling brushes."

Her eyes glistened at the memory. "He was handsome and smooth-talking and a whole lot older than me. I was pretty in those days and looking for a Prince Charming to carry me away from the drudgery of the farm. We started courting and fell in love, and I knew I'd found my man. But one day he up and left, no word, nothing. He left me with a broken heart and a baby in my belly. That baby was you, Luke.

"One day this man came back to Fort Wayne and I showed him his baby, and we fell in love all over again. He made lots of promises, but he never talked about marrying me. That's when I began to suspect he was already married. I didn't ask. I didn't want to know.

"For several years this man was in and out of my life, here a spell, then gone again. I considered him my husband. I took him as he was, no questions asked. Five years after Luke was born, I bore him a daughter. That was you, Bethany Rose."

"Stop, Mama. I don't like this story. It can't be true!"

"Hold your tongue, girl, and let me get it all out. Then you can have your say." Laura swallowed her tea, then wiped her mouth with a corner of her apron. "As the years went by my man spent more and more time here on the farm with me. He never carried me away like Prince Charming, but when he wasn't out selling he helped tend the farm and raise the kids. Then one day when Bethany Rose was about five years old, he says to me, 'Let's get married,' like it had just occurred to him. I figured then, if he was married before, somewhere along the line he must have got a divorce. So we were married, and he came to live on the farm full time, except, of course, when he was out on the road selling his brushes or vacuum cleaners or encyclopedias. That man I fell in love with and finally married was Tom Henry, the man in that bedroom."

Cath shook her head. "There's a glaring mistake here. The man in that bedroom is not Tom Henry. He's Tom Herrick, my father."

Laura lifted her chin defensively. "Yes. I found that out when Tom had a heart attack last autumn. We thought he was going to die. In his delirium he called out names I didn't know. *Catherine. Knowl.* I knew it was time I learned the truth and put things in order. So Luke and I went through Tom's private papers."

Luke broke in. "We found out Papa was Tom Herrick from Willowbrook. He had all these old pictures of you, Cath, and your brother, and faded clippings about your art shows, and an old *Saturday Evening Post* cover you painted."

"I knew then I was wrong to pretend Tom never had another family," said Laura, "so I sent Luke to Willowbrook to find out about you."

"That was the time last fall when I saw you watching me and you followed me home," said Cath.

"It was," said Luke. "Mama didn't want me telling you who I was. She figured the shock might be too much."

"Tom rallied and got better," said Laura, "so we decided to leave well enough alone. But several months ago Tom got worse again. Doctors said his heart was failing fast. I knew Tom had to make peace with his other family before the good Lord took him."

"That's when I came to Willowbrook and found you painting in the park," Luke told Cath. "I figured if I got to know you, I'd get some idea how you'd feel about seeing your papa again. And if I won your trust, maybe you'd come home with me. I bided my time for weeks, working odd construction jobs, but our papa was getting sicker and sicker, and finally I knew I just had to pick you up and bring you here, no matter what."

"I thought you were a maniac," said Cath ruefully. "I was sure you were going to kill me."

"I never meant to scare you, Cath. You're my sister."

"She is *not* your sister," said Bethany shrilly. "*I* am!" She jumped up from the table, nearly toppling her chair. "You're all lying! Papa wouldn't do such awful things! You're making up ugly, ugly stories!"

"We are not," said Luke. "It's all true. Tell her, Mama."

"No! I don't want to hear it!" Bethany covered her ears with her palms and ran out of the room. A moment later the radio blared from her bedroom, spewing out the jolly, gravelly voice of Arthur Godfrey.

"Turn it down!" Luke shouted.

Laura gravely shook her head. "I should have told her sooner. I knew how hurt she'd be."

Cath stood up shakily, her hands gripping the table edge. "I'm not handling this too well myself," she murmured. She felt like the fabled Alice tumbling down the White Rabbit's hole into Wonderland, where nothing and no one made sense. Like Alice with the Queen of Hearts, Cath wanted to brush these people aside like a pack of cards, dismiss their bizarre claims, and restore sanity in her life. But this wasn't Wonderland. That man lying sick in the bedroom was her father, and nothing she said or did could change that fact.

"Are you all right, child?" asked Laura, standing too.

"No, I'm not," said Cath. "My head hurts. I can't think straight. My mind is reeling. Perhaps what you've told me is true, but I have to hear it from my father."

"I know." Laura took her arm. "First, come sit down on the davenport and rest."

Cath allowed herself to be escorted to the living room, where she settled on the lumpy couch and put her head in her hands. Perhaps if she simply drifted off to sleep, she would wake up and realize this was all a dream.

But her reverie was broken by Bethany's startled exclamation from the hallway. "Mama! Luke! On the radio they reported a woman missing in Willowbrook. The police are looking for her kidnappers!"

Laura stared at Luke. "Did they mention the woman's name?"

"Yes, Mama. It's Catherine Herrick!"

Laura swatted her son's arm. "Look what you did, boy!"

He raised his hands defensively. "Well, I got her here, didn't I?"

Cath looked up urgently at Laura. "I've got to call my family and tell them I'm okay."

"The telephone's on the wall in the hallway."

With trembling fingers Cath dialed the familiar number. She prayed Knowl wouldn't answer. She wanted to tell him in person about their father's secret life, his other family. It rang once, twice. Knowl would be at work, of course, unless he was waiting by the phone for a call from her kidnappers.

Finally an answer. Cath sighed with relief. Her mother's voice. She assured Betty she was fine and added, "I'll explain everything when I get home. Don't cry, Mama. Is Robert there? No, not Knowl. I've got to speak to Robert."

Minutes later Cath returned to the living room where Laura Henry waited with her two children. Cath stared at Luke and Bethany as if seeing them for the first time. Was it true they were her father's own misbegotten offspring?

"Did you reach home?" asked Laura.

Cath nodded. "A friend is driving over from Willowbrook. He should be here in a couple of hours."

"How come you didn't ask your brother to come?" said Luke. "Our papa needs to see his other son before he dies."

Cath shivered. "There's still time, isn't there? I need time. I don't know how to tell Knowl."

"Nobody knows how much time Tom has," said Laura. "Some days he's better, some days he's worse."

"You're going to see him again before you go, aren't you?" asked Luke.

Cath averted her gaze. "I don't know."

The late afternoon sun streamed in through the windows when Cath heard Robert pull up outside the farmhouse in Knowl's Dodge sedan. She flew to the door, lest Luke Henry hold her back. It was an irrational fear—she realized that now—but a remnant sensation of terror remained nevertheless. But, thank God, her beloved rescuer had come. She flung open the door and ran into Robert's arms as he came striding up the walk.

To her surprise, his passions were as heightened as hers. He wrapped his arms around her and held her so close she thought her ribs might crack. He kissed her hair, her forehead, her cheeks, pulling back just before his lips touched hers. Instead, he breathed against her mouth, "My darling Catherine. I feared you were dead. I feared I'd never be able to hold you in my arms again and tell you how much I . . ."

Cath was about to say, *Oh, Robert, I love you too,* but he let his words drift off, unfinished. She stepped back, quelling a momentary twinge of disappointment, and led him into the house to meet the Henry clan. During the next hour, for Robert's benefit, Laura Henry recounted the extraordinary tale of Tom Herrick's other family, concluding with Tom's near fatal heart attack and Luke's bungled, imprudent attempt to reunite Catherine with her father.

"That was a stupid thing to do," Robert told Luke, "forcing Catherine to come here against her will without telling her the reason. Half the police this side of Chicago were looking for you until I called and told them it was a false alarm."

Luke scowled. "I didn't mean her any harm. She knows that."

"I didn't know it last night," Cath retorted.

Robert reached across the davenport for her hand. "When you didn't come home last night, we were beside ourselves with worry. Then, when we found your easel and paints still set up in the park, we thought the worst. We were up all night talking with police, praying for you, and telephoning people who might have seen you."

Cath patted his hand. "As you can see, I'm fine—at least physically. Emotionally, I'm still numb with shock. I can't believe my father deceived us all these years."

Laura looked off toward the hallway. "My poor Bethany Rose can't believe it either. She's locked herself in her room."

Cath studied Laura for a long moment. "I don't understand how you could live with my father all these years and not know about his past. Why didn't you make him tell you?"

Laura's chin quivered slightly, then stiffened with conviction. "Maybe that's why Tom loved me. I accepted him as he was. He didn't have to explain, or apologize, or justify himself to me. Don't you see? His past didn't matter."

"It mattered to me," said Cath. "And it mattered to my mother and brother."

"I didn't know about you," said Laura.

"I know," said Cath. "You never asked."

Robert spoke up. "Catherine, would you like to head home to Willowbrook now?"

She nodded. "Suddenly I'm exhausted."

Laura stood up. "I'll check on Tom. If he's awake, he'll want to say good-bye."

Cath was about to protest, but Laura was already heading down the hallway. She returned a moment later. "He wants to see you, Catherine. He's more alert than he's been in days."

Cath looked at Robert. He squeezed her hand. "You don't have to see him if you're not up to it."

"Please," urged Laura. "You might not have another chance."

"All right. But only if you'll come in with me, Robert."

He agreed and followed her down the hall to the tiny darkened room. A knot of panic and revulsion twisted in Cath's stomach as she opened the door. Nausea rose in her throat. What could she say to the man who had abandoned and betrayed her and her mother and brother? What vestige of affection could she summon for the father who had left her as a child feeling unloved and unlovable?

Because of him, her entire life had been a painful paradox. Driven to find love, she was convinced no one could ever love her. How different her life might have been had she not felt compelled to win Chip Reed's love at any cost, or had she not relinquished her fatherless child to Annie out of misguided fears of rejection and feelings of inadequacy.

"Cath, are you all right?"

157

She looked up at Robert. "Yes. Why do you ask?"

"You're standing here in the doorway, but your mind is a thousand miles away. Your father's waiting. Have you changed your mind?"

"No, of course not." Last night she had experienced the wonder and sweetness of Christ's unconditional love. Wouldn't He give her the strength to face her father now?

Squaring her shoulders, she approached his bedside and touched his hand lying limp on the blanket. He opened his eyes and gazed up at her. "Papa," she asked softly, "are you feeling better?"

His mottled brow furrowed. "Did Laura tell you—?"

"Yes, Papa. I know the whole story."

His eyes glistened with unshed tears. "I—I'm sorry."

Cath drew closer to the bed. "Tell me, Papa. I need to hear it from you."

He closed his eyes for a moment, as if drawing from untapped reserves of strength. Then he opened his eyes and fixed his gaze on her. "Betty and I—we were no good together. We clashed constantly. She turned to alcohol. I—I found comfort in other women. Both of us were miserable."

"I remember those days," Cath admitted.

"The only time I felt like a man was," he continued haltingly, "when I was closing a deal. Only trouble was—" He paused, sucking for air. "I couldn't close a deal with my family. You all expected things I couldn't deliver. Your mama wanted us to be rich like the Reeds around the corner, but my schemes always fell through. I felt worthless, like a shriveled up old man."

He began coughing, so Cath handed him a glass of water with a straw. His fingers trembled as he clasped the straw and sipped. A rivulet of water trailed from his chapped lips. "Then I met Laura," he said, the lines in his face relaxing. "She made me feel ten feet tall. Accepted me faults and all. I couldn't let her go."

"Why didn't you tell us?" asked Cath.

"Your mama's a spiteful woman. She would have broke us up."

"So you lived a double life all these years! You even changed your name to Henry! Why, Papa?"

He sighed heavily. "I didn't want either family knowing about the other, so I took the name from Reverend Henry. *Henry, Herrick.* Similar, but different."

Tears of anger welled in Cath's eyes. "Didn't you ever think about how Knowl and I would feel? You abandoned us, Papa!"

He turned his head away. "I've lived with regret every day, daughter."

"But not enough regret to make things right," she retorted.

He looked at her, his eyes luminous, urgent. "Is it too late, Catherine? Can you forgive me?"

She drew back. "Forgive you? Papa, you gave me a lifetime of pain. Words can't change that. Words can't change what I feel inside. Words can't undo all the damage."

He closed his eyes, his jowls sagging with resignation. "I know, daughter. I've had my last best shot at life, and lost. God will have the last laugh."

Cath blinked back her tears. "He's not laughing, Papa."

The old man coughed again. His breathing was labored. "Remember, daughter, I always loved you."

A sob convulsed in Cath's chest. "I never felt it, Papa. Oh, God, I wish I had!"

Robert slipped his arm around her shoulder. "Maybe we'd better go."

She nodded and leaned over and touched her father's forehead. His skin was clammy. With effort he lifted his hand to her. "Tell Knowl to come. Let me see my son once more."

"I'll tell him," Cath murmured. She was feeling faint. The airless room was closing in on her, oppressive as a cave. *Oh, God, I'm holding on for dear life. Don't let me collapse now!* With a whispered good-bye to the broken man in the bed, she gripped Robert's sturdy arm and fled.

17

ON THE DRIVE home to Willowbrook, Cath sat in the darkness of the Dodge sedan beside Robert, silent at first as the tires made a rhythmic whirring sound over the pavement. She vowed not to speak of this day, nor to acknowledge this new bizarre truth about her father, lest speaking of it give it validity and substance.

But how long could she keep silent? The numbness was slowly wearing off even as pent-up emotion swelled within her chest. In an effort to neutralize her feelings she fidgeted with the folds of her skirt. She sighed over and over again but couldn't seem to catch her breath. Her throat felt tight; a lump was growing there, making it hard to swallow.

She rocked back and forth, her distress mounting. She felt confined; this vehicle was too small, its doors and windshield and seats boxing her in. Her legs felt jumpy; she wanted to kick, hit something, scream. The lump in her throat was a massive sob, so full and hard she might not survive its force were she to release it. She would not cry, not now, not here, not in front of Robert.

"Are you all right?" he asked, casting her a sidelong glance.

"No," she managed in a small voice. "I'll never be all right."

"You can cry if you want to. They say it helps."

"I don't want to cry."

"But isn't that what women do when . . ."

"When they're upset?" Cath finished with a note of sarcasm.

"I didn't mean to sound patronizing. I just thought—"

"I don't want anyone at home to know I'm upset. If I cry, my eyes will be red and my face blotchy."

Robert gave her a long questioning glance.

"Watch out," she warned. "You're weaving."

He turned his gaze back to the road, but his concern was obviously still focused on her. "You're going to have to tell them, you know. Knowl and your mother will have to know the truth about your father."

"I can't. It would kill them."

"No, it won't. They'll survive just as you will."

"You don't understand," argued Cath. "Knowl has worked so hard to make something of his life. You know how he is. He works twice as hard as any other man to prove he's nothing like our father. He's lived his whole life in the shadow of our father's sins. I know my brother. Knowing what Papa has done would devastate him."

"You can't keep this to yourself, Catherine. It's too big."

"I have to, Robert. The truth would destroy my mother too. After all these years she's finally stopped drinking. How long do you think her sobriety would last if she knew about Papa?"

"Do you really think you can go home and pretend that nothing happened?"

"I have to try." She seized his arm. "Promise you won't tell."

"It's not my place to tell, Catherine. It's yours."

"Give me time. Please, Robert! Time to get my bearings."

"Of course." He squeezed her hand. "You know I only want the best for you."

"The best for me?" A sob tore at her throat. "God has certainly given me the best, hasn't He? I prayed to have my father back, and now that I have him I learn he has two lives, two wives, and two sets of children. I got more than I bargained for, didn't I? God certainly has a sense of humor!"

Robert's voice was gentle, yet firm. "Don't blame God for what your father has done, Catherine. It wasn't God's will that your father sin."

Her eyes welled with unshed tears. "I know about God's love and mercy, but I'm afraid I can't be as forgiving as He is. I'll never forgive my father for what he's done."

In spite of her resolve to keep back her tears, Cath could no longer staunch their flow. Her shoulders heaved as anguished sounds erupted from her throat. It shocked her to realize the noises were coming from her own lips.

Robert pulled the automobile over to the side of the road and turned off the engine. Tenderly he pulled Cath against him and held her head against his chest. She wept until her sobs turned dry and a fit of hiccups sent spasms through her chest.

"Get it all out," Robert whispered against her ear. "Kick, scream, hit something if you must. It's what I did for months after I was wounded at Pearl Harbor."

Her breathing still labored, she moved from the shelter of his arms and slammed her fist against the solid dashboard. It stung, but she hit it again, and again, and again.

A part of Cath remained at a distance watching and monitoring the out-of-control Cath as she screamed and pounded her fists against the dashboard. The distant, silent part of her felt relief wash in even as the sobbing Cath finally collapsed against Robert again in exhaustion. They sat that way for a long time, neither of them moving a muscle, except for their own separate, rhythmic breathing.

At last she stirred. "You do know how I feel, don't you?" she whispered in the darkness.

He pressed his cheek against her damp, tangled hair. "Yes, Catherine. My losses were different, but the pain was just as intense."

She looked up at him. Lights and shadows played across his face, giving his chiseled features the contrast and drama of an El Greco painting. "Knowl or Chip would have told me to stop crying," she murmured. "They would have been afraid of so much emotion."

Robert chuckled. "We're very much alike, Catherine. I told you that before, but you didn't believe me."

She wanted to believe him, yearned for him to kiss the salty tears from her lips and offer not just arms of comfort, but the embrace of romance. But she could not risk Robert's rejection. If love were to blossom between them, he would have to make the first move.

But instead of seizing the moment Robert suddenly disengaged himself from her and turned on the engine. The warmth in his voice turned to caution. "Well, Catherine, we'd better get you home before everyone thinks you've been spirited away again."

She settled back in her seat, disappointed. For an instant the torment over her father's double life gave way to a new pang—the thought that her love for Robert might never be returned.

It was after nine when Robert pulled the vehicle into the familiar driveway on Honeysuckle Lane. As he opened the door for her, Cath hoped everyone might be in bed, but naturally everyone was waiting up to welcome her home. Betty, Anna, Knowl, and Annie promptly surrounded her, greeting her with eager hugs and sighs of relief. Even little Jenny had refused to go to bed until she could give her Mama Cath a big hug and kiss.

"I'm fine. I'm perfectly fine," she assured everyone as she headed for the kitchen for a cup of hot tea and a bowl of Anna's chicken soup.

"You don't look fine," said Annie. "You've been crying."

Cath sat down at the table while Anna poured the tea. "It's been an upsetting experience," she conceded.

"What happened?" demanded Knowl. "Are you all right? I want to know every detail."

"She wouldn't tell me a word on the phone," Betty complained. "She would only talk to Robert."

Knowl turned to Robert, who was helping himself to a bowl of Anna's chicken soup. "How about it? Have the police made an arrest?"

"No," Cath broke in.

"Why not?"

"Because I wasn't abducted."

"Then what happened? Where were you?" quizzed Annie.

Cath lifted her hands placatingly. "Please, everyone, no more questions. I don't want to talk about it tonight. I just want to finish my soup and go to bed."

"I think that would be best," Robert interjected. "There will be plenty of time for questions later."

But in the days that followed Cath carefully avoided all their questions, heightening the mystery of her disappearance with her cryptic responses: "I'll tell you the whole story someday . . . I can't talk about it now . . . I'll explain when the time is right."

"Did someone attack you?" Annie asked her privately. "The night you came home, I noticed your hands were bruised."

Another time Knowl drew her aside and asked, "Who are you trying to protect? Someone hurt you, didn't they? Tell me, so I can make things right."

Even Anna in her delicate, genteel way probed Cath for answers. "You've changed since you came home, dear. You're so serious and introspective. I see you sitting for long periods of time staring into space. Wouldn't you feel better if you talked about what happened?"

And, of course, Cath's mother, Betty, made no bones about how she felt. "I know something bad happened to you that night, girl. Come on, tell your mama. It's not right for a daughter to keep something like this from her mother. Did you run off with some man and find out it wouldn't work? Are you in trouble again? I figured you would have learned your lesson after Jenny. 'Fess up, girl."

Cath's blood boiled. "No, Mama, I didn't run off with any man and I'm not in a family way! Just let me be!"

"Have your own way. You've always been secretive and independent and stubborn as a jackass. Your willfulness comes from your father's side of the family. You certainly didn't get it from me!"

Only little Jenny allowed Cath any peace. For days after Cath returned home Jenny would curl up in her lap, lovingly pat her cheek, and murmur, "You stay home now, Mama Cath. Don't go away again. You stay here with me, okay?"

"I will, sweetheart," Cath assured her with a big squeeze. If anything good had come out of her misadventure, it was this new closeness she felt with her daughter.

And, of course, there was Cath's new relationship with Christ. The memory was still fresh of that night alone in the barn and the brokenness she had felt over Christ's sacrifice for her. Golgotha had become a reality. Redemption was personal, accessible, hers to claim. She was aware of this new dimension in her life—the presence of Christ's Spirit within her.

But in many ways the relationship remained a mystery. What exactly did it mean to know God? Most of the time she felt like the same person she had always been. Was the experience real or just a figment of her imagination? Did God really inhabit her being or had she merely had an emotional reaction to a desperate situation?

When the doubts came, Cath answered them with the only reality she knew. She was the same person, and yet not the same. Even in her rage and despair over her father, she was conscious of a presence within her—a quiet voice that came to her in the eye of the storm, spoke to her in the silence, and assured her she was not alone. This new spiritual dimension was a marvelous, incredible paradox. The One who had died for her lived within her. The voice in her soul was no longer hers alone. Now His voice was there, His love, His being. This truth changed everything, and yet it was too immense to digest except in hairbreadth fragments.

Constantly the questions whirled in her mind, spinning out new questions, new possibilities, all without answers. What did it mean to experience God? How could she fathom His truths? How could she comprehend such love? She kept the questions to herself just as she kept her new faith to herself. How could she find the words to convey something so imponderable to those she loved? They might say, *Go to church, join the choir, put on all the accoutrements of traditional Christianity.* She wasn't ready to step into someone else's religious trappings, lest this secret treasure become routine and commonplace.

One sunny July afternoon Cath strode out past the gazebo in the backyard to the garden studio that had sat boarded up for months. During her recuperation from the accident it had fallen into disrepair and become a catchall storage shed. But now she was ready to do some serious painting, so she carted away the junk and debris and scoured the shed until it was spanking clean. Then she moved in all her art supplies from her makeshift studio on the back porch.

For the next several days Cath spent long hours at her easel. She was obsessed with the desire to capture on canvas what she had experienced that night in the barn. If she could make Golgotha as vivid to others as it had been to her, perhaps they would catch a fresh glimpse of Christ. With new vigor and passion she painted the panels of Jesus for Reverend Henry. No longer was Luke Henry her inspiration, although the resemblance was there in the physical features. Now she longed to portray the inner man of Christ, His light, His passion, His very Spirit.

Working every day from dawn until dusk she completed the panels one by one—the life of Christ from His birth to His ascension. But most dramatic, most gripping, most heartrending were the panels depicting Calvary.

Cath refused to let anyone see the panels until they were completed. When Reverend Henry asked how the paintings were coming along, she assured him she was proceeding on schedule and the works would be ready for viewing by September 1.

She was glad her work occupied her time, keeping her mind off her father and his other family. She had made no contact with them since leaving Fort Wayne, nor had they telephoned her. She couldn't be sure her father was even still alive, although she supposed Laura Henry would have notified her if Tom had died.

Thinking of their father dying without seeing Knowl pricked her conscience more than she cared to admit. She had promised Tom she would send Knowl to see him. Now, weeks had passed and she still kept Tom's terrible secret from her family.

Robert kept urging her to tell Knowl and her mother the truth, but how could she risk their happiness for the sake of a dying old man who had betrayed them all?

Cath was only vaguely aware of the events occurring in the lives of the rest of her family. She knew Robert and Knowl were proceeding with their plans to purchase the publishing facility on Van Buren. They were often off consulting their attorneys and bankers and publishing colleagues. Or else Robert was on the phone taking care of Sanders and

Browne business. In fact, Robert had become a permanent fixture around the house. Although he had made a token effort to find an apartment of his own, the few apartments in town were already occupied by veterans and their rapidly growing families. But Cath suspected Robert was just as happy to stay on as a guest in the Herrick house where he could be close to Annie.

During the first week of August Cath realized just how out of touch she had become with her family. The truth hit home after dinner one evening when Knowl stood up and proposed a toast. Everyone looked up questioningly except Annie, who sat with a pleased little smile on her lips.

"Annie and I have an announcement to make," he declared, raising a crystal goblet of Vernor's ginger ale as his dark eyes crinkled with merriment. "My darling Annie and I are expecting a baby sometime around Christmas, and we trust you will join us in thanking God for His wonderful gift!"

Everyone uttered exclamations of delight, except Cath, who sat staring at Annie, stunned. "I never guessed! Why didn't you tell me?"

Annie beamed. "You were so busy with your painting, dear heart. I didn't want to distract you."

Cath went over to Annie and drew her to her feet. "You must be nearly five months along, and I never even noticed!"

Annie pulled her full skirt tight across her blossoming middle. "See? The right garments can disguise almost anything, for a little longer, at least."

The two friends embraced. "I'm so happy for you," Cath told her earnestly. "You and Knowl deserve every happiness."

"How about a hug for the papa?" said Knowl.

As her brother swept her up in his arms, Cath stole a glance at Robert, expecting to see a look of disappointment on his face. But, surprisingly, he looked genuinely pleased with Annie's news. Cath wondered, had he finally put away his romantic feelings for Annie, or was he merely showing himself to be a very good actor?

Turning her attention back to Annie, Cath asked, "Why did you keep your good news a secret for so long?"

Annie's expression took on a sudden wistfulness. "After the miscarriage, we decided to wait a while before telling anyone about this baby. You understand. We wanted to be sure. . . ."

Cath embraced Annie again with a little sob in her throat and whispered, "If it hadn't been for me, there might not have been a miscarriage."

Annie held Cath at arm's length. "Don't ever say that, dear Cath. It was an accident. That baby wasn't meant to be born."

Cath's eyes filled. "I wish I could believe that."

Annie smiled lovingly. "You can. Just be happy for us now."

"We're all happy for you, dear girl." Anna came over and gave her daughter a generous hug, then winked knowingly at Betty Herrick. "We grandmothers had our suspicions a long time ago, didn't we, Betty?"

"We spotted the signs," Betty agreed. "It was those gallons of milk she was drinking and the tiny booties she was knitting."

Annie laughed. "I didn't know anyone was watching!"

Robert stepped in, taking his turn to give Annie a congratulatory hug and a kiss on the cheek. "Looks like my favorite author will be busy with other things for a spell."

"Don't worry," she assured him with a wink. "My new book will be ready for Herrick House as soon as you close the deal on the Van Buren facility."

"Let's not get the cart before the horse," warned Knowl. "Robert and I have a lot of options to explore before we can sign on the dotted line."

"Son, if you want my opinion," said Betty, "you'd better hold on to your job at the newspaper, especially with the baby coming."

"I never said I was giving up my job," replied Knowl.

"Well, I think it's plain foolishness," snapped Betty, "buying a publishing house in these unstable times. You're going to end up just like your father, Knowl, chasing dreams and following schemes that will leave you penniless."

"I'm not like Papa, Mama," Knowl countered hotly. "I'm nothing like him. I've taken care of you since I was a boy, and I've taken good care of my wife. Remember, it was my investing in the newspaper that allowed me to buy this house back for Annie after her family sold it. And if I decide it's right for us to invest in this publishing house, that's what we're going to do!"

Betty offered a stiff, conciliatory nod. "Whatever you say, son. I'm sure you know best."

Anna broke in discreetly. "Listen, everyone, let's have dessert in the parlor. I made Annie's favorite—floating island pudding. So get your-selves comfortable, and I'll bring along a fresh pot of coffee."

"No dessert for me," said Betty, sounding a trifle peeved. "I'll take Jenny up to bed and read her a story."

"I'll tuck her in tonight," offered Cath.

"No, daughter, you stay and visit with Annie." Betty took Jenny's hand. "My granddaughter and I have our routine all set, don't we, Jenny?"

The child nodded vigorously, her auburn curls bobbing. "Grandma Herrick rocks me and we play the radio."

"We listen to *The Great Gildersleeve* or *Baby Snooks,*" said Betty. "Then we read a story and have a drink of water—"

"Then I say my prayers and go right to sleep," said Jenny brightly. "But Grandma always leaves a little light on to keep the monsters away."

"Don't you worry, sweetheart," said Cath, giving her daughter a bear hug, "no monster will ever get you. You're too sweet." She touched the tip of Jenny's nose. "And, wherever you go, God will always have His angels watching over you."

Everyone took turns kissing Jenny good night, then headed for the parlor as Betty took her granddaughter upstairs. Annie settled beside Knowl on the velvet love seat; Cath and Robert took the nearby wing chairs. "Cath," said Annie with a smile, "Jenny has done wonders for your mother."

"Yes, it's hard to believe how much Mama's mellowed."

"The fact that she hasn't had a drink in ages helps," mused Knowl. "I hate to think what would happen if she ever hit the bottle again."

"Don't even say such a thing," admonished Cath.

Annie ran her fingertips over the cuff of her husband's shirt. "Knowl, I'd like to continue our discussion about buying the publishing house. Are you having second thoughts?"

"No, darling. I'm just not sure yet what my role is going to be in this venture—whether just a financial investment or a career change as well."

Annie studied his expression. "I don't want you to do this just so I can have my book published."

"I'm not, Annie. I'll make my decision based on what I feel is best for this family."

"I'm very optimistic about this investment," said Robert. "We couldn't ask for a better time in our nation's economy. Industrial production, wages, and corporate earnings have reached new heights."

"You're right, Robert," Knowl agreed. "With wartime controls off and exports booming, everyone has money and wants to spend it. The question is, Will they spend it on books—inspirational books, at that?"

"Joshua Loth Liebman's *Peace of Mind* is on the Best Sellers list," noted Cath. "And that's an inspirational book."

"But for every best-seller, there are hundreds that fall by the wayside," said Knowl.

"Reprints are doing well this year," noted Annie.

"True," said Robert. "The twenty-five-cent paper-bound books are selling like hotcakes, but look at the big names they're touting. Penguin-Signet's list claims Faulkner, James Joyce, and Erskine Caldwell."

"Well, Annie's established her name too," said Cath.

"And I'm already a has-been."

"That's not so," said Robert. "Okay, the sales of *Pacific Dawn* have slowed considerably, but it's still selling well for a first novel. And I think your second novel offers a refreshing alternative to the costume romances they're cranking out these days."

"But can you make a go of this new publishing venture if Knowl remains with the newspaper?" asked Annie.

Robert and Knowl exchanged cryptic glances. "Naturally I'd like Knowl on my editorial team, but I'll respect whatever decision he makes."

Annie slipped her hand into Knowl's. "My husband loves his work. He thrives on knowing what's happening in the world almost before it happens. Isn't that right, darling?"

"That sums it up rather well."

"Anyone for coffee or dessert?" Anna entered with her serving tray of steaming china cups and crystal goblets of creamy, meringue-peaked floating island.

When everyone had been served, Robert sipped his coffee, then said wistfully, "I'm going to miss service and food like this."

"Miss it?" said Cath, a bit too quickly. "You're not leaving Willow-brook, are you?"

"No, I'm staying right here, Catherine." He glanced over at Annie. "I just figured with the new baby coming, Annie and Knowl might need my room for a nursery."

"There's always the sewing room," said Annie.

Robert grinned. "You think I might be able to squeeze in beside your trusty old Singer sewing machine?"

Annie chuckled. "I meant the sewing room for the baby!"

"You know, Robert," said Knowl, "if you're getting cabin fever around here, I know of a house on the market. It's a fixer-upper, but it's going for a good price."

Robert's brows arched with interest. "Where's it located?"

"Right around the corner. It's the house Cath and I grew up in. It's been vacant for months now and is badly in need of repair. But it's structurally sound. Annie's grandfather built the house around the turn of the century, about the same time he built this place."

"Sounds intriguing. I'll have to take a look at it."

"Like I said, it needs a lot of work. You'd have to find yourself a good carpenter."

"What about that young man who posed for you, Cath?" suggested Annie. "Didn't you say he's a carpenter?"

The blood drained from Cath's face. "Who?"

"You know. That man who posed for you in the park."

Cath's hand jerked slightly so that her coffee sloshed over into her saucer. "I'm sorry. I—"

"I thought he was your inspiration for those early sketches of Jesus," Annie persisted.

Cath set her cup and saucer on the mahogany table between her chair and Robert's. "Uh, his name? I really don't—"

"Wasn't it Luke something? Yes, I remember. He had the same last name as Reverend Henry."

"If he lives here in town," said Knowl, "Robert could get in touch with—"

"Robert doesn't even know if he's interested in our old house," protested Cath.

"Cath's right," said Robert quickly. "It's quite premature for me to think about buying a house right now."

"Except for a certain publishing house on Van Buren," said Knowl.

Robert grinned. "Yes! That's the house on my mind these days—if we can just come up with investors and a staff."

Annie looked over at Cath. "Dear, you look deathly pale. Are you feeling all right?" Suddenly she smiled. "Oh, I know what your problem is."

Cath's mouth went dry. "Robert told you, didn't he!"

"No, dear. I figured it out by myself." Annie went over and knelt by Cath's chair. She patted Cath's burnished ringlets and looked around from face to face. "Next month our Cath will be having her first art exhibition since her accident. Think of it! She'll be unveiling her lovely panels of Christ's life. Reverend Henry is planning a wonderful reception for the entire town. Art connoisseurs will be here from around the country. And yet here we sit talking only about ourselves and our publishing venture. How selfishly we're behaving! Will you forgive us, Cath?"

Cath looked away, blinking back her own guilty tears. *Will any of you be able to forgive me when you find out how I've deceived you?*

18

YOU ARE CORDIALLY invited
to a Preview Art Exhibition
featuring twelve paintings of "The Life of Christ"
by renowned Willowbrook artist Catherine Herrick
at the Willowbrook Christian Church
Willowbrook, Indiana
at 2 p.m., Saturday, September 6, 1947
Reception following

It seemed half of Willowbrook ventured out for the unveiling of Cath's paintings, not to mention a number of art enthusiasts from out of town and out of state. The church had never had a larger crowd swelling its walls and swarming over its premises. Old Reverend Henry was ecstatic. "Everyone is here," he told Cath excitedly, "the mayor, ministers from Chicago and Indianapolis, newspaper reporters, and representatives from several of the most prestigious galleries and museums in the country!"

Cath herself, her auburn hair in a fashionable chignon and wearing a striking queen's blue and emerald green suit with matching tam, was amazed at the interest her show had generated. Artists and dealers journeyed from neighboring states—Illinois, Michigan, Ohio. Art critics and religion reporters came representing midwestern newspapers and journals. And several colleagues and instructors from the Chicago Art Institute made their appearance, bringing back nostalgic memories of her freewheeling days at the Institute. But, more than memories, they offered her an invitation to display her work in their upcoming exhibition of contemporary American art.

But that was only the beginning. A suave young man with pronounced Roman features introduced himself as Marcus Casella and told Cath he was a representative from the Whitney Museum of American Art in New York City. "I have followed your career since you studied at the Art Institute before the war," he told her with the hint of an accent. "Your portrayal of *Mother and Child* on the cover of the *Saturday Evening Post* possessed a powerful artistic essence that overshadowed many of the provincial Rockwell covers."

Cath flushed with pleasure. "Thank you, Mr. Casella. I'm flattered."

"I was disappointed that I did not see more of your work." His intense dark eyes fixed on hers. "Then I learned of your accident and understood why we had not seen more paintings from you."

"It took me more than a year to gain back my skills," Cath told him. "And even then I wasn't sure I could do it."

"Ah, but you have succeeded beyond your dreams, Miss Herrick." Marcus raised his hands in tribute to her work. "These paintings of the life of Christ transcend all that you have done before. They are masterful, capturing both the ethereal grace of our Lord as well as His gritty earthiness. They breathe realism and yet shimmer with celestial light. They are stunning, riveting, particularly the portrayals of Golgotha. Never have I experienced the events of the Crucifixion with such a sense of personal involvement." He closed his eyes and crossed himself. "You made me weep, Miss Herrick."

Cath felt tears well in her own eyes.

Marcus smiled. "And now, Miss Herrick, I hope to have good news for you. We may be interested in your work for one of our Whitney

Biennials. Of course, the final decision will be up to our curator, Lloyd Goodrich. It is his great desire to educate the public about what important artists of our day are doing."

Cath could scarcely catch her breath. "I would be honored to have the Whitney Museum exhibit my work, Mr. Casella."

He took her hand and kissed it lightly. "We will be in touch, Miss Herrick."

While Cath was still recovering from the shock of Marcus Casella's proposal, an older, paunchier man, with a gleaming bald head and shrewd black eyes, handed Cath his card. "I'm Alex Shubin, art dealer from New York, and I think we can do business, young lady."

Before Cath could respond, he asked, "How would you like to see your work displayed at New York's Museum of Modern Art beside the paintings of Ben Shahn and Georgia O'Keeffe, or at the Corcoran Gallery of Art in Washington, D.C., or at the Boston Museum of Fine Arts?"

Cath finally managed a reply. "I'd be delighted, Mr. Shubin, but what makes you think those galleries would—"

"Want you?" finished Shubin, rubbing his double chin. "I'll tell you the truth, Miss Herrick. I have an eye for what interests art directors and curators like Alfred Barr and Dorothy Miller. You've heard of Miller, of course."

"Yes—"

"She curates the Modern's exhibitions of up-and-coming artists. I think she'd like your work. In fact, her husband would like your work. Holger Cahill. Ran the artist projects of the WPA during the Depression."

"Oh, yes," said Cath. "The American Scene painters."

"Right. Cahill prefers realism over some of this new abstract stuff. I agree. I think American artists should leave abstraction to the Europeans with their impressionism and postimpressionism. So, like I say, if you're interested in representation to some of the best galleries around, I'm your man."

"Thank you, Mr. Shubin," Cath said politely. "I'll certainly keep you in mind."

As Alex Shubin padded off to the refreshment table, Cath turned to Robert. "Can you believe it? Shubin and Casella talked with such confidence about my work appearing at some of the most prestigious galleries in America!"

Robert slipped an arm around Cath's waist. "It's what you deserve, Catherine. Your work is stunning."

Her eyes searched his. "Do you think so? Do you really like what I've done?"

"Like it? Dear Cath, that doesn't begin to express my reaction." He drew her to him, his face so close to hers she could feel his warm breath on her lips. "I'm amazed by your portrayal of Christ. You've gone far beyond the sketches of Luke Henry. I see something in your work I'm almost afraid to hope for."

She stared questioningly at him. "What, Robert? What do you see?"

His voice grew tremulous with emotion. "I see a woman who captured the Spirit of Christ because she knows His Spirit personally. Am I wrong, Cath? Tell me I'm not wrong."

Cath smiled deeply. "No, Robert, you're not wrong. I wanted to tell you sooner, but I didn't know how. I suppose I was afraid to tell. I didn't want anyone pushing me into a religious mold I wasn't ready for or turning something so fresh and beautiful into a rigid set of rules and regulations."

"Why would you even think that, Cath?"

"Because that was all I saw of Christianity when I was growing up—the dos and don'ts, the rituals and routines. I don't want to lose the joy and wonder of Christ's presence."

Robert grinned. "They're not antithetical, you know, dear girl—a personal relationship with Christ and traditional Christianity. They are one and the same, or at least they can be. You'll see that as you come to understand the Scriptures."

Knowl and Annie interrupted then, offering embraces and effusive words of praise and congratulations. "I knew you could do it, little sister," Knowl enthused, "but I didn't realize until now how big your talent is."

"Dear Cath, this is your childhood dream come true," said Annie with feeling. "I'm so proud of you!"

Robert squeezed Cath's hand and said, "We'll continue our conversation later. May I escort you home after the show?"

"Of course, Robert. I'd be honored."

It was nearly six before the last guests left. Reverend Henry, lumbering slowly now with weariness, remained the perfect host, shaking hands and thanking each person for coming, while adding a sly, "Hope to see you in the morning for services."

Even Betty Herrick, with little Jenny in tow, offered Cath a rare compliment. "You did yourself proud, daughter. Didn't know you had it in you, girl. You choked your ol' mama up with some of these paintings."

Jenny squirmed at Cath's side, holding her arms up for a hug. "Paint me a picture too, Mama Cath! Paint Jesus watching over me when I go to sleep."

Cath scooped her child up in her arms. "I'll do that, sweet pea. I'll paint Jesus holding you in His arms, like the Good Shepherd held His sheep."

"But now it's Jenny's bedtime." Betty took the child from Cath. "Wave bye-bye to Mama. That's a good girl."

Cath was still throwing kisses to Jenny when Robert ambled over and squeezed her shoulder. "Are you ready to go home, too, or would you like one more glass of punch?"

Cath laughed. "As much as I'd love to hold on to this magical day forever, I'm ready to go home." She glanced down at her three-inch platform shoes and wiggled her toes. "I've been standing all afternoon. My feet hurt like the dickens."

Robert offered her his arm. "Then shall we go?"

She looked up at him. "But how? Knowl is driving the family home in his sedan. Won't he expect us too?"

Robert's eyes crinkled with amusement. "No, I told him to go on without us. I have a taxi waiting."

"A taxi? How thoughtful. But just one more moment, Robert." Holding his arm, she stepped out of her shoes and picked them up in one hand. In stocking feet she circled around her paintings one last time, her gaze taking in each one. "It's really happened, hasn't it, Robert? I'm back. Whole again. My career is on track, stronger than ever. My dreams are really coming true this time."

Robert nodded. "God has blessed you with a rare and special talent, Catherine."

With a grateful smile, she took his arm and they walked out of the church together, stopping in the narthex to bid Reverend Henry a good evening.

In the taxi on the way home, as a salmon-pink sunset settled on the horizon, Robert slipped his arm around Cath's shoulder and drew her close. "We need to talk, dear girl. I've paid the cabby an extra dollar to drive us around a while, along a country lane or through a lovely wood, so we can chat privately a spell. Now tell me the story of how you came to know our Savior."

Cath told him about her night alone in the barn and how real Golgotha had seemed in that terrifying darkness. "For the first time I caught a glimpse of how Christ suffered," she told him, "and I suddenly realized He would have died for me even if I'd been the only one who had ever sinned. I realized His gifts were personal, from Him to me—His love, His forgiveness, His Spirit. I couldn't turn away from such love any longer."

In the quiet closeness of the cab, Robert turned Cath's face up to his and whispered, "There's another love I hope you can't turn away from, my darling."

She looked into his eyes, her lips parted with an unspoken question. But before she could speak he kissed her lips, gently at first, then deeply. Within moments she was returning the kiss, releasing the passion she had held back for so long.

Against her cheek he whispered, "I've wanted to hold you like this for months, dear girl, but I couldn't take to my heart a woman who didn't share my faith."

"I thought you still loved Annie," she replied breathlessly.

"No, I care for her as a friend, but I never loved her the way I love you."

"I was afraid to hope for your love," Cath murmured. "Everyone I've ever loved has hurt me, or I've hurt them."

"Hurt is what we risk when we love," said Robert.

"I thought you said you would never love again, after the woman you loved broke your heart during the war."

Robert kissed the tip of Cath's nose. "I was wrong, dear heart. I know now I never loved until I loved you."

"Nor did I," said Cath softly.

He looked closely at her. "What about Chip?"

She was thoughtful a moment. "He was my first love. We were young. There was a war on. I'll never forget him, but he's part of the past."

"And what about us, Catherine?"

She studied him intently. "I don't know, Robert. Is love enough? Even love that has Christ as its inspiration?"

He looked away, but still held her close. "Time will tell whether what we feel will endure. I pray it will. Someday I would like to invite you to be my wife."

Her heart skipped a beat. "Your wife?"

"I realize it's too soon to speak of such things. For now, let me ask a lesser question. Will you allow me to court you, the way a gentleman ought to properly romance his lady?"

Cath smiled playfully. "Yes, Robert. I would like very much to be courted by someone so handsome and dashing as you."

"Then we will consider this the beginning of our courtship." He leaned forward and said to the driver, "You may take us home now to Honeysuckle Lane."

When they arrived, the house was quiet. Everyone had gone to their rooms for the night, except Anna, who was puttering in the kitchen. "We had only a light supper tonight," she told Cath. "Soup and a salad. I could fix you two something, if you'd like."

"Thank you anyway, Anna," Cath told her, "but with all the cake, punch, and finger sandwiches at the reception, neither of us is hungry."

"Then I'll just go on up to bed, children." Anna paused, removed her apron, and kissed Cath good night. "It was a beautiful exhibit today, Catherine. You've done a wonderful thing, donating such glorious paintings to our church. The Lord will reward you bountifully."

"He already has," Cath replied, stealing a glance at Robert. When Anna had gone upstairs, Robert took Cath in his arms and kissed her again. "I could make quite a habit of this," he told her with a mischievous smile.

"So could I. I think kissing could take the place of breakfast, lunch, and dinner."

"And midnight snacks," he added.

"Especially midnight snacks," she teased. She was about to say something about never being hungry again except for his love, but the telephone startled her with its jangling ring. "Who could that be at this time of night?" she wondered aloud.

Robert shrugged. "Another well-wisher wanting to congratulate you on your exhibit?"

Cath grabbed the receiver before the ringing woke everyone in the house. For a moment she didn't recognize the woman's voice. "Catherine, is that you?"

"Yes. Who's this?"

"It's Laura Henry. I hope I didn't wake you up."

"No, I was still up. What is it?"

"It's your papa. He's dying. He wants to see you and your brother right away."

"Papa? Dying?"

"The doctor says it could be any time. He needs you, Catherine. You and Knowl. Please, come."

"I—I don't know," Cath stammered. "It's too late tonight."

"I know. Please come tomorrow. Promise me you'll come."

Cath's heart raced as the old anxieties and pain washed back over her. Suddenly she was suffocating, drowning. "I can't, Laura," she cried. "Knowl doesn't know. I'm sorry. I'll call you in the morning and see how Papa's doing."

"Don't call," pleaded Laura. "Just come!"

19

Aᴛ ʙʀᴇᴀᴋꜰᴀꜱᴛ ᴛʜᴇ next morning Cath and Robert exchanged private glances across the dining room table. She knew what he was thinking. *You've got to tell your family about your father. You can't put it off any longer. They need to know!*

She knew he was right. But with everything going so well in their lives lately, how could she risk her family's harmony and her mother and brother's well-being for a man who had shown such careless disregard for their feelings?

Papa's dying. That changes everything.

Robert drilled her with his gaze, his jaw set. Surely he would speak up if she didn't. She had no choice but to tell the truth. She looked around the table, tucking this pleasant, ordinary Sunday morning into her memory lest it never come again.

Anna was pouring coffee. Betty was buttering Jenny's toast. Annie sipped a glass of milk and gazed dreamily out the window as an inquisitive squirrel scampered up the oak tree through leaves already turning the vivid colors of autumn. Knowl picked at his ham and eggs while scribbling notes for an upcoming editorial—something about Truman's volatile relationship with Congress and how it might affect the presidential election next year. *The Eternal Light* was drifting faintly from the parlor radio. In an hour the family would leave for Reverend Henry's morning service.

Cath winced. How could she shatter this tranquility? She glanced again at Robert. His eyes seemed to be saying, *Go ahead. I'm here for you.*

She cleared her throat and began. "I—I have some news."

Eyes glanced curiously her way. Anna asked, "You mean, reviews of your art show?"

Knowl answered for her. "No, it's too soon for reviews."

"What then?" asked Annie.

Cath drew in a breath. "News about Papa."

"Papa? *Your* papa?" asked Betty. She handed Jenny her toast, but her eyes remained locked on Cath.

"Yes, our papa. He's—very ill. He's living in a farmhouse outside Fort Wayne."

The lines in Betty's face grew taut. "How do you know this?"

"I saw Papa myself," Cath admitted reluctantly. She was digging a hole, burying herself. There was no turning back now.

"You saw him? How?" asked Knowl. "No one's seen or heard from Papa in over seven years!"

"I know. But I met someone who knows him."

"Who?" demanded Betty.

Cath sat in her chair growing more miserable by the moment. In a small voice she answered, "Luke Henry."

There was a long, discomfiting silence in the room, except for the distant laughter and cheerful patter from the radio.

"How would Luke Henry know our father?" demanded Knowl, his brows furrowing behind his wire-rim glasses.

Finally, haltingly, Cath spoke, letting the words spill out about Tom's secret family. She could see the incredulity and shock building in everyone's eyes, especially Betty's and Knowl's, but she pushed on anyway, carrying the terrible tale to its wrenching conclusion. "And that's about it," she finished, her voice wavering with emotion. "The night I disappeared was the night Luke Henry took me to see Papa."

Knowl's face was bleached white. He took off his glasses and wiped them with his handkerchief. "I knew Papa was capable of vile deeds, but nothing so cruel and deceitful as this!"

"I don't believe a word of it!" exclaimed Betty, her face reddening as swiftly as her voice turned shrill. "These people are telling you a tale, taking advantage of a sick old man who's too ill to defend himself. We should have the lot of them arrested!"

"But it is true, Mama," said Cath. "I saw Papa. I heard the story from his own lips."

"Well, he's crazy then. Your papa was married to me until you were nearly grown. He couldn't possibly have a son who's twenty-two!"

Knowl stood up and paced the room. "What you're saying is that Papa has had two families all these years, and neither of us knew about the other?"

"Laura Henry suspected," said Cath, "but she never asked. She didn't want to know."

Knowl pummeled his fist against his palm. "This is inconceivable! I can't believe Papa would do something like this! How could he possibly have kept up the pretense with none of us suspecting?"

"I don't know," said Cath, her own misery mounting afresh as she felt Knowl and Betty's pain and confusion. "Papa was gone more than he was home. We should have made him tell us where he was all that time."

Betty stood up and gripped the back of her chair. "I'll tell you where he was! He was flitting from woman to woman, sowing his wild oats like the no-good louse he was. It wasn't in him to settle down and have kids with some other woman. He already had a home and a wife and kids. Why would he start the same thing all over again some other place?"

"Maybe he didn't plan it, Mama," said Cath. "Maybe it just happened and he didn't know how to stop it."

"No!" declared Betty. "It didn't happen! Nothing you say can convince me this terrible thing happened."

Robert got up and went over to Betty and put his hand on her

185

shoulder. "I'm sorry, Mrs. Herrick, but it's true. I was there. I heard the story directly from your husband."

Knowl paused and stared hard at Robert. "That's right! You drove to Fort Wayne to get Cath. You knew about this all along."

Robert solemnly met Knowl's gaze. "Yes, I knew."

"And yet you said nothing all these weeks?"

Robert's jaw tightened. "I felt it was Catherine's place to tell you about your father."

"Really? Catherine's place? And that removed all responsibility from you, is that how you see it?" Knowl's face flushed and his nostrils flared. "We're about to enter into a very important business venture, Robert. We're going to be partners. Don't you think we should at least be honest with each other? What do we have if we don't have trust between us?"

"He wanted to tell you," Cath interjected, "but I wouldn't let him. I wanted to be the one to break the news."

Knowl paced the floor. "Well, I'm glad you finally got around to telling me, little sister. But why now? Why not keep Papa's ugly little secret forever?"

Cath's throat tightened. "Because Papa's dying. If we want to see him alive, we've got to go to Fort Wayne today."

There was a momentary hush in the room. No one moved or spoke as this new reality sank in. Finally Knowl strode over to Cath and looked her squarely in the eyes. "You said Papa was ill. You said nothing about him dying."

Tears rolled down Cath's cheeks. "Laura Henry called last night. She said we should come right away. Papa's heart is failing."

Knowl threw up his hands in futility. "This can't be happening. It's too much! I've got to get out of here and think!" He strode out of the room and down the hallway. Cath heard the door slam moments later. She looked at her mother.

Betty glared back. "You should have held your tongue, daughter. Your papa won't be happy until he's destroyed this family."

"You don't mean that, Mama."

Betty leaned close to Cath and waved her finger under her nose. "I do mean it, girl! And if you and your brother go off to Fort Wayne to see your papa, you can count your mama dead! It will kill me to have you two visiting that old man after what he's done."

Anna came over and held her arms out to Betty. "Come, dear. We don't want to upset little Jenny, do we? Let's take her for a walk in the garden and sit for a spell in the gazebo. We won't have many nice days left before winter sets in."

Annie went to Cath and they embraced. "What can I do, dear friend? How can I help?"

Cath choked back a sob. "I don't know how to fix this, Annie. It's going to hurt everyone I love, and I can't stop it."

"I'll go find Knowl," Annie promised. "No matter how hurt he feels, he's got to go see his father. He'll never forgive himself if he doesn't."

That afternoon Knowl, Cath, and Robert drove to Fort Wayne. Cath sat in the middle, between Robert and her brother. Knowl was silent most of the way, except for an occasional outburst of anger or self-deprecation. "I must be a fool to think I can go face the old man and pretend everything's fine. If he thinks we can patch up this mess on his deathbed and be one big happy family, he's got another think coming."

Cath shook her head. "I can't forgive him either, Knowl. I've spent my whole life longing for a father to love me, and here he was off being someone else's papa!"

Knowl kept his eyes on the road, but Cath could see the tendons tighten in his jaw. "You know what I've spent my life doing, Cath? Trying to distance myself from that man and everything he stood for. I've tried to be an honest, upright, decent citizen, a faithful husband, and a loving father to Jenny, even when you took her back to raise yourself. I took care of Mama and paid the bills and saw to it you got to study art at the Institute. I've bent over backward to make up for what that man did."

Cath squeezed her brother's arm. "I'll always be grateful for all you've done for Mama and me, Knowl."

"And you know what our papa did for us?" Knowl went on heatedly. "He made us live in shame. From the time I was a little boy I heard people talking about Papa and his women. I pretended it wasn't so. I wanted more than anything to believe Papa was an honorable man."

"All I wanted," murmured Cath, "was for Papa to love me."

Knowl tightened his grip on the wheel and drew in a deep, shuddering breath. He seemed to be speaking to himself now. "I remember one time when Chip and I were out riding our bikes with some boys from school. I saw Papa walk into a bar with his arm around some strange woman. One of the boys said, 'Hey, Herrick, ain't that your old man?' And I said, 'Naw, never in a million years!' But later Chip says to me, 'You lied. That was too your papa.' And I said, 'He *was* my papa, but he's not my papa anymore.' And that's the day I stopped wanting to be like that man."

"Don't talk about it, Knowl," said Cath. "You'll just get more upset."

"Your sister's right," said Robert, his arm around the back of the seat, mere inches from Cath's shoulder. "I know how a weakness can overcome a man when he doesn't know the Lord. I became a falling-down drunk after Pearl Harbor, but when I stumbled into that Salvation Army mission in Los Angeles, the Lord picked me up and put me back on my feet."

Knowl ground his teeth. "I know you mean well, Robert, but I think we'll all be better off if you keep your nose out of our family's business."

"How can you say that?" cried Cath. "Robert's practically a member of the family."

"Since when did you become Robert's champion, Cath? I thought you two maintained a friendly rivalry." Knowl glanced at Robert. "We've taken you in like one of the family because it was what Annie wanted. Frankly I've kept my feelings to myself about your friendship with Annie when she was in California. I know you behaved yourself properly with my wife, but I also know you would have pursued her if she hadn't been married. When you came here in good faith as Annie's editor, I resolved not to hold any bad feelings against you. Then, as we discovered so many common interests, I figured we could form a profitable partnership and accomplish something for the Lord."

"I still think we can," said Robert.

"Maybe, maybe not. Right now I can't even think about the future."

An uncomfortable silence fell over them. No one said anything for the next several miles. Robert removed his arm from the back of the seat and turned his gaze out the window. Cath felt a cloud of gloom settle over her spirits. It all came back to Tom. Just when she had finally found a good man's love, success in her art career, and even peace with God, she was brought back to this—the defining relationship of her life that had tainted every other relationship. And it would end with her father dying in a shabby house with people alien to her—a woman Tom loved and a boy and girl who were somehow her kin. Unthinkable that Tom's blood pumped in their veins just as it pumped in hers and Knowl's. How could she and Knowl and Betty ever live with that awful reality?

It was nearly three when Knowl pulled into the driveway of the antiquated farmhouse outside Fort Wayne. "This is where Papa has been living all these years?" asked Knowl incredulously. "And I thought the house we were raised in in Willowbrook was run-down!"

The three got out of Knowl's sedan and walked in strained silence up to the door. Cath knocked. After a moment, Laura Henry opened the door. "You came! Thank heaven! Tom has been asking for you all day."

They entered, and Cath made brief introductions. Knowl said little, offering only a perfunctory nod, but then what could he say to the woman who had taken his father from his mother?

"How is Papa?" asked Cath. Perhaps Laura had only said Tom was dying to get them here. It was the sort of ploy Tom would have used.

But Laura quickly dispelled that notion with the gravity of her expression. "He's not good," she said, stifling a sob. "The doctor says he's already living on borrowed time. Doc figured he'd die yesterday, but for some reason he's still holding on even though his heart's about given out. I think he's just waiting to say good-bye to the two of you."

"Where is my father?" asked Knowl, glancing around restlessly. Cath could see his distaste for these drab surroundings and the fact that he had to be here.

"In there." Laura nodded toward the closed door down the hall. "Luke and Bethany Rose are with him now. I'll fetch them and give you two some time alone with your papa." She left and was back a minute later with Luke and the solemn young woman who had retreated to her room the day Cath was there. Again, introductions were made—stiff, abbreviated, and stressful, as brother and sister silently scrutinized brother and sister.

"I told them they could spend some time alone with Papa," Laura told her children. Luke nodded and trudged out of the room without a word. Bethany moved impassively across the room and lingered in the doorway just long enough to cast a reproachful glance at Knowl.

"I'll wait here," Robert told Cath. She nodded.

Laura Henry stepped in front of Knowl and touched his arm. "I want you to know," she said with raw, hard emotion, "I love your papa. I have always loved him. He is a good man."

Cath waited in the hallway, watching Knowl for his response, but he simply moved on past Laura Henry with a purposeful stride and met Cath beside the closed door. As she gingerly opened the door, Cath scoured her mind for words to warn Knowl about this stuffy, stinking box of a room and the frail, broken man in the bed. But even as they stepped inside she knew words said too little.

She could feel Knowl's revulsion without even looking at his face. She heard it in the way he caught his breath, the way he stopped for a moment in his tracks before proceeding to their father's bedside.

The old man was already lifting his head and extending his hand, and no doubt straining his eyes for a glimpse of his progeny. He rasped, "Knowl—is that you?"

For a moment Knowl took his father's hand without speaking. Cath suspected her brother was fighting back tears. At last he said, "Papa? It's been seven years."

Tom nodded, allowing his head to sink back on the pillow. His eyes closed. Cath thought she saw tears squeeze from his closed lids.

"Seven long years, Papa," Knowl repeated, his voice sounding strangled. "The world's changed, Papa. We've changed. A whole world war's come and gone since we were together. Why, Papa? I thought you were dead, and you were right here in Fort Wayne?"

Tom opened his eyes and gazed imploringly at Knowl. "Forgive me?" he whispered.

"Why did you do this, Papa? If you had someone else besides Mama, you could have told me. You could have told Cath. Look at you, Papa! You have grown children. When I was just a boy, you had another son. How could you keep that from me, Papa?"

"I'm sorry." Tom held out his hand again. Cath noticed the knuckles, how knobby they were, and the fingers, how gnarled. Her father had always had attractive, manicured hands, a salesman's carefully groomed hands. Now, little of her handsome, golden-tongued father remained in this tortured shell of a man, except the eyes. He still had Papa's eyes.

"Tell me why you lived this lie, Papa," Knowl pleaded. "Help me make sense of it! Why, Papa, why!"

Tears rolled down her father's cheeks. "I don't know."

The answer seemed to infuriate Knowl. "You don't know? If you don't know, who on earth does? That woman out there? Her misbegotten children?"

Cath put a calming hand on her brother's shoulder. "You'll upset him, Knowl."

"Upset him? Why shouldn't I? *I'm* upset!"

"I—I never meant to hurt anyone." Tom's chest heaved as he forced out the words. "I wanted you—to be proud of me."

"Proud of you?" Knowl threw his hands up in exasperation. "You had some way of making me proud!"

Tom coughed and sucked for air. "I wanted the best for you money could buy. A fancy house, nice clothes, the best schools."

Cath moved closer to the bed. "We only wanted *you*, Papa."

"Every venture failed," he lamented. "I was never smart enough, or fast enough, or good enough."

"Those are excuses," said Knowl, "to justify your walking out on us. They won't do anymore, Papa. It's too late."

Tom nodded, his face sagging with resignation. "Yes. Too late. I'm dying. I can't make it right."

Knowl stepped back from the bed. Cath looked at him. She had never seen such an expression of desolation on her brother's face. "I can't take this," he told her.

"Don't go!" It was Tom's voice, deep and resonant with torment. "Please, son, don't let me die alone."

Knowl returned to Tom's bedside and took his hand, but his voice remained remote. "It's okay, Papa. I'm right here."

Cath approached and put her hand over both Tom's and Knowl's. "We're both here, Papa."

His eyes darted from her face to Knowl's. His fingers tightened with urgency. "I'm afraid to die. The devil's waiting for me. I've seen him. Is it too late? Can God forgive me? Can you forgive me?"

Knowl turned away again. He walked over to the door and pressed his hands against it. A dry sob heaved in his chest. Cath went to him and put her arms around him. "Tell him," she whispered. "Tell him how to be forgiven."

Knowl stared at her as if she'd uttered an oath. "Can *you* forgive him?"

Tears of frustration sprang to her eyes. "I don't know, but we can't let him die like this—without hope, without peace."

"I can't forgive him, Cath. Don't ask me to."

"I'm not the one asking." She reached up and took her brother's face in her hands. "I realized something just now as I watched Papa asking you to forgive him. I'd lived this moment before, Knowl, only I was the one asking for forgiveness."

Knowl's brows arched. "You?"

"Weeks ago I asked God to forgive me, and He did, and for the first time in my life I felt free, at peace with myself."

Knowl took Cath's hands in his. "You never told me."

"I was afraid—that it wouldn't last, or that it wasn't real, or that the old Cath would come back. The old Cath would never forgive Papa."

Knowl's eyes searched hers. "And now you're saying you can forgive him?"

"No, I can't. But perhaps God through me . . . In my head my voice says no, but His voice says yes. If God is willing to forgive me, how can I refuse to forgive Papa?"

Knowl held Cath's hands tight against his chest. She felt his breathing, deep and heavy, with a slow, solid rhythm. She waited, silent, tears washing her cheeks, her nose running, mixing with her tears. She felt Knowl's struggle, felt the forces of emotion waging war inside him. The same battle raged within her—the anger, the bitterness, the hurt. Through the years those feelings had played inside her like a phonograph needle stuck in a record's groove, playing the same destructive message over and over. But now she was learning to listen to a new voice with a message of hope.

Knowl's eyes met hers. She couldn't read his expression, but she knew something had been resolved. He removed his glasses and wiped the lenses with his handkerchief. Then he took her hand and walked her back over to Tom's bedside.

"Are you leaving now?" Tom asked.

"No," said Knowl. His voice was as gentle as Cath had ever heard it. "Papa, Cath and I want to talk to you. About forgiveness."

20

Iт was AFTER nine when Knowl's Dodge sedan finally pulled into the driveway on Honeysuckle Lane. Cath expected all the lights to be out and everyone to be asleep, but instead, lamplight spilled out of the living room and parlor windows.

"They must be waiting up," noted Robert.

"That's not like Annie," said Knowl as he unlocked the door. "Now that she's expecting, she's usually in bed by dark."

"Mama's probably waiting up to find out about Papa," said Cath as they entered the marbled foyer.

"Yes, she was as mad as hornets when we left." Knowl smiled dryly. "Let's hope she's had a chance to cool off. Mama on the warpath is not a pretty sight."

In the living room Cath was surprised to encounter Anna on the telephone and Annie thumbing through an address book. She looked from one to the other. "What's going on?"

Annie looked up fretfully. "Oh, Cath, it's your mama."

"What about Mama?" asked Knowl as he crossed the room and greeted his wife with a kiss on the cheek.

"She's gone, Knowl." Annie's lower lip trembled. "We think she left in a taxi, but we don't know where she's gone."

"We've called everyone we know," said Anna, "but no one's seen her. She's simply disappeared."

"Where would she go?" asked Cath. "She has hardly any friends and no family except us. Did she pack any clothes?"

"No," said Annie. "She left her room untouched."

"And she didn't say a word about where she was going?"

"Nothing," said Anna. "Oh, we knew she was upset about you children going to Fort Wayne to see your father. She stewed about that all day. But the last we saw of her she was sitting in the parlor listening to her radio programs. It was right after *The Fanny Brice Show* that I realized she wasn't sitting there anymore."

"We looked in the garden and everywhere," said Annie. "But she was gone."

"And she never came home for dinner," said Anna. "And you know how your mama doesn't like to miss a meal."

"That's when we started getting really worried," said Annie. "Oh, Knowl, what if she's met up with some terrible calamity? She could be lying in a ditch somewhere hurt and bleeding!"

Knowl sat down and wrapped his arms around Annie. "That's your writer's imagination, sweetheart. Don't upset yourself. It's not good for the baby." He looked up at Anna. "Of course, to be on the safe side, have you called the police?"

"Yes, and the hospital too. No one's been found or admitted matching Betty's description. And it's too soon to file a missing person's report."

Robert spoke up. "Knowl, would you mind if I took your car and went out looking for your mother?"

Knowl looked quizzically at him. "Suit yourself, old man. In fact, I'll come along."

"Not necessary," said Robert. "You're needed here."

"Well, *I'm* coming with you," said Cath, "and that's final."

Robert grinned. "You'll get no argument from me. Come on."

Minutes later, as Robert turned off Honeysuckle Lane onto Maypole

Drive, Cath, sitting beside him in the darkness, remarked, "You think you know where my mother is, don't you?"

He kept his gaze fixed on the road. "I have a hunch."

"Mind telling me?"

"You'll see."

He drove a mile or two, then pulled up beside a seedy brick building with mullioned windows and a flashing neon sign that read SPIVAK'S PUB.

Cath stared at him. "You think Mama went to a bar?"

Robert met her gaze. "Hasn't that crossed your mind?"

"Oh, Robert, she's been sober for so long! She hasn't had any alcohol since she's lived with us. Anna doesn't even allow cooking sherry in the house."

Robert reached over and rubbed Cath's shoulder. "Well, Catherine, you ask any reformed alcoholic and he'll tell you he's always just one drink from disaster. You set up the right—or maybe I should say the *wrong*—circumstances and put enough pressure on a person and he may buckle and take that drink."

Cath saw the gravity in Robert's gray-blue eyes. "Is that how it is for you?" she asked softly. "Do you feel you're always one drink from disaster?"

A muscle tightened in his cheek. "That's the name of the game. The stakes are high. You weaken once and you can lose it all."

Cath took Robert's hand from her shoulder and locked her fingers with his. "It's still hard for you, isn't it? The temptation is still there."

He made a chuckling sound low in his throat. "If you're asking if I'm constantly thinking about booze, I'm not. But if you're asking, Do I think about how good it would feel going down my throat and how quickly it would smooth the rough edges of some tough times, well, yes, I think about it sometimes. The temptation will always be there, Catherine, but let's just say God and I meet it together."

She pressed his hand against her lips. "I want to help you too, Robert, in any way I can."

He leaned over and lightly kissed her lips. "You, dear heart, are all the intoxication I need."

While her head still whirled with his closeness, he opened his door and stepped out. "I'll just be a minute."

"Wait! You're not going in without me!" She flung open her door, scurried out, and followed him into Spivak's Pub. The lights were low, bathing the narrow room with a hazy orange glow. The dark paneled walls were covered with boxing posters of Joe Louis, Rocky Graziano, and Sugar Ray Robinson. The air was thick with cigar smoke and heavy with the fermented aromas of barley and yeast.

"A bunch of beer guzzlers here," noted Robert. "Your mama liked her wine."

"She liked whiskey too," Cath murmured as memories of those dark days peppered her mind like buckshot.

"Stay here," said Robert. "I'll check with the bartender." He was back a moment later. "Let's go. Your mama hasn't been here."

"Where are we going?" she asked as he ushered her out the door and back into the sedan.

"We're going to check all the taverns in town until we find your mama."

In the next hour they visited the Golden Rooster, Comiskey's Saloon, the Starlight Cocktail Lounge, and the Old Watering Hole. But there was no sign of Betty. Finally they pulled up to the curb beside Ben's Bar in the old section of Willowbrook, where elegant houses built around the turn of the century had fallen to neglect and disrepair. Red neon signs flashed BEER AND ALE. Thick bottle glass windows gave the place an aura of menace and secrecy.

Cath looked wearily at Robert. "Don't you think we should give up? It's almost eleven. Maybe Mama's home by now."

Robert nodded. "If she's not here, we'll head home."

It was so dark in the small barroom that Cath blinked several times before her eyes grew accustomed to the shadows. Only a few patrons sat at the bar, all of them men. "She's not here either," Cath whispered.

"I'll just check with the bartender," said Robert.

Cath watched as the paunchy, bald man behind the bar nodded and pointed toward a corner booth. Robert motioned for Cath to join him. Panic rose in her throat as they approached the stooped figure sitting alone in the murky shadows. "Mama?" she asked, sliding in across from the woman.

The haggard face looked up. A faint stream of bluish light cut across her angular features. It was Betty Herrick, nursing a shimmering glass of ale. "You looking for me, Catherine?"

"Oh, Mama, no!"

Robert sat down beside Cath and, leaning toward Betty, asked quietly, "How many have you had, Mrs. Herrick?"

"Enough," she snapped.

"What? Whiskey? Gin?"

Betty sat forward and folded her hands like a child pleased with herself. "Whatever they gave me. I drank it all."

Robert reached carefully for the glass and moved it out of her reach. "It's time to go home now, Mrs. Herrick."

She shook her head. "I'm not ready."

"But the bartender wants to close and we have the car waiting," Robert said patiently.

"I'm happy right here," Betty announced. She lurched back against the seat, swayed unceremoniously, and raised her elbows like wings in an exaggerated effort to steady herself. "So, daughter, did you go off to Fort Wayne to see your papa?" she asked, her words thick and slurred.

"Yes, Mama. Knowl and I spent several hours with him."

"Did you now?" Betty's voice slithered out barbed with sarcasm. "I suppose you and your brother and your papa made up, just like all those lost years didn't even matter. Now all is forgiven and the lot of you are just brimming with sweetness and light."

Cath could feel the old animosities rising deep inside her. Why did Mama always have to pit Knowl and her against Papa? Why couldn't she for once just let things be? "It wasn't quite that simple, Mama," she said over a sudden groundswell of emotion, "but yes, Knowl and I made our peace with Papa, and Papa made his peace with God."

Betty reached awkwardly for her drink, but Robert diverted it. "So everybody's happy. You're happy. Papa's happy. I'm happy. You and your brother have that old womanizing roustabout, and I have my trusty bottle!"

Cath's fragile composure finally crumbled, giving way to a geyser of seething rage. "Why, Mama?" she demanded. "Why did you start drinking again? Wasn't it enough that Knowl and I had to deal with one crisis today? You want equal time, is that it? You want us to see what a mess *both* of our parents made of their lives?"

Robert seized Cath's hand and gripped it firmly. "Stop it, Catherine! You'll only make matters worse!"

She stared at him in astonishment. He sounded like a parent correcting an obstreperous child. "I'll say what I please," she shot back. "She's my mother, and she's being destructive and self-indulgent!"

Robert gripped her shoulder until she winced. His deep voice boomed, "Let me handle this, Catherine. Your mother needs help, not condemnation!"

The hint of a smug, pleased smile on her mother's lips sent a lightning bolt of indignation shooting through Cath's veins. What was there about this woman that forever drove Cath to the edge of madness? With fury short-circuiting her mind, she turned her wrath on Robert. "What is this?" she shrilled. "One drunk standing up for another?"

The words burned on Cath's lips. She regretted them the instant she said them. Robert looked stunned. He recoiled as if he'd been slapped. Cath herself flinched at the sudden, stark pain in his eyes. It was the expression of a man betrayed. He recovered quickly, turning his attention back to Betty, but Cath knew the damage had been done.

All the way home in the car, while Betty squirmed and complained beside her, Cath struggled to keep back her own desolate tears. How could it be that her sweet victory with Papa today had so quickly degenerated into this devastating scene with Mama? Why couldn't Cath emotionally disentangle herself from her parents' failures? And why had she allowed Mama's venom to infect her relationship with Robert?

He would never want to court her now. She felt the weight of estrangement like a physical presence between them. It was as if they were all in separate rooms clawing on walls that had no doors. In fact, sitting in this vehicle between her mother and the man she loved, she felt more like an orphan, alienated and abandoned. It always came back to that—being abandoned by those she loved. By Chip at Pearl Harbor. By Papa, who was dying. By Mama, who had become a drunk again. And now by Robert, who had caught a glimpse of how cruel and sharp-tongued she could be.

Whenever she came close to the intimacy she yearned for, it was inevitably snatched away. For a few tenuous moments this afternoon she had actually felt close to her father. Did something as final as death have to threaten before such closeness could be hers?

No one slept much in the Herrick household that night. Anna tended to Betty's needs and got her safely to bed, but Knowl and Robert took turns checking on her to make sure she didn't wander off in her alcoholic delirium. Cath went to bed, but slumber eluded her. After spending an emotionally draining day in Fort Wayne with Tom and a harrowing night rescuing Betty, she was too keyed up to relax. But one thing she vowed— first thing in the morning she would try to make amends with Robert.

True to her resolves, Cath gathered her courage and knocked on Robert's door before breakfast. When he called "Come in," she was stricken with sudden misgivings, but steeling herself, she entered his room with her chin high and determination intact. But her courage gave way to dismay when she saw that he was packing. "Where are you going?" she asked in alarm.

"New York," he said without looking up.

"Back to Sanders and Browne?"

"Yes. I've been away long enough."

Cath's despair deepened. "But I thought you were planning to move here and start Herrick House with Knowl."

Robert tucked several pairs of socks in beside his undershirts. "That's not official yet. We still have investors to line up and contracts to negotiate."

"Oh, Robert, are you leaving because of me?" Tears of contrition rolled down Cath's cheeks. "I never meant to say such a spiteful thing last night, especially to you!"

Robert tucked another pair of socks into his suitcase, then turned to face Cath. He took her hands in his and pulled her against him. "Silly girl, I'm not leaving because of you."

She stared up wide-eyed at him. "You're not?"

"Of course not. I've been away from Sanders and Browne entirely too long." He chuckled with amusement. "I need to go back and close the pages on that chapter of my life, by turning in my resignation."

"Then you are moving to Willowbrook?" she asked excitedly.

"I hope so—if the deal for Herrick House goes through. If not, I'll probably head for California and pick up my work at the rescue mission. Whatever I do, I've got to be in ministry."

Cath jutted out her lower lip. "Then you're still thinking of making California your home?"

"Let's call it a backup plan." With a hint of whimsy in his eyes Robert traced the outline of her mouth with his fingertip. "Don't pout, dear heart. It's not because I'm angry with you."

"But you have every right to be." The words tumbled out before she lost her courage. "What I said last night was hateful. I always speak too impulsively, Robert. I wish I could be like Annie. She's always tactful and kind. But I'm not like Annie, and if that means you don't want to court me after all—"

"Whoa!" exclaimed Robert. "Who said I don't want to court you?"

She lowered her gaze. "I saw how much my words hurt you."

Robert gently lifted her chin. "Yes, at the moment I felt a trifle wounded, but then I thought to myself, *Robert, old man, you are a drunk, so what's the big deal? If that girl's willing to love you as you are, you'd better be willing to love her as she is too!*" He grinned broadly at her, his blue eyes sparkling. "And I do love you, my sweet, impulsive, passionate Catherine—no matter how many times you stick your foot in that pretty mouth."

Cath's legs felt suddenly weak. She sank against him, deliriously happy. "Oh, Robert, I love you too!"

"Then would you like to take a walk with me in the garden?"

"A walk? This early in the morning? Why?"

He flashed her a marvelous wink. "Because I'm about to make this the shortest courtship in history. And because a gentleman doesn't ask for a lady's hand in marriage in his bedroom with his socks and underwear in plain view."

21

CATH COULD HARDLY wait for Robert to return to Willowbrook. For five days she had wondered if those romantic hours in the gazebo last Monday morning had actually occurred, or had they been merely a sweet concoction of her imagination? Had Robert actually proposed marriage? And had she truly accepted?

For five days she had kept their secret to herself—a rare feat for a young woman who loved to talk as much as Catherine did. But now, at last, it was Saturday and Robert was coming home. Together they would make their remarkable announcement to the family.

But what was keeping him? The train from New York was scheduled to arrive in Willowbrook at noon. Allowing him time to collect his luggage and hail a taxi, Robert should have been striding up the walk an hour ago. For the tenth time that afternoon Cath peered out the bay window, craning her neck to look up and down the street.

"Still no sign of Robert?" asked Annie from the doorway.

Cath whirled around as if she'd been caught with her hand in the cookie jar. "Not yet. I'm just keeping an eye out for him."

"I notice. Since when have you been so concerned about Robert Wayne? I remember a time when you weren't too fond of him."

Cath felt her face flush. "That was a long time ago."

Annie came over and walked her fingers over one of Cath's long red curls. "We've been friends for a long time, haven't we?"

Cath smiled. "Best friends, through good times and bad. I'll always be grateful for the home you and Knowl have given Jenny and me."

"You're our family, Cath. You always will be. I hope you'll—" Suddenly Annie flinched and her hand flew to her middle. "Oh, my goodness, feel this," she said, taking Cath's hand and placing it on her rounded abdomen. "My baby's kicking!"

Cath squealed with delight. "My heavens, what a powerful kick! He's going to make the world stand up and take notice!"

Annie nodded, her mood turning serious. "Our children will need all the spunk and grit they can muster, won't they, Cath? It's a different world than what we knew as children. Everything's moving so much faster since the war. Do you feel it?"

"Yes, I do, but it's not necessarily bad, is it? Our children will have opportunities we never had."

"And so many more choices, and temptations."

"We've survived. So will they."

Annie studied Cath with an unsettling intensity.

"What is it, Annie? Why are you looking at me that way?"

Annie leaned close to Cath's ear. "I've noticed such a light in your eyes lately. Will you tell me the truth?"

"Of course. We're best friends, aren't we?"

"Indeed! In my Bible I still have our blood pact we made as youngsters. So tell me. Are you in love with Robert?"

Cath felt her face burning. "Is it that obvious?"

"Oh, you truly are!" Annie enveloped Cath in her arms as much as her ample middle would allow. The two hugged until a knock sounded on the door. Together they exclaimed, "Robert!"

They greeted him with impish smiles; he met them with hugs, with an especially generous one for Cath. "I've missed my girl," he whispered as he nuzzled her ear.

"Annie has guessed our secret," Cath announced as he removed his overcoat and hung it on the hat rack.

"Has she now? She knows about our engagement?"

"No!" cried Annie. "She never told me you were engaged!"

"I told her we're in love," said Cath. "I was afraid I had dreamed the engagement."

"Well, I have proof you didn't," said Robert with a twinkle in his eyes. "But perhaps I should save it for a romantic evening with candlelight and music."

"It's too late," said Annie. "The secret's out."

"Yes," said Cath breathlessly, "let's see your proof!"

Robert reached into a pocket of his striped gabardine suit and produced a black velvet box. "My proof comes in a very small package," he said softly. "But I'll be the happiest man on earth, my darling, if you'll accept this tiny token of my love."

With trembling fingers Cath opened the box and uttered a gasp of surprise as her eyes settled on a radiant diamond ring. "Oh, Robert, it's the loveliest thing I've ever seen."

"No, Catherine," he said, gathering her into his arms, "*you're* the loveliest thing I've ever seen."

Cath's ecstasy over her whirlwind engagement was dampened only by her concern over her brother's reaction. Would Knowl welcome Robert into the family, or would he continue to nurse his resentment toward him for keeping her father's secret? When Knowl arrived home from the newspaper office, Robert invited him into the parlor for a private talk. Mystified, Cath waited in the hallway for several minutes, hoping to catch a few words through the open door. She heard Robert ask about Tom's health and heard Knowl say his condition hadn't changed. Then, maddeningly, Robert shut the door and their voices were too muffled to hear, so Cath ambled restlessly into the dining room and helped Anna set the table for dinner.

When the two men finally emerged from the parlor, they were both smiling. Cath felt immediate relief. No black eyes, no ripped shirts or mussed hair. Knowl strolled over to her and took her in his arms. "May I offer my best wishes to my kid sister?" He went on to tell her, "Frankly

I was shocked when Robert asked me for your hand in marriage, but after we talked a while I realized he'll be good for you, so I gave him my blessing."

Cath looked at Robert in surprise. "You asked Knowl for my hand? What if he had said no?"

Robert just chuckled and gave her a sly peck on the cheek.

Dinner that evening turned out to be an impromptu but cordial celebration. Anna served a succulent beef roast with browned potatoes and carrots and, for dessert, a four-layer chocolate cake with white icing. On top she had painted a red heart with food coloring and written in scrolled letters, "Robert loves Catherine."

After dinner, as Anna cut the cake, Knowl stood up and said, "Attention, everyone, I would like to propose a toast." He turned to Robert. "I admit I had some misgivings about you, old man, but last week you stuck by our family through a difficult time. You went with Cath and me to see Papa and you helped Cath find Mama and bring her home. The way I see it you're one of the family." He raised his glass with a flourish. "To my sister Catherine and her future husband. May they share a lifetime of happiness and blessing as they serve the Lord together."

Even little Jenny entered into the festivities with a crayon drawing of a wedding cake with a stick-figure couple on top, which she presented to Robert with a little curtsy after they'd had dessert.

He looked genuinely touched. "May I give you a kiss?"

To everyone's surprise, Jenny climbed up on Robert's lap, flashed a crinkly-eyed smile, received her kiss on the cheek, then asked, "Are you going to be my papa, too, like Papa Knowl?"

Robert's voice filled with sudden emotion. "Yes, Jenny. I'd be very honored to be your papa too."

She patted his cheek. "Then you're my Papa Robert."

Everyone laughed and applauded while Jenny, the coy little center of attention, scurried into Cath's open arms.

Cath gave her daughter a big bear hug, then looked around the table. "It's been a perfect evening, everyone. Thank you." Within minutes everyone had left the room, purposely giving Cath and Robert a few moments alone in the candlelight. He drew her close and whispered, "It has been a perfect evening, Catherine. And I hate to bring this up now, but one person was glaringly absent from our celebration. Is your mother ill?"

"I'm not sure," Cath admitted. "Mama's been withdrawn and depressed all week. She stays in her room all day listening to the radio, starting with *Queen for a Day* in the morning and ending with *Burns and Allen* at night. She even insists on eating her meals in her room and refuses to see anyone except Jenny. Jenny's the only one who brings Mama joy anymore."

"Have you thought about sending her back to the sanitarium?"

Cath shook her head vehemently. "Oh, Robert, I can't!"

"I know how you feel, but she may be sneaking drinks. She may have bottles stashed in her room. She needs help, Cath."

"I don't want to think about Mama now."

"All right, we'll talk about it later."

Cath looked up and kissed Robert's lips. "This is *our* night."

He returned the kiss with exquisite tenderness. "Tell me, Miss Herrick, how do you feel about becoming Mrs. Robert Wayne?"

She thought a moment. "Deliriously happy, excited, scared."

"Scared? Why are you scared, dear heart?"

She searched his eyes. "Tell me the truth, Robert. Will it bother you to marry a woman who had a child out of wedlock?"

"Does it bother you to marry an alcoholic? My darling girl, God has brought together two imperfect people whom He loves."

Cath ran her finger along Robert's collar and savored the feel of his warm, shaven skin. "What about Jenny? How will you think of her? How do you feel?"

He smiled. "She's a part of you, Catherine, your own flesh and blood. I adore her already, and if she allows me to, I will love her as my own child."

Cath sighed. "That's just the problem. Jenny's five years old, and I still don't know whose child she is—Annie's or mine. What will happen when we marry, Robert? Will Jenny come with us or stay with Knowl and Annie? What will happen when she has to choose between Annie and me?"

"That's the hundred-dollar question, isn't it?"

Cath massaged the back of Robert's neck with a solemn preoccupation. "I couldn't stand to be without her, Robert. When Jenny was born I gave her to Knowl and Annie so she'd have a real home. But I stayed on for months suckling her, and I knew then she would always be my heart, my soul, my self. I sculpted her, made her, built her out of my own bone and sinew and flesh. And Chip's. She was our creation."

Both Robert and Cath lapsed into silence as they watched the flickering candlelight. At last Cath spoke again, her voice hushed with wonder. "Robert, do you know what it's like to be an artist and create something that's uniquely yours, that in some wonderful way bears your own image, so that when you look at it you see yourself, only better? It's that way when I paint. Sometimes I catch a glimpse of my hopes and dreams, my very future. That's how I feel when I look at Jenny."

"Does Annie know how strongly you feel about the child?"

"I don't know. We don't talk about it. To be honest, I haven't tried to take care of Jenny the way a mother should. I'm afraid she'll reject me. It's easier to remain at a distance."

"Your concerns are understandable. You've never had a normal mother-daughter relationship—with your mother or your daughter."

"You're right. Life hasn't been what you would call normal. And look at Jenny—how unsettled her young life has been. First, Annie raised her while I pursued my art career. Then I took Jenny back and Annie ran away to California. Then Annie came back and I had my accident. Annie was forced to be mother to both of us. Now that I've recovered from the coma and have my life back, I don't know where that leaves Jenny and me."

"Perhaps you should talk to Annie about it."

"I—I'm afraid to. Jenny's been the only divisive thing between us. I can't bear to open old wounds."

"Well, you're going to have to, sweetheart." Robert nuzzled the curls around her ear. "If our venture with the publishing house falls though, you and I will be heading to California."

Cath turned her face to him. "Oh, Robert, I couldn't bear to go so far away without Jenny. But how can I expect her to leave the home she's always known and the family she loves?"

Robert pressed his cheek against hers. "Those are problems we'll have to resolve before we can begin our life together."

"But what if there are no answers? Whatever we do, someone will be hurt. Annie and I can't both have Jenny."

"You're right, darling." Robert's eyes grew serious. "So you'll have to decide whether you love me enough to come with me with or *without* Jenny."

22

THROUGHOUT SEPTEMBER TOM lingered at death's door. He was in a coma now, according to Laura Henry, and had been hospitalized in Fort Wayne. "He's already gone to us," Laura lamented over the phone to Cath. "My Tom's already sleeping the sleep of death. I just thank the Almighty he got to make his peace with his children."

Cath was glad too, although she knew she would never resolve all of her feelings about Tom. They cut too deep and traversed too many areas of her life ever to put them completely behind her. But lately, when the shards of anger or resentment struck, she closed her eyes and silently relinquished them to the Holy Spirit.

She wished she could feel victory in other areas of her life as well, such as with Betty. The woman was becoming increasingly reclusive, combative, and stubborn. Everyone in the house knew Betty was getting liquor somewhere, but how? She spent most of her time in her room with her radio blaring; she refused to socialize with the rest of the family; Anna, Cath, and Annie took turns keeping an eye on her to make sure she didn't wander off again. But in spite of their efforts Betty's room was beginning to smell like a brewery, and her breath reeked of whiskey or wine.

"Where is Mama getting the stuff?" Knowl shouted one evening in consternation. "We haven't caught her sneaking out at night, and no one comes to the house except the postman, the milkman, and the delivery boy from the A&P."

Cath and Annie looked at each other. "It couldn't be the milkman or postman," said Cath, "but what about the delivery boy? He's always bringing sacks of groceries for Anna. Maybe he's making some extra deliveries on the side."

After a little investigation and a brief interrogation, Knowl found his guilty culprit. The delivery lad confessed. Betty had been paying him a dollar tip for every bottle of booze he smuggled in to her.

Once Betty's supply of alcohol had been cut off, she became more disagreeable and unpredictable than ever. Several times Cath awoke in the dead of night to hear a taxi pulling away from the house, taking her mother on another of her drunken binges. Finally Knowl telephoned the city cab company and insisted that they send no more taxis to his address except at his request. They assured him their cabbies would cooperate.

One afternoon Cath tried reasoning with her mother. She entered the small airless room filled with the scent of lavender talcum, which Betty no doubt hoped would hide the heavier stench of whiskey. "You worked so hard to get sober, Mama," Cath lamented, trying to remain calm. "Why are you throwing it all away now?"

"Because it doesn't matter anymore," snapped her mother. She was sitting in her overstuffed armchair beside her table radio, listening to her usual melodramas. Amid background static and melancholy strains of a violin a woman was sobbing over a long-lost love. *Oh, George, George, how can I live without you?*

"Why doesn't it matter?" Cath sat down on the unmade bed and spoke over the radio commotion. "Is it because of Papa?"

Her mother stared off into space, expressionless. "I always thought he would come home some day," she murmured idly. Her words trickled out with a slow, singsong monotony. "I thought after everything was said and done, something would be resolved. I'd have a chance to face him, look him in the eye, and say all the things I've rehearsed in my mind all these years, all the arguments I've played in my head, so real I can hear the sound in my ears. There'd be a proper ending. Like closing a door. And I'd know why it all came to this, and I could be done with it. But now I know it'll never be done. I'll never have my say. The old fool didn't even ask to see me. When I wasn't even looking, that scoundrel won the game."

"It isn't a game, Mama. There aren't any winners. Just losers. Don't you see that?"

Her mother pulled her rumpled robe around her with a detached, self-contained air. She looked straight at Cath, one bristly eyebrow arched higher than the other, and her eyes small and hard as steel ball bearings. "Your papa won. He had it both ways. He lived as he pleased and got you and God to forgive him. But not me. I'll hate him till my dying day."

Cath stood up with a sigh of resignation. "Would you like a cup of tea, Mama? Tea and a slice of toast with Anna's jam?"

"No, daughter. No tea. Just go and let me be!"

As September gave way to October, Cath realized there were other pressing issues to deal with in addition to Betty's drunkenness. Knowl came home one evening that first week of October with bad news about the publishing venture. "I talked with the bank today," he said when he had gathered Robert, Cath, and Annie in the parlor, "and even with the investors we've lined up we're still thousands of dollars short of what we'll need to buy the facility on Van Buren. And that doesn't even take into consideration the money we'll need to renovate the building and upgrade the presses for printing hardcover books."

Robert met Knowl's words with obvious disappointment. "I was really counting on this venture, ol' boy. I've got my heart set on settling here in Willowbrook. Cath wants to stay here too. Is there anything we can do?"

"Pray," said Knowl. "If God wants us to have Herrick House, He'll work out the fine print."

"You said something before about taking out a mortgage on the house," said Cath. "Is that still a consideration?"

Knowl's forehead furrowed grimly. "We could, but if our venture fails, we could lose the house." He looked at Annie with sudden wistfulness. "Even when your Grandfather Reed lost all his wealth in the Crash, he managed to hold on to this house."

Annie nodded. "After my papa died, Mama sold it in her grief, but, thank God, you bought it back for me, Knowl. It's my dream to keep this house for our children and our grandchildren."

"That's my dream too," said Knowl.

Robert stood up and cracked his knuckles, his cavalier tone hiding his agitation. "Well, then, it looks like Herrick House will be a memory before it was even a reality. But I suppose that's best in the long run."

"Why do you say that?" asked Annie in surprise.

"Because I don't think your husband is ready to commit himself totally to Christian publishing," Robert said matter-of-factly. "His loyalty lies with his newspaper, and that just may be where God wants him to remain."

Knowl removed his glasses and rubbed the bridge of his nose. "You've hit the nail on the head, Robert. My loyalties are still divided. I want Herrick House; I see the need for the voice of Christian publishing here in the Midwest; and yet I feel God has given me a unique voice through the *Willowbrook News*. As managing editor I'm able to keep my fingers on the world's pulse and let people know what's going on. I don't relish surrendering that opportunity."

Robert nodded. "I understand, Knowl, but you need to understand that money alone won't be enough to get Herrick House up and running. We'll need manpower too. Sure, a full third of the present employees are willing to stay on because they don't want to move out of state, but most of those people work the presses. We need people with leadership capabilities to step into management, marketing, and editorial."

Cath coughed to clear the lump in her throat. "It sounds like Herrick House was an impossible dream all along."

Annie went to Knowl and clasped his arms. "I don't believe God gave us this dream just to let it die. We've got to find a way to make it happen, Knowl, and I'm not saying that just because Robert wants to publish my book. I think this is a ministry our whole family can become involved in. Look at Cath with all her artistic ability. Imagine what an asset her talent could be!"

Cath joined Annie's side. "She's right, my dear brother. I can help. I want to help!" Cath's mind raced, grasping for the wildest idea imaginable. "What if we published a book about the life of Christ and illustrated it with the panels I painted for Reverend Henry? Look what publicity the paintings have already received from some of the best art critics in the business. And people are flocking to see them. Wouldn't people buy such a book so they could have their own copy of the paintings?"

Cath could tell by Robert's expression that the idea excited him. Knowl, too, looked more than a little intrigued. "It could work," said Robert while Knowl examined his spectacles and nodded. For several minutes the two batted ideas back and forth about the feasibility of such a book, but finally Robert said, "There's no sense discussing this until we know where we stand with the publishing house."

Knowl conceded that fact. "The truth is," he said solemnly, "the denomination that owns the Van Buren facility wants our decision by the middle of the month. They need the money for the purchase of their new facility out of state."

"That soon?" echoed Cath in alarm. "How can we possibly decide that soon?"

"Indecision will mean a no decision," said Robert. He looked squarely at Knowl and Annie. "You realize that if Herrick House doesn't fly, Catherine and I will be heading for California as soon as we're married."

Cath felt a sudden instinctive urge to shout, *No, Robert! I can't bear to leave my home and family and all I have here in Willowbrook, not even for you!*

But that wasn't true. She would leave if it came to that, because she loved Robert with all her heart. She would follow him anywhere, wouldn't she? But silently she prayed, *Oh, God, please don't force me to choose!*

Other worries nagged Cath when she thought about moving to California. Would Robert expect her to work in the rescue mission the way Annie had? Would he make unfavorable comparisons between the saintly, traditional Annie and the eccentric, capricious Cath? Would the old familiar mission setting make him miss what he had shared there with Annie during the war?

These questions led to still others. Would Robert expect Cath to conform to his ideas and become something she wasn't in the name of ministry? Or would he allow her to soar free in her own creative pursuits as she felt God leading her? In painting the panels of Christ's life Cath had had a taste of using her talent for a higher purpose. She had experienced the marvelous conviction that this was what she was born for—to create paintings that would help people catch a glimpse of her Savior. Would Robert let her pursue that calling if he returned to the mission?

Cath's concerns about leaving Willowbrook and moving to California faded swiftly when she received a phone call the next day from Laura Henry. "Tom passed on this morning," the woman said, her voice expressionless. "We'll be having the funeral on Friday. You and your brother are welcome to come."

"Yes, of course we'll be there." Would Knowl agree to go?

"Only thing is," continued Laura in a slow, ponderous voice, "we don't have a preacher. Luke said you might know someone."

"Yes, I do. Our Reverend Henry knew Papa. I'm sure he'd be willing to officiate."

"We don't want any fancy eulogy. Just a few respectful words will do."

After Laura Henry's phone call, Cath went directly to her mother's room, where her mother sat rocking, listening to the radio. Cath turned down the volume and said softly, "Mama, Papa's dead."

Betty stared straight ahead and said cryptically, "Tom's dead? I'm dead too."

"We'll be going to the funeral on Friday," said Cath. "Do you want to go with us?"

"Will that woman be there with her mongrel offspring?"

"Laura Henry will be there with her children, yes, Mama."

Her mother finally looked her in the eye. "You say you and your brother are going to the funeral?"

"Yes, Mama. I am. I can't speak for Knowl, but I assume—"

Betty made a scornful growl low in her throat. "Sure, go on! Pay your respects! Honor that man who never gave you an ounce of love or the time of day!"

Cath pushed back a stray ringlet from her forehead. "I can't live with hate in my heart, Mama. I tried. Hate destroys the one who makes room for it. If you can't forgive Papa, can't you at least stop hating him now? He's gone. It's over, Mama."

"It's almost over, but not quite, daughter." Her mother shuffled over to the bureau and picked up an old photograph in a handmade frame. The faded picture showed the Herrick family in better days—Betty and Tom standing arm in arm and looking young and hopeful, their smooth, smiling faces wearing an innocence that time and disillusionment soon replaced with spiteful furrows and frowns. Cath was just a toddler holding on to her mother's skirts, and Knowl stood waist-high to his father, straight and proud as a little soldier. In those days Knowl still wanted to grow up to be like Tom.

Betty slammed the portrait face-down on the bureau's white linen doily and said again, "It's not quite over, daughter!"

Cath nodded. "But with Papa's funeral, it will be over."

As it turned out, on Friday morning Knowl drove Cath, Robert, Annie, and Reverend Henry to Fort Wayne for Tom's funeral. Anna stayed home to care for Jenny and keep an eye on Betty.

Only a handful of mourners gathered for the graveside service at the little country cemetery. As Cath looked around at the grassy slopes covered with autumn leaves, she noticed all the small white uniform crosses for the Civil War dead and the newer bigger crosses in long neat rows for soldiers who had died in the two world wars.

Her Chip was like those young men cut off in their prime because people waged wars and couldn't get along. But how could she expect nations to get along when families warred among themselves, when people like her own mama and papa, who had promised to love each other, ended up turning all the promises to pain?

Even as she stood listening to Reverend Henry invoking the Almighty's mercy on Tom's soul, Cath prayed that she and Robert would never hurt each other or bring shame and calamity on their children. Unlike her parents, she and Robert had God's Spirit of love to keep their hearts pure and tender.

Reverend Henry kept his remarks brief and ended with an admonition for Tom's children. "Don't dwell on your loss, and don't live with regrets. Don't fret over what might have been. Even out of the weaknesses of men God will bring forth good." The old minister moved his venerable, unsteady fingers through the tissue-thin pages of his large, worn Bible. "The Good Book promises God will not leave you fatherless," he intoned in his deep husky voice. "Listen to what the Scriptures say in Second Corinthians 6:18: 'I will be a Father unto you, And ye shall be my sons and daughters, saith the LORD Almighty.' I echo our Lord's sentiments. To each of you I say, Remember how Christ loved the widows and orphans. Now, in your great sorrow take to your bosom the love of your Father God."

With that Reverend Henry offered a closing prayer, then held out his hands and declared, "Let us sing 'Blest Be the Tie that Binds.' " The faltering voices sounded small and of little consequence under the expansive dome of a slate-gray sky. Cath noted that Knowl had tears in his eyes and the muscle along his jaw twitched and throbbed as he worked to keep his chin from quivering. Laura Henry wept softly in the arms of her son while Bethany Rose stood alone, her lips silent, her brown eyes glazed and distant.

Then, as quickly as it had begun, the service was over and the grave diggers were back to finish their job. They lowered Tom's plain pine casket into the black earth under the twisted limbs of a scarred, hoary oak. Cath stood with the rest of the mourners, watching motionless and silent as the coffin disappeared into the dark narrow gash spaded out of the hardpacked ground. She watched the brawny men in their rolled sleeves shovel the pungent, sweet-smelling soil back into place, making Tom one with the earth.

Afterward, Laura Henry placed a modest bouquet of daffodils and carnations on the loose grassy tufts of earth, then collapsed in sobs on Tom's grave. Luke Henry went to her and drew her up into his arms and nuzzled her head with his chin as she wept brokenly.

As the two families stood facing each other, Cath felt a painful discomfort settle between them like a woman's mourning veil. They had been strangers during Tom Herrick's life. Should they remain strangers at his death? After a long moment of indecision Cath stepped forward. The other mourners joined her with a slow, synchronous motion, offering one another awkward embraces and uttering muted words of condolence.

Cath hesitated before the bleak, steely presence of Bethany Rose thin as a windlestraw in her ill-fitting black dress, her cascade of auburn curls wound in an untidy bun. She looked as cold and unapproachable as an ice princess, but Cath stifled her pride and forged ahead anyway, remembering the specter of her own grievous past. Opening her arms, Cath embraced her startled, unmoving sister and whispered, "I know how much you're hurting. I loved him too."

Bethany Rose stared back wordlessly and without expression, except for two large tears that slid down her pale cheeks.

The drive home to Willowbrook was the longest of Cath's life. A vital chapter had been closed, and yet everything seemed so unfinished. She had a brother and sister she hadn't known about before. Would her injured heart allow her to forget them, pretend they never existed? And what about Knowl, who prided himself in championing truth and justice? Would his conscience let him put these odd, troubling siblings out of mind?

When Cath had exhausted herself with unanswered questions, she slipped into an uneasy slumber, her head lolling against Robert's shoulder as Knowl's sedan jounced over endless narrow country roads. Bone-weary, they arrived back at the house on Honeysuckle Lane shortly after eight that evening.

But before they crossed the sprawling front porch, the door flew open and Anna came running out. She stared beseechingly from one face to another, her hazel eyes wide and glistening with horror. "Oh, merciful heavens," she wailed, "the unthinkable has happened! Betty has run off again in a drunken rage, and this time she's taken little Jenny!"

23

Everyone spoke at once, filling the room with a cacophony of alarmed voices.

"Betty took Jenny? Where? When?"

"You're sure they're gone?"

"You say she was drinking?"

"Have you looked everywhere?"

"Did you call the police?"

Anna, usually so composed and serene, was in a state of near hysteria. She sank down on the sofa and shook her head despairingly. "I shouldn't have left them alone. It was only a few minutes. I thought it was safe."

Knowl sat down beside her. "Tell us exactly what happened, Anna, right from the start."

She wrung her hands. "Betty was deeply distressed over the four of you going to Tom's funeral. I've never seen her so upset. I knew she was drinking. I even slipped into her room and looked for the bottle, but I couldn't find it. I tried giving her a sedative to calm her nerves, but she just got more and more agitated. Kept talking about this being the end of things for her. I wasn't sure what she meant, so I said, 'Betty, you're still going to have a nice long life, if you'll just let the wounds heal. You've got your health and your family.'

"But she didn't take any stock in my words. Just kept grumbling on about the cruel prank life had played on her. Said she had nothing left except Jenny. Everyone else had forsaken her. The only time she would quiet down was when Jenny crawled up on her lap and the two rocked together in the parlor listening to the radio. After dinner—around six—I left them there listening to Fred Waring—or maybe it was Hoagy Carmichael. I went to the kitchen to clean up—I wasn't gone more than twenty minutes—and when I came back the radio was still on, but the two of them were gone."

"Perhaps they just went for a walk," said Robert. "Have you called the neighbors?"

"I've called everyone we know. No one's seen them. I called the cab company, and they've sent no taxis to this address. I've even called the bars in town, and they've seen no one tonight fitting her description. And of course she wouldn't be fool enough to take Jenny into a bar, would she?"

"Who knows what she would or wouldn't do!" cried Annie.

"What about the police?" pressed Cath. "Are they looking for Mama and Jenny?"

"No," replied Anna. "The police say there's nothing unusual about a grandmother taking her granddaughter on an outing. They said to call them back if they're still missing in the morning."

"By then it'll be too late!" Cath protested shrilly.

"Let's go out and look for them," said Annie, pulling her coat back around her shoulders. She took a step toward the door, then swayed a little, and grabbed hold of a wing chair to steady herself.

Knowl went quickly to her side. "Are you all right, darling?" He helped her over to the sofa and sat her down.

Annie folded her arms across her ample middle. "I—I'm having some pains. False labor, I think."

"The baby's not due for two months yet," said Anna, sitting bolt upright and fixing her gaze on her daughter.

"I know, Mama. These cramps will pass. I'm just terribly worried about Jenny."

"Well, we're not taking any chances." Knowl lifted her up in his arms. "We're going to get you up to bed and bring you some tea." He glanced back briefly as he headed for the stairs with his charge. "Catherine, call Dr. Galway!"

"What about Mama and Jenny?" Cath asked urgently.

From the top of the stairs he called with an edge of desperation, "Robert, would you and Cath take the car and drive around the neighborhood? I've got to stay with Annie. Mama can't have gotten far on foot with a child in tow."

"Knowl's right," Robert told Cath minutes later as she settled into the sedan beside him. "We'll find your mother and Jenny and bring them home. Everything will be okay."

"I wish I could be as certain as you," she murmured as he pulled onto the cobbled street. Her eyes were already searching the darkness, skimming over neighboring homes with winding driveways and manicured lawns, taking in the shadowy forms of porches and pavilions, chimneys and cupolas, balconies and gables. There were so many places Betty and Jenny could hide. In sprawling yards with fancy terraces and promenades; behind white trellises covered with vines. Still, most of the houses on Honeysuckle Lane were surrounded by imperious hedges or wrought iron fences to keep intruders out.

"See anything?" asked Robert as he turned the corner onto Maypole Drive.

"Nothing out of the ordinary."

On Maypole Drive, where Cath had grown up, the houses had always been poor, sorry imitations of the affluent residences on Honeysuckle Lane. From Cath's earliest childhood, she had known that to live on Maypole Drive was to be inferior to the moneyed families around the corner. Betty had always dreamed of living in one of those opulent homes, so close and yet so far, but ironically, now that she did she was more miserable than ever.

"Everything looks quiet and peaceful," said Robert.

Indeed, rosy lamplight spilled out of windows; people were cozily at home enjoying themselves. *Everyone except us,* Cath thought ruefully. *First the funeral today, and now this!*

"Why does trouble always come in bunches?" she asked aloud.

"A little like bananas?"

She smiled dutifully at his feeble attempt to cheer her. "This is the last straw, isn't it, Robert? You were right. Mama will have to go back to the sanitarium now."

"For her safety and your family's."

"If it's not already too late." She shivered as the chill October air seeped through her light tweed jacket. Her classic navy suit with its sheer white blouse had been warm enough during the day. But now a brisk wind was coming up, sending pine needles skittering like whirling dervishes and brown leaves scudding over dry grass.

"This is the street where I grew up," she said with a bittersweet stab of nostalgia. "My house is just down the block—1334 Maypole Drive. It's set a little apart from the others. See, there it is. You can't see much in the shadows. Everything's dark and dreary. It's been empty for months now."

"I know," said Robert. He pulled over to the curb across the street and stopped. He gazed with mild curiosity at the house. "Remember, your brother said I should take a look at it. Thinks it would be a good buy, if a fellow doesn't mind putting in a little work to fix her up. It's not a bad-looking place, is it? A roomy two-story with a fair-sized porch, lots of windows with fancy shutters, and plenty of character in her lines. What do you think of the idea, Catherine?"

"Living in my old house? I'm not sure. There are so many ghosts. Even if we were to restore the place, I'm not sure I could shake off the past." She shivered again, this time not from the cold.

"Are you all right, Catherine?" Robert reached over and clasped her hand. "You're cold. Your hand's like ice."

"Something just came over me," she murmured, "more than a chill. I felt it in my very soul. It left me feeling weak and frightened. Oh, Robert, where do you suppose Mama and Jenny could have gone?"

"I don't know."

Cath stared out the window again at the shadowed monolith across the street. It looked so bleak, like an ancient relic rising up against a raven-black sky. It was surrounded by twisted oaks with shorn, spidery branches that reached out like starved, desperate, bony, imploring fingers.

Cath's heart started pounding. "Robert, what's that in the upstairs window?"

"Where?"

"On the left."

He craned his neck. "What, Catherine? I don't see—"

"I thought I saw a light—faint, flickering."

"Maybe it's just the moon, or your imagination."

"You're right. The house is empty. There's no electricity." She gazed at the murky window, the latticework still hanging just as it had when she was a girl. "That was my bedroom once," she told him. "I used to stand in that window looking out and dreaming of the world beyond. In those days I wanted so desperately to get away from Willowbrook."

"And now?"

"And now I want desperately to stay. I've seen what the world has to offer, and everything I want is here."

"That's just how I—"

"Look!" Cath seized Robert's hand. "I did see something. Do you see it? The faintest flicker of light behind the lace curtains. I didn't imagine it!"

Robert opened his door. "I see it, Catherine. I'm going to investigate."

"Not without me," she cried. She opened her door, stepped into a bed of decaying leaves, and hurried around to his side of the car. Together they crossed the leaf-strewn cobblestone street. Robert opened the creaking iron gate, and they ran up the broken sidewalk to the porch with its bric-a-brac trim and rusting swing.

Weeds and nettles had sprung up in the yard, wild and unattended, and were crowding the porch and shooting up through the floorboards. Cath sidestepped a tangle of thistles and sniffed the crisp autumn air. There was the piquant smell of chimney smoke and the zesty aroma of burning leaves.

Robert tried the door. "It's unlocked." He opened it slowly. As they stepped through the doorway, they found themselves entering a cave of darkness, the air scant and stale with must and mildew. As Cath's eyes became accustomed to the darkness, she could make out furniture covered with dusty sheets. The pale white shapes gave the room an aura of being haunted, like something out of a Bowery Boys flick. She reached instinctively for Robert's hand.

"Where are the stairs?" he whispered.

She led the way slowly, painstakingly, remembering which steps creaked and which did not, as if it had been yesterday. When they reached the landing Cath turned her gaze down the hall toward her room and saw a hazy glow emanating from the doorway. Her pulse quickened. She moved stealthily down the carpeted hall and held her breath as she stepped into the familiar room.

There, surrounded by the flickering glow of candlelight, sat her mother rocking a slumbering Jenny. Candles had been placed strategically on the linen-draped furniture to form a wreath of light around the rocking pair, and the tiny spirals of flame cast a gauzy, glimmering light on the walls and ceiling that undulated in a silent ballet. The stench of whiskey weighed heavy in the airless room.

"Mama, what are you doing here?" cried Cath.

Robert tightened his fingers around her wrist as if to say, *Take it slow and easy. You don't know what condition she's in.*

"Mama, did you hear me?" Cath persisted. She heard it now. Her mother was crooning a lullaby under her breath. Singsong, off-tune, heartfelt. She gazed up at Cath, put a finger to her lips, and whispered, "Silence, daughter. Jenny's sleeping."

More softly Cath asked, "Why did you come here, Mama?"

Betty's words emerged thick and slurred. "This is my home. It's where you were born and raised."

Cath took a tentative step toward Jenny. She was wearing the red taffeta dress Anna had sewn for her. Her lacy petticoat showed from under her skirt. "Don't you remember, Mama?" said Cath. "We don't live here anymore. We live around the corner on Honeysuckle Lane. You always wanted to live there, Mama, and now you do."

Her mother shook her head. "No, this is where I belong. With my sweet baby." She gazed down at the sleeping child.

"Jenny's *my* baby, Mama, remember?" Cath glanced back at the doorway, where Robert remained in the shadows.

Should she ask her mother to surrender the child, or simply step forward and seize Jenny before her mother realized what she was doing? She decided the tactful approach was safer. "Mama, it's time for Jenny to go home to bed. Will you let me take her?"

Betty drew the child closer against her bosom. "She is home, daughter. This is where we're staying."

Cath tried another tactic. "Are you doing this because you're angry with Knowl and me for going to Papa's funeral? Are you trying to get even with us, Mama?"

"No, daughter." Betty's gaunt rawboned features took on an unexpected softness in the candlelight. Her voice grew wistful. "I thought about your papa today. I remembered how he looked when he courted me. All the girls were jealous. He was very handsome in those days." She laughed mirthlessly. "Did you know he once told me I was the prettiest girl in the world?"

"I'm sure you were, Mama."

Betty's voice turned petulant. "When did it change, daughter? Where did those people go—the people we were then?"

"I don't know, Mama."

Betty stared up at her, her pupils like nails. "Did you know you could love someone and hate him at the same time? That's how I felt about your papa. Oh, he could be a charmer, and then I'd find the lipstick on his handkerchief."

Cath took another step into the room. "Let's not talk about Papa. Let's just get Jenny home to bed."

Betty held the child closer. "It's too late for that."

Panic danced along Cath's spine. "Why, Mama?"

Betty shook her head. "Jenny won't wake up anymore."

"Of course she'll wake up," said Cath, her throat tightening with alarm. "Come on, Jenny, wake up, sweetheart!"

The child didn't move.

"Anna gave me pills to help me sleep," said Betty. "I gave them to Jenny to help her sleep."

"Dear God, the sedatives? How many did you give her, Mama?"

"Until she stopped crying." Betty pressed her cheek against Jenny's burnished curls. "I didn't want her to cry. That's why I lit all the candles. So she wouldn't have to sleep in the dark. Jenny hates the darkness."

Cath sensed Robert behind her now. She felt the tension in his body. He was ready to leap out and end this bizarre charade. Time was of the essence. Jenny could be dying. Or dead.

In one swift motion Cath sprang forward and grabbed the motionless child from Betty's arms. At the same time Robert darted across the room and seized the startled woman. But even as he gripped her arms, she heaved her body backward, momentarily disengaging herself. Before he could snatch her again she stumbled backward amid the shrouded nightstands and bureaus and blundered into a dressing table. She reached up, caught the corner of the linen covering, and pulled the burning candle onto the pinewood floor.

Cath stood mesmerized, clutching her motionless child to her breast as fire raced up the linen cloth and leapfrogged to the curtains. Hungry flames devoured the organza and finespun lace and climbed the wall, spreading to the velvet drapes framing the window. Robert lunged into the darkness, tore the drapes from their brass rod, and began smothering the capricious flames. Breathlessly he shouted, "Catherine, take Jenny! Get out of here!"

She ran with the limp child down the carpeted hall, lurched blindly down the darkened stairs, and staggered outside into the cold night air. Her heart hammering, she laid Jenny in the overgrown grass beside the porch, then pulled off her coat and tucked it under Jenny's head. Her beautiful daughter lay unmoving, her porcelain-white face peaceful with slumber. Cath stooped down and listened at Jenny's chest.

God help her, her child wasn't breathing!

24

CATH AWOKE IN her own bed in the rosebud room as sunshine streamed through filigrees of lace at the window. Robert sat in the oak rocker by her bed, his sturdy brow furrowed, his blue eyes fixed on her face. "Good morning, sleepyhead," he said softly.

She tried to speak, but her lips felt stiff, her mouth dry. Finally she managed, "How did I get in my own bed?"

"I carried you. You fell asleep beside Jenny's bed."

She sat up, holding the downy eiderdown quilt up around her shoulders. "Jenny, my baby—how is she?"

Robert's eyes crinkled in a smile. "Jenny's fine, darling. Dr. Galway was with her most of the night. Remember?"

"Yes. He kept reassuring me. But I was so afraid. I thought we had lost her."

"Well, she's awake and quite chipper this morning. The sedatives wore off several hours ago and she apparently has no bad memories of last night."

"Thank God. And you, Robert—are you all right?"

He held up bandaged hands. "Fine, except for a few superficial burns."

"Oh, Robert," she moaned in sympathy. "Thank you for putting out the fire. It could have burned down the house."

He smiled. "Your old bedroom on Maypole Drive will need some new wallpaper and drapes, but that heavy baroque decor didn't suit my tastes anyway."

"Nor mine," said Cath, returning his smile. She lapsed into silence, then ventured to ask, "What about Mama? What's going to happen to her?"

"Dr. Galway says he'll keep her in the hospital, under observation, until Knowl can make arrangements for her to go back to the sanitarium."

"Poor Mama. But what else can we do? She needs more help than we can give her." Cath paused. "Did anyone find out how she got into the house on Maypole Drive?"

"Apparently she still had a key. No one ever changed the locks, so she just walked in and made herself at home."

Cath shook her head, marveling. "That's Mama for you." She felt too weary and drained to think any more about Betty now. But another question gripped her with fresh alarm. "How is Annie this morning—and her baby?"

"They're fine, my sweet little worrywart. It was false labor, as Annie suspected. Dr. Galway says her body is just practicing for the big day. But he wants her to get a lot of rest in the next two months. He thinks the baby could come early, before Christmas."

"It'll be an exciting Christmas," said Cath. She tossed back her quilt and slipped one long leg out of bed, then realized she was wearing her flannel nightgown. And with Robert perched by her bed conversing as if she were entertaining him in the parlor! She burrowed back down under the covers, her face flushing warmly. In a small voice she asked, "Robert, who got me ready for bed?"

"Anna, of course. Who else, dear girl?" Smiling at her discomfiture, he tucked the quilt snugly under her chin. "Catherine, we could make Christmas even more exciting, if you'd like."

Her eyes widened. "What are you saying, Robert?"

"What would you think of a Christmas wedding?"

"Christmas? You mean I'd be Mrs. Robert Wayne before the year is out?"

"Would you like that?"

She sat back up, pushed away the quilt, and swung her legs out of bed. "Oh, Robert, it would be divine—except for one thing. I want Annie to be my matron of honor. I'm not sure her baby will cooperate with our schedule."

He thought a moment, looking a tad professorial. "Well, then what about the first Saturday in the new year?" He stood up and looked at the wall calendar, following the little numbered squares with his index finger. "That would be January 3, 1948."

"That has a nice ring to it," said Cath, standing beside him. "Close enough to Christmas to be festive, and yet long enough after to have its own special significance."

Robert gathered her into his arms, flannel nightgown and all. "I adore you, Miss-Catherine-Herrick-soon-to-be-Mrs.-Robert-Wayne. Now tell me truly. Can you plan a proper wedding in just three months?"

"Indeed I can," she assured him. "Just watch me!"

And plan it she did. With Annie's help—and Anna's—she prepared a guest list, selected engraved invitations, shopped for a lovely satin wedding gown, and hired a caterer and musicians. Anna made matching green velveteen dresses for the bridal party, which included Jenny as the flower girl and, to everyone's surprise, Annie's older sister Alice Marie, popular girl singer with the American Stardust Dreams Orchestra. "The band will be in Chicago from Christmas Eve through the New Year," Alice Marie wrote in one of her rare letters home, "so I might as well catch a train to Willowbrook for the wedding and attend the dedication of my new little nephew or niece as well."

As the middle of December approached, both Cath and Annie began to wonder when that blessed event would occur. Annie's former hourglass figure swelled to enormous proportions so that simply navigating about the house became intolerable. "Dear Cath, now I know why you complained so much when you were expecting Jenny," Annie lamented one evening as she attempted to remove her shoes from her swollen feet.

"Let me do that," said Knowl, bending down to untie her laces. He glanced over at Cath, then back at his exhausted wife and quipped, "Who knows? Maybe we're going to have twins!"

Cath laughed. "Maybe you're going to have an entire baseball team!"

On the third Thursday in December Annie woke Cath at dawn and announced, "This is it. Call Dr. Galway. Tell him Knowl and I are on our way to the hospital!"

With a whoop of victory Cath threw off her covers and exclaimed, "Wait for me! I'm coming too!"

While Knowl paced nervously in the father's waiting room, Cath insisted on seeing Annie through her labor, just as Annie had done for Cath five years before. Dr. Galway didn't argue. "I brought both of you girls into the world, and I know how stubborn you can be," he said.

But around noon, when Annie's bearing-down pains came, the physician shooed Cath out of the room. Half an hour later he stepped into the waiting room with a pleased smile on his lips. "Well, Knowl," he boomed, "your wife has given you a healthy seven-pound baby girl with lungs like Kate Smith!"

Knowl jumped up, twisting a dog-eared copy of *Life* magazine in his hands. "Is—is Annie okay?"

"Go in and see for yourself," said Dr. Galway with a wink. "She's giving your daughter her first meal, and, if you ask me, Annie's the most radiant new mother I've seen in a long spell!"

Ten days later, on December 28, Knowl and Annie brought home their dimpled, rosy-cheeked princess, Margaret Kate Herrick. When asked how they'd picked that name, Knowl replied simply, "We named her after Harry's daughter."

"And," said Annie with unabashed pride, "I expect our Margaret to grow up to *be* the president!"

With all of the excitement over Margaret's homecoming—or *Maggie,* as she came to be called, to Annie's consternation—plans for the wedding just a week away took a momentary backseat.

Robert did inadvertently let it escape that he was taking Cath to

New York City for their honeymoon. The secret came out when the headlines for the *Willowbrook News* proclaimed:

RECORD-BREAKING SNOWSTORM PARALYZES NORTHEAST

Robert seized the newspaper and scanned the story in a fit of dismay. "This can't be!" he thundered. "Over twenty-five inches of snow fell on New York City, and I've got tickets next week for the Annie Oakley musical, *Annie Get Your Gun*. With Ethel Merman! On Broadway!"

"Well, now we know where you're spending your honeymoon," mused Annie as she discreetly nursed little Maggie. "It should be lovely, if you don't mind a bit of cold weather."

Cath smiled at Robert. "I'm not at all worried. I've got my love to keep me warm. And," she added with a mixture of whimsy and wistfulness, "if it turns out we settle in California, we'll enjoy the sunshine while all of you dig yourselves out from under sky-high snowdrifts."

The subject of Cath and Robert moving to California came up again two days before the wedding, as the Herrick household relaxed in the parlor after one of Anna's succulent pork roast dinners. Annie sat rocking Maggie; Cath and Robert occupied the love seat; Knowl sat in a wing chair, balancing a steaming cup of coffee on his knee. A cozy fire crackled in the fireplace. "Annie, you're the picture of contentment," Cath declared. "And you, too, Knowl. I've never seen the two of you happier."

Annie nodded. "Knowl and I are very much at peace with the Lord and each other. We wish the same happiness for you and Robert."

Robert pulled Cath close. "I'd say we're off to a good start, wouldn't you, darling? We don't know what's ahead, but with God's help we'll face it together. Right now it looks like we'll be singing, 'California, here we come!' "

Annie's expression clouded. "There's something we haven't talked about. I suppose I keep putting it off because I don't want to face it, but time has run out. What will we do about—?"

"Jenny?" finished Cath softly. She looked into Robert's eyes for strength, then, with a sigh of resolve, gazed back at Annie. "We've been best friends all our lives, Annie. In so many ways I owe you my life, my sanity. No one else could have brought me back from the coma the way you did. For nearly a year you were mother to both Jenny and me." Cath's voice broke. "I can never repay such a debt."

"I don't expect you to," said Annie. "I did it because I love you."

"And I love you too, Annie, with all my heart." Cath spoke over a growing lump in her throat. "That's why it's so hard to say this. It's time for me to accept my role as a wife and a mother. If I'm ever going to raise my daughter, I have to begin now. I know Jenny may not understand why she has to leave her home here in Willowbrook, but Robert and I have decided. Wherever we go, Jenny will go with us and be our daughter."

Annie's chin quivered and she held her baby a little closer to her breast. "I understand how you feel, Cath. I won't fight you on this. But I hope you'll also understand why I must pray with all my heart that you never take that child from this house. This is her home. We're her family. It would break my heart not to be part of her life."

"That's how I feel too," said Cath. "Jenny's my flesh and blood, and I won't go to California without her."

Knowl set down his coffee cup and turned to his sister. "Cath, you have every right to raise Jenny as your daughter, and if that means taking her to California, so be it. But I—well, I—oh, for crying out loud, I'm going to have to spill the beans on this one."

Annie stared in bewilderment at her husband. "What are you talking about, Knowl?"

He sat forward with a sly, conspiratorial air. "I wanted to save this for a wedding present, but it looks like I'd better come clean with it now."

"What is it, Knowl?" urged Cath. "You're talking in riddles. I feel like Alice at the Mad Hatter's tea party!"

"She's right. Come on, ol' man," said Robert, "fill us in."

Knowl's face took on a flushed, animated intensity. "All right, here are the facts. I took a mortgage out on the house, so we now have all the capital we need to purchase the Van Buren facility."

Annie stared at her husband. "Knowl, you mean—?"

"That's right. As soon as we sign on the dotted line, we've got ourselves a publishing house!"

Cath clapped her hands. "Then we can stay in Willowbrook!"

"Marvelous! And Annie will be our first Herrick House author," said Robert expansively. "If all goes right, we'll have her book out in time for the spring list."

"But, Knowl," said Annie with sudden concern, "I thought you didn't want to risk the house on a publishing venture."

"I didn't," he said, his tone turning serious. "But the other night when Mama and Jenny were missing and our old homestead almost went up in smoke, I realized a house is only a building. It's the people who make it a home." His dark eyes took on a beatific sheen. "The truth is, I want to build something lasting on this earth, not just wood, hay, and stubble. I want to help people. And I think publishing Christian literature will do that."

"Hear, hear!" declared Robert. "God knows our world needs a voice for Christ during these turbulent days. We're halfway through this century, and what have we got to show for it? Two world wars, the Depression, Communism spreading like wildfire, and the atom bomb."

"Exactly," said Knowl. "If we Christians don't take a stand and risk something today, where will we be by the end of this century?" He grinned sheepishly. "I didn't mean to turn this into a sermon, but there it is. I may not be a Truman or a Churchill or a Rockefeller, but I'm determined to do what I can to turn things around in the next fifty years."

"We're with you, old man," said Robert heartily. "To quote Dickens's Tiny Tim, 'God bless us, everyone!' "

"Darling, I don't mean to play devil's advocate," said Annie, "but what about your work at the newspaper? Surely you're not planning to juggle two careers. Maggie will need lots of her daddy's time. Jenny too."

"I've thought of that." Knowl retrieved his coffee cup and took a leisurely swallow. "I've talked with the owner of the paper and I'm resigning my position as managing editor. But he's agreed to let me stay on as a freelance columnist after I've assumed my duties at Herrick House."

"Oh, Knowl, that's wonderful!" said Annie.

"I've already picked out a name for my column. 'A World's Eye View.' I'll be able to continue commenting on what's happening in Willowbrook, the state, the nation, and the world. In fact, since I'll no longer be editor of the paper, I'll have more freedom to express my personal opinions."

"Sounds like it's right up your alley," said Robert. "Tell you what. Right after the honeymoon we'll have to sit down together and work out the details of our publishing venture."

"I'll be ready whenever you are," said Knowl. "In fact, while you're in New York I'll get in touch with our bankers and lawyers. They can start the paperwork."

Robert rubbed his hands together. "I can't wait."

"Hold on," said Cath. "I'm getting married in two days and I want to savor every moment. No more business talk tonight. The only subject of conversation I'll allow is our wedding."

Annie put Maggie on her shoulder and rubbed her tiny pink back under her kimono. "Cath, the big question is, are you ready? You've had so many distractions, with my being in the hospital ten days, and Christmas to celebrate, and then Maggie and me coming home. Are you forgetting anything important?"

"I hope not." Cath thought a moment. "My wedding gown is ready. Anna's finishing my veil and hemming the bridesmaids' dresses. The church is reserved. Reverend Henry will perform the ceremony. We'll come back here for the reception. I've sent out all the invitations. Tell me, what have I forgotten?"

"What about Mama?" asked Knowl meaningfully.

Cath felt a chill go through her heart. "What about Mama?"

"Is she going to attend your wedding?"

"How can she?" cried Cath. "She's in the sanitarium."

"They might give her permission to leave for a few hours," said Annie. "I think it would mean the world to her."

"Dr. Galway might be willing to pick her up and take her back," Knowl continued. "He could see that she behaves herself."

Cath looked at Robert. "Did you know about this? They're making plans for Mama to be at our wedding! How can they think of such a thing? She could have killed Jenny!"

"But she didn't," said Robert. "She's been off the booze for two months; it was the liquor that made her crazy."

"She could spoil the entire wedding. You know how she is!"

"I've seen her, Cath," said Knowl. "All she talks about is you and Jenny and the wedding. I've talked to her doctors, and they say she's showing real improvement. They'll give her a pass for the day if you're willing to have her come."

Cath bit her lip to keep back the tears. "You're all conspiring against me. I can't! What if she humiliates us all?"

Robert leaned over, nuzzled her ear, and whispered with a tender seductiveness, "Come on, dear heart." He winked playfully. "What's one more drunk at our wedding?"

She stared at him in astonishment. "Oh, my love, I never thought of it that way! You think if I can't accept Mama with her weakness, I won't be able to accept you either!"

"It is something to think about," he mused.

Annie cleared her throat. "While we're on the subject of people who weren't invited—"

"Who else?" exclaimed Cath. "We've invited half the town!"

Annie's voice took on a solemn note. "I've thought about this for weeks now. What about your brother and sister?"

Now it was Knowl's turn to protest. "You think we should invite Papa's other family?"

"It's just a thought," said Annie. "They are your kin."

"Only because Papa couldn't stay home where he belonged!"

Annie gave Knowl a sly glance. "What were we saying about accepting people with their weaknesses?"

"It's called unconditional love," said Cath. "It was the only way I could find wholeness. It's still a mystery. Christ accepted me just as I was."

Knowl looked hard at her. "Are you saying you'd consider inviting Papa's mongrel children to your wedding? I believe in doing the Christian thing too, Cath, but what kind of message would that send? That we can just overlook the terrible things Papa's done? That we can all somehow be one big happy family?"

"I don't suppose they'd come anyway," said Cath. "Especially Bethany Rose. She doesn't like us or trust us."

"Well, I'm not especially fond of her either," said Knowl. "And I certainly don't trust Luke Henry, the way he forced you to go with him to Fort Wayne. He's impulsive and unpredictable."

"Like me?" said Cath with a wry little smile.

"No, nothing like you. He's like no one I ever knew."

"So what do we do?" asked Cath. "Pretend they don't exist?"

"Okay, I admit it," conceded Knowl. "Maybe I have a blind spot where those two are concerned. I think they have their lives and we have our lives. I don't see any reason to welcome them as family."

For several moments silence weighed heavy in the room. All that could be heard was Maggie sucking her fist and the crackling of a few remnant flames lingering over dying coals.

Finally Cath said, "Maybe we should welcome them because Christ welcomed us as family when we were unlovely and unacceptable and misbegotten." Where were these thoughts coming from? Not herself, surely. These were *His* thoughts, Christ's Spirit speaking to her spirit.

"Are you serious, Cath?" asked Annie. "You'll consider inviting your brother and sister to the wedding?"

She stood up, walked to the window, and gazed out at the black starry sky. Frost had etched intricate designs on the window panes. Through nature's mystical prism the world was suddenly a hazy, glazed wonderland. Lamplight glowed from slumbering houses and street lights glimmered like friendly beacons. Crystal-white flurries wafted downward, floating silent as goose-down feathers.

"Look, it's snowing," said Cath with the wonder she felt as a child at winter's first snowfall. "Look, do you see? A fresh white blanket is covering the earth, making everything clean."

"You could telephone them, Cath," said Annie. "Just extend the invitation. If they come, they come. If not, at least you've done your part."

Robert got up and joined Cath at the window. He stood behind her and slipped his arms around her waist and pulled her back against him. With his chin he nuzzled the top of her head. "It's up to you, sweetheart," he said. "Don't let any of us talk you into doing something you're not comfortable with. It's your wedding."

"*Our* wedding."

She sighed deeply, savoring Robert's closeness, the warmth of his arms. "I just thought of something," she said, her voice hushed as the snowfall. "Someday, when Mama's better, I want to take her to Fort Wayne to see Papa's grave. I want her to tell him all the things she never got to tell him. It'll be good for her, don't you think?"

"Yes, I think so." He was breathing in and out slowly now, matching her breath for breath.

"And about Jenny," she said, her voice rising with a strange urgency, "she'll be happy with us, won't she? She may be reluctant at first, but she's young and resilient. She'll come to realize she needs to be with her real mother. Don't you think so?"

Again Robert nodded. "I'm sure you're right, dear girl."

"And if we live close to Honeysuckle Lane, she'll be able to come home whenever she wishes. Just as I've always done. This house has always been here for me, Robert. I want it to be here for Jenny too."

"It will be."

"We could buy the house on Maypole Drive," she rushed on, a bit breathless now. "We could renovate it and make it a grand house filled with love just like this one. It would be the house it never was when I was growing up. And all our family could find healing and wholeness there, just as I've found here on Honeysuckle Lane."

"*All* our family?" he echoed, his voice unexpectedly pensive.

She turned her cheek against his powerful chest. "People are all little mysteries, aren't they, Robert? Perched on their own little rocks in a vast ocean, all alone and sometimes angry, with pieces of themselves broken off and missing, so they can hardly stay afloat.

"And then God spins webs of love and forgiveness binding them to one another and binding them to Him, so that they never have to feel lost and alone again."

Outside the window, the flurries were thickening, swirling and dancing in a celestial ballet. "I wonder about this girl, Bethany Rose," she said suddenly. "I wonder if she'll come to the wedding. Perhaps she'll think it odd she didn't receive an invitation. I'll apologize for the oversight."

Cath was speaking more to herself now than to Robert. "I would think she wonders what it's like to have a sister. I do. How odd it would be to say, 'My sister and I are going to lunch. . . . My sister and I would love to join you. . . . My sister and I . . . my sister and I . . .'"

She gazed out the window at the stars and snow and street lights and lamp glow of Willowbrook, at the frozen blue world that shimmered beyond the frosty glass. In the hush of the moment, in the warmth of her beloved's arms, she sensed that this time and place had been imbued with a touch of the eternal. Never before had she felt so whole and alive and eager to embrace the mysteries, the tantalizing future God was writing just for her.

About the Author

Carole Gift Page, considered one of America's best-known and loved Christian fiction writers, writes from the heart about issues facing both adults and teenagers. She has written more than 30 books and is the recipient of two Pacesetter Awards and the C.S. Lewis Honor Book Award.

Carole is a fiction columnist for *The Christian Communicator* and founder of the Inland Empire Christian Writers Guild. She has published countless articles and poems in Christian periodicals, including *Virtue, Moody, Decision, The Christian Home,* and Focus on the Family's *Brio* and *Breakaway.*

She has taught creative writing at Biola University and served on the advisory board of the Biola Writers Institute. In addition, she is a frequent speaker at conferences, schools, churches, and women's ministries.

Carole and her husband Bill have three children and live in Moreno Valley, CA.